Misfitz Tavern

Matthew Lee & LaTasha Lee

Cover art by Kendall Hart.
Interior layout by Edward Gehlert.
Beta Reading by Genna Branson and Eva Gehlert.
Editing services provided by Edward Gehlert.
Editorial support by Eva Gehlert.

Happy Duck Publishing
PO Box 607
Belle, MO 65013

Genre: Fantasy
ISBN: 978-0-9861182-4-1
First Edition.

To Professor Rev. Richard Knudsen
1933-2014

Who spent endless hours teaching us of World Religions and Philosophy, who took the time out of his day after class for our theological debates one-on-one, whose eyes lit up once he saw the family we had become, and who was always an unbiased ear to our views and questions.

You helped us form the mortar of the Misfitz Tavern. Wish you were here to read it.

ACKNOWLEDGMENTS

First and Foremost, we would like to thank our editor, friend, and family member, Edward Gehlert. Without you, your knowledge, and your constant persistence and badgering that we keep writing this would not even be an option for us. Thank you for everything!

To Zayne, Bria, and Johnathan thank you for allowing us the time to write. We know how difficult independent play can be. For being patient when you ask us questions and we continue to stare away at the screen before turning to answer them, and for listening with wide-eyes and eager smiles as we read to you portions of the book. You three were there for all of the editing process and we couldn't have done it without you. We love you all so much.

To Tasha's parents, Ron and Tammy Jones, who welcomed the news of the book being published as if it were another grandchild in the family, understanding the time, love, and devotion that we put into it. For all that you have ever done for both of us, standing by our side no matter what the situation, through good and bad, and knowing that we both had great potential to be the very best we could. Without you guys, no guarantees of where we would be writing this from or how we would ever get ourselves out of some of the predicaments we put ourselves into. We love you. Thank you, Mom and Dad.

To Matt's parents, blood is thicker than water, but love is thicker than blood. Thank you for teaching the valuable lessons that helped to guide us in our endeavors.

To Woo, for never giving up on us. Ever.

To Mem and Pop, for believing that we always had it in us even when we didn't.

To the patrons of Josie's Tavern and Cheers. You know who you are.

To Steve, haha, didn't think you would make it into the book, did ya'? Thank you for exposing us to the hardwood floors, the glass chandeliers, and the cold beers of the Misfitz Tavern, where only Karma is law.

To Chris, Chan, Johnney, Kyle, and Amanda: each with their own favorite characters, thank you for the 3 a.m. messages asking us to send you another chapter, begging us for more, and religiously questioning us on when the book would finally be in print. Thank you for laughing, crying, and screaming with us at the characters. Thank you for being our first true fans.

To all those who choose to hide in the shadows, remaining unnamed; the beaten, the battered, and the tired. Thank you for helping us with some of the questions we had. Thank you for telling us of your darkness, your bitterness, and your pain. You know who you are and may you one day embrace your sobrieties, may you one day move on past your anger. May you one day find peace.

To Sasha, wherever you are out there honey. You have talent and beauty. Keep your head up.

To Jodi Picoult, with a single email you motivated us. You cheered us on and now, here it is. Thank you my friend and now fellow author. May we one day be able to meet face to face.

To any other author of any book we have ever read. From Dr. Seuss to Steven King, from Shel Silverstein, Dan Brown, and Simon R. Green to Nathaniel Hawthorne. To everyone in between, of all genres, who spilled their souls onto paper. We raise a glass to you.

To anyone wanting to write a book, you can. Write, write, and write some more. Write until it hurts to not write. We are the future.

To Grandma Lorton, thank you for introducing us to the beautiful, wonderful world of books; for guiding us through our first letters, our first words, and the everlasting "just one more chapter."

To anyone we may have forgotten. There are too many of you to name, but you know who you are. To friends. To family. To Misfitz.

And to Nanny, who without her unconditional love for us both, we never would have even considered ourselves as anything more than everyday people. Who laughed with us, cried with us, and prayed for us; who was there as a warm hug or a late night phone call. Who, though it wasn't her type of book, eagerly awaited the day she could hold it in her hands. Who asked daily for updates on the writing, editing, cover art, and publication date. We love you Nanny! Thank you for everything! Please don't read this until it's a *New York Times* bestseller.

CHAPTER ONE

MISFITZ TAVERN

Chara stormed into the back door of the tavern, careful to not let the door slam too hard. This place had been her home for the past two years and wasn't the same cold building that Will Pearson had first inherited. The building before had paint peeling away around the large windows that lined the far wall, where a small elf shared a drink with a giant at the tall tables that replaced the once dry-rotted booths.

As distant travelers stopped through the small magical town in Nebraska, business had picked up for Will and his tavern. Chara couldn't deny that her rent, now nearly three hundred gold for the single bedroom, had risen with the improvements of the rest of the pub.

Chara also couldn't deny that the small town with a population of some two hundred people was not what she had originally had in mind for a resting place. Passing through the town on her way to Nevada, one of the only places still available for magical beings to make their stand, she had stopped in for the night. Now, it had become a home. Although Will complained that Chara spent over an hour longer than any other customer in the bathroom, her rent was always paid on time and the consistent company in the pub was quite nice.

She passed by the pool tables, ignoring the usual stares of the wizards who had recently gotten off work. She stormed past the bar, ready to dart up the stairs and hide in her room from her nightmare of a day when she saw the tavern owner pouring drinks.

He was certainly easy on the eyes. *No,* Chara reminded herself. He was devilishly handsome. Chara fought against the urge to stare at his business suit. It fit the clean-shaven man nearly as well as his title did. He held his head up with pride, laughing with a green-skinned goblin that sat across from him. She bit her bottom lip against the smile before being brought back to reality.

She needed a job, some way to pay the rent if she had any intention on continuing to stay there. Chara's old beater of a car had broken down, and made her late for work, causing her to lose her job at the local coffee shop not more than two hours ago. Yes, another job wasn't optional. It was mandatory.

"Umm... hey Will," she turned back to face the man, "Are... Do you need any extra help?"

"Well that depends, Legs."

The curves that shaped her muscular calves were exposed beneath her regular skirts. It was enough to drive any man or creature wild. Referring to her familiar nickname the former barista had been christened with was a good sign.

"Do you know how to mix strange and unusual concoctions?" He smiled, tossing a shaker in his hands. Cracking it open, he let the drink spill into a glass on the bar in front of the horned goblin that licked its lips in want.

Chara should have known this was coming. Will never could give a straight answer. She watched as he waved his elderwood wand, causing the drink to form into a tornado of liquid rising a foot from the glass and landing perfectly back into the highball container. The goblin clapped its hands, laughing at the show before taking the drink from the bar and leaving Will a hefty tip.

Will tossed a stained towel over his shoulder. Leaning against the cooler, he looked her up and down. "We get all kinds in here and we don't discriminate. So, everybody gets good service like they're at home whether you like them or not. Can you handle that?"

"Will," she couldn't hide a deep sigh, "I've lived here for two years. I know how you treat the customers."

There hadn't been a dwarf, alien, gypsy, or faerie that hadn't been treated with respect in his pub. Once they walked through the heavy oak door, it no longer mattered if the customer participated in dark or light magic, nor did the number of deaths they had caused, the light within their blessings, or the amount of gold warranted on their head. In Will's pub, they got respect with their beverage.

"As for the fancy drinks…" She looked past Will to the cooler and extensive drink selection. She bit her bottom lip while glancing at the foreign labels on bottles of blue, yellow, and green glass. "I can learn my way around."

She grinned at him. *How hard could it be?* She had worked with coffee. Alcohol couldn't be that difficult.

"Okay, you start tonight. Want me to pay you or we can call it even on your rent and you can keep your tips?"

He liked the idea of giving her options to work with. She'd been a great tenant and with her long black hair, pale skin, and petite figure she was easy on the eyes. Tips would not be difficult for her to earn.

Chara thought about it as she brushed her hair back from her face. Her emerald eyes lit up with a charming smile. She knew how to treat a customer, but also knew how busy the bar could get. She also knew how much overtime Will demanded of Kritter. It was a tough decision.

"Umm… Can I think about it?"

Will smiled at her and nodded. "Be here at six and I'll give you a crash course in drinks. Kritter will update you on the menu. Dress to sell."

He winked at her in boyish charm before turning back to restock the cooler. "Let me know how you want your pay to work tonight when you come in."

Chara squealed in delight, unable to hide her excitement. "I won't let you down!" Her green eyes glowed with relief as she quickly ran up the stairs.

Will smiled. He watched her skirt rise and fall with each step, barely hiding the soft curve of her behind. It was a good thing the old bar rose to his naval as he discreetly adjusted his pants to hide his erection from the excitement of watching the young woman before sliding a bubbling blue liquid to a diminutive fellow across the bar.

"Two silver, Ernie."

***

Chara sprinted down the stairs of the inn at 5:45, freshly showered and ready to start the evening's work. She had dug through the old trunks in her room, tossing clothes here and there before finally settling on a black knee-length skirt she didn't even remember owning and a white button down shirt with a deep purple cardigan. Her straight, dark hair was pulled back in a tight ponytail.

Unsure what kind of shoes would complete the professional look she knew Will was going for, Chara finally decided on a pair of black heels. She held her head high with an unexplainable sense of pride the moment she put those shoes on. She was no longer a clumsy girl in dangerous heels, but a powerful woman.

"I'm ready to work, sir." Chara rounded the bar with a smile before inspecting the bottles.

"Not all of these are—" She stopped and glanced down at a neon green liquid in a dark brown bottle. "Dragon's juice?"

"Don't call me 'Sir'. We already have someone who carries

that name and I'm most certainly not him. As far as the bottles go… some of our customers have more discerning tastes. And no," he added, knowing the next question weighing on her mind, "Not all of them are legal."

Seeing her standing there in a black skirt and white button up blouse sent his pulse racing. She looked both sexy and professional, which was exactly what he had wanted.

"You look… great," he smiled his approval at her wardrobe decisions.

"Thank you," she blushed, looking down. "What… umm… what do I do if someone asks for something—"

She stopped herself, already knowing the answer. "I send them to your office."

Will's royal blue eyes flashed at her remark. "Yes. If anybody asks for something of a questionable nature send them to me, both at the bar and when I'm in my office. Speaking of which, stop by my office before you knock off for the night."

"Yes, si— Will." Chara nodded her head. She felt slightly out of her element.

Will turned back to the bar and continued straightening up bottles and glasses. He scanned a section of the liquor before calling out towards the back room, "Kritter!"

A small pixie dashed out from the kitchen. Her spiked orange wings were tucked neatly in close to her four-foot tall frame; leaf-shaped ears comically a bit too large for her body.

"Master Will? Master Will called for Kritter. What can Kritter do? Does something need cleaning?"

The pixie's high pitched voice and fast talking always made Will smile. "No, Kritter, as always the place looks fantastic. I want you to teach Miss Chara the menu and the normal drinks that get ordered. Dinner starts in an hour. You've got until then to teach her the basics."

Will pointed behind the bar to the attractive woman. Kritter's gaze followed the motion and she quickly nodded several times at Chara.

Out of the corner of his eye Will caught sight of Fawn as she walked back into the pub. The bulges in her clothing indicated she had more stock heavily lining her pockets. She smiled when she saw him. He nodded his head toward his office and turned back to the pixie and his newest employee. "I've got some business to attend to. I'll be back to check on you in a little while."

Without waiting for Kritter to reply, Will stepped from behind the bar and walked into his office. He didn't bother to look behind him to see if she was following him. He knew Fawn would be eager to finalize the sale.

"Does he do that often?" Chara asked Kritter in a hushed whisper, looking over the menu after Will walked off. She could still feel a flutter in her stomach at his compliment.

"Does he do what, Mistress Chara?"

"Wander off like that?"

The pixie shrugged her shoulders and glanced back at the office door Will had just closed. "Sometimes Master Will does. Kritter asked once if Kritter should clean Master Will's office and Master Will said no. Master Will just handles business back there sometimes."

Kritter shrugged again. "Kritter take care of Mistress Chara. If Mistress Chara needs help, just call for Kritter."

"I will." Chara smiled at the diminutive pixie before turning back to the bar. "Thank you."

***

"Check out that Glock!" Fawn leaned over the bar, batting her eyelashes as she tucked a strand of her cotton candy colored hair behind one of her pointed ears. The gills that lined the woman's neck flared up with excitement. "Damn!"

Her eyes never left Will's sidearm. The black metal gleamed

back at her with teasing of what a few moments alone might have in store.

"Don't be jealous Fawn. I've got spares in my office that I can loan you. Unless you've got something to offer in trade, sweet cheeks?" Will was willing to flirt back with the tanned beauty as the rest of the guys at the bar laughed and snickered to themselves. He raised a questioning eyebrow as his blue eyes shone from beneath them, a simple flirtatious gesture towards a regular customer.

"I might have something to interest you!" Fawn leaned over the bar. "A refill dear?"

Will knew the woman was an accomplished trader. She was from Caly, the same realm as his friend Worvacs. Fawn and Worvacs had been running together for years, her willingness to help Worvacs sell his loot from hunting or mining anytime the market didn't seem to be working out in his favor. Worvacs had money in his wallet right now and had no need for the beauty who used her charm, as well as her body, to sell whatever might be sitting in her pockets.

"Of course," Will reached under the bar for the blue glass bottle containing her liquor of choice. "For you, the drinks are on the house. The guns, however, are not."

Grinning wickedly, he poured himself a shot and clicked it against hers before downing it.

"To big rewards and high stakes," Fawn answered, toasting her drink and swallowing it one gulp before leaning forward, hoping for business.

She opened her palm, nearly childlike in size, to expose a red and white pill. "A loot pill. Picks up your earnings for you. You play poker?"

Her mind was all business now, and selling whatever she could to get her hands on something of equal or, hopefully, higher value. Most realm jumpers were cruel. Fawn couldn't always count on a reliable teleport that wouldn't expose her for every bronze in her pocket, but with Worvacs willing to provide, she could cross realms to a place where the returns were high.

Will picked the pill off the bar, rolling it over in his calloused palm, feeling its weight. "What do you mean a loot pill?"

Fawn laughed. "A loot pill. You take it with a glass of water, give it about twenty minutes and you're ready to go. Any loot, or earnings, you make don't need to be collected. Once the prize is yours, it immediately goes into your inventory. They are great for hunting."

Sounds like one'd be great for more than just hunting, Will thought to himself. He knew many of his customers had deep pockets that evening and the fact that they were all drinking just made it that much easier for money to come up missing and them only to think they spent too much drinking the night before.

"How effective is it? And how long does it last?"

"Fifty feet," Fawn answered firmly, "For an hour and a half. If that's not quite what you're looking for..."

She looked him up and down, her purple eyes trying to feel out the handsome bachelor with a firm jawline and stern chest. His blonde hair stood out against the bright blue of his eyes, the dark green of his suit only adding to the look of an appetizing man with expensive tastes. She could just see him taking her to his oversized room, where his money was exposed in luxuries and his boxers were...

"Silk. You look like a silk man." She pulled two blue syringes from her pouch and held them up for Will to examine. "Works with any animal hide, magical, and common. I have a set of gold moontooth sheets at home."

Will smiled with a seductive wink in return at her accuracy of his taste in silk. "This should cover part of it. I'm sure you can use those blue syringes on my sheets upstairs to change them into something beautiful and the loot pill should cover the rest of the cost. If not, I'm sure we can settle up the rest while you're changing them over."

Will guided the inter-realm traveler through the crowded bar to his personal office. He waved his right hand in a series of quick magical gestures that ended with his door opening.

Fawn followed Will into his office with eager curiosity, waiting until the purple stained glass door was closed before letting out a gasp at the beauty of the room.

When she had read him as a silk man, this was not what she had envisioned. A warm fireplace made of polished cobblestone sat along a back wall, surrounded by dark green shelves lined with numerous books of all shapes and sizes. The floors were a highly-waxed cherry, a difficult wood for even her to come by in large quantities, with a matching spiral staircase taking up the center of the room with purple carpet lining the stairs to an upper level.

Will didn't give the woman a chance to be too awed before sitting behind his large desk. "Sit, please." He motioned to the chair across from him before gazing out of the red, see-through wall that gave him full view of the pub.

Fawn regarded the one-way window. *No wonder nothing that happened in the room where brownies and gremlins came to drink surprised him, he can see it all from the privacy of this office.*

This was nothing like the common streets or random wooded areas where Fawn's business usually took place. She was more accustomed to secrecy and deception, not this higher level of elegance.

"Very impressive, reminds me of the flats on Fomar, minus the view." A contented sigh escaped her before walking over and sitting on his desk.

Unzipping her jumpsuit she revealed the a bit more cleavage as she kicked off both her boots. "But, I think we have a misunderstanding. It will take at least a hundred and fifty extractors for your sheets, not including hides. The transfer rate, transportation fees... what kind of gun are we talking about here?"

"It's a standard Glock .45 with a few... homemade adjustments that should make it worthwhile in any realm you happen to find yourself in. Blessed and cursed ammo for those pesky angels and demons you may find yourself fighting. Also, it will only fire for you once you're imprinted on it."

"Unable to steal," Fawn nodded her head in thought. "Yet also unable to resell. Continue."

"Self-targeting guarantees a center mass shot every time, no matter how small your target. Trust me, it's worth every bit and more of what you should offer. So, it looks like we may have to meet in the middle on something." Will concluded as he stood and walked around his desk to her. He fingered the zipper of her jumpsuit while eyeing her up and down.

"I think that may be possible," Fawn grinned, looking down at her zipper before stretching her legs around his waist. Using her legs, she pulled Will closer as she ran her hand down his toned chest. "How does it handle in extreme weather?"

"Phenomenal. It'll never jam on you or leave you wanting more..." Will replied. He grinded forward into her, making sure she felt every inch of him and all his possibilities. "I'm sure that with a test run, you'll feel the same way."

***

Waving his hand, Will caused the office door to swing open nearly an hour later. He smiled at his business associate while motioning her to follow him. "Any last-minute suggestions?"

He led Fawn back into the main room of the bar and turned to her with his hand extended. Fawn gripped it, shaking it firmly while glancing at Chara.

"Keep the legs behind the bar," Fawn's purple eyes sparkled. "Sex sells."

Legs bent over the bar with one knee on the cooler, twirling a dwarf's goatee around her forefinger. She was whispering something in his ear that caused the burly man to drop the bag of gold on the counter he'd been holding onto, his eyes going wide.

Her slender figure was draped across the bar, her skirt stuck up in the air in a way that was both tempting and begging the customer. Will's gaze fell on her long, beautiful legs. She twirled a high heeled shoe on her toe in a rhythm matching the twirling of her finger. Will looked at the dwarf to see his eyes flicking back and forth between her fingers and her toes.

"Thank you." She took the money bag slowly from the counter, her voice steamy as she walked back over to the register.

Humming to herself, she added double the coins to the register, pocketing her tip before returning to the dwarf. Will saw her mouth the words “Next drinks on the house” in the dwarf’s ear before seductively flexing her legs as her hair brushed down across his beard.

Will had to catch himself from chiding the new employee. Hiding his concern with a smile, he strolled behind the bar and started counting the till.

"I think I have been doing the math right," Chara explained as the dwarf left the bar. "I promise anything we are short, I will make up by the end of the night," she insisted nervously.

Will smiled as he listened to her apologizing, realizing all the money was accounted for in the drawer. She had to be taking the 'free drinks' from her tip jar, which was also heavily stocked with gold and silver coins. "It's not a problem."

"Kritter cleaned behind the grills and oven. Kritter wiped down all the tables and bar fourteen times. Kritter did four loads of dishes, swept the kitchen floor nine times, swept the bar floor three times, cleaned all bathrooms and beds are made, Master Will. Kritter also got the two spare rooms booked for two days each, Master Will." The pixie listed with pride, rushing up behind Will from the kitchen.

"Good. Finish cleanup and then you're off for the night." At the sudden look of disappointment on the pixie's face, Will crossed his arms before saying, "Fine and you can dust... something." He waved his hands in exasperation. The look of sudden glee flashing across Kritter's face made him chuckle.

"Thank you, Master Will. Kritter will clean out the chimneys tonight!"

CHAPTER TWO

OVER A CUP OF COFFEE

Angel walked into the cafe with a smile covering her face. There was something about the small building that always helped put her mind at ease. Perhaps it was the fireplace in the corner, a perfect little reading nook for anyone just wanting a moment of warmth and relaxation. Or maybe it was the fresh smell of vanilla and coffee beans that overwhelmed her senses as soon as she opened the door. Whatever it was, it was comfort. Warm, safe, and sweetened with sugar and cream comfort.

A small dwarf greeted her at the counter with pen in hand, ready to take her order. She made a small pretense of looking at the options on the menu before vocalizing her go-to drink. "A double iced mocha with a caramel twist please."

She turned from the counter and scanned the establishment for familiar faces. Sir and Pet were present. The stern older man sat outside next to the window reading a paper dressed in his usual tailored black suit. Pet was pretending to do the same. Angel noticed the girl was toying with her hands as she stared at her lap. Her dark hair draped down her back in a tight braid of submission.

What's on her mind? Angel wondered as she scrunched her brow. She didn't even look at the dwarf when she took her drink from him as she studied the typically stress-free woman's looks of concern and worry through the window. She slid into an empty booth and took a sip of the frosty concoction.

***

Worvacs quickly stepped across the street. Not that he had anything to worry about in such a small town. The traffic in Knowhere was the equivalent of any other small town in America, non-existent except for the occasional car driving the sluggish speed limit.

Pulling open the heavy glass door, he entered the small coffee shop with hopes of a small boost of caffeine to help clear his mind of the fog from the evening prior. Stepping up to the counter, he eyed the short man with long gray beard and pointed ears with keen interest before asking, "Did you choose to be that tall in this realm or was it just the way you were born?"

His voice was barely above a whisper and full of undisguised curiosity. He knew that sometimes traveling from one realm to another allowed a traveler choices in their appearance.

"I'm a dwarf, dumbass! We're all this height. Now whadda' ya' want?" The dwarf tugged at his scraggly, navel length beard.

"A quadruple shot of espresso with extra caramel."

Worvacs shrugged off the dwarf's attitude with indifference as he waited for his drink. He never took his eyes off the creature, in case the cranky shortened man decided to try and jip him out of one of the four shots... or spit in his coffee.

Angel turned around at the sound of the dwarf's frustration. Her vision was assaulted as the large man with orange hair blurred. The illusion of pale skin fell, revealing his natural cobalt blue color. Her mouth dropped open in shock at the familiar face.

"Walter Worvacs Korvacs!" She was thankful to see the old familiar face back in town. "And here I thought you had moved back to Caly for good!" Laughing, she stood up to hug the large man.

Worvacs turned at the sound of his name being called. Noticing Angel staring back at him caused a smile to spread across his unshaven face. Her auburn ringlets hung gently around her soft face and her smile helped to light up any room she entered. "Angel! Are you kidding? You can't get rid of me that easily."

"Here's your caffeine. I hope it makes your heart explode you overgrown blue booger," the dwarf mumbled while sliding the small cup across the counter to Worvacs before huffing and turning back to the now-rattling espresso machine.

Ignoring the dwarf's name calling, Worvacs grabbed the small cup and moved over to where Angel stood waiting. After a quick embrace, he took a plush seat across from her. "How have you been? Business is good I hope?" he asked intrigued.

"It's not Vegas, but it's steady. How do you get away with walking in broad daylight without the no-mags noticing? I mean standing out in New York is one thing, but here… don't people question your bold appearance?" she asked with a laugh, still unable to believe her old friend had entered the coffee shop.

Her smile, warm and friendly, was impossible to wipe from her face as she stared at Worvacs. He was a sight for sore eyes, the foreign man who traveled to distant realms. She had run across him multiple times over the years, and yet still found herself shocked to see his blue skin standing out against the hustle and bustle of Knowhere's magical creatures.

"Oh you know how it is. Ancient spells and old magic. Will told me it had something to do with the Misfitz Tavern. Knowhere was built around the tavern, not the other way around. So the entire town is affected by it. If you don't already know about magic, about the beings, then you're protected by the illusion of normal. If you do know, then you can see the truth. No-mags see Knowhere the same as everywhere else. I'm the same as everyone else, normal. But people like us, we are different. We know magic is real so we can see each other. Like this, like we really are. Now enough! Tell me all about business!"

"Well, I can't expect to find Vegas in Nebraska I suppose. It pays the bills but when they bills reach the skylights it gets hard to keep up. You know how it is. What about you?! How was Caly? Tell me everything! Did you strike it rich?" She leaned closer to him putting her chin in her hands, ready for one of his elaborate tales.

"Oh gods, if only I could get so lucky. Not yet unfortunately, or at least no more than usual. It's great having a realm like Earth where my currency exchange is good coming in. It just sucks when I have to transfer it back out."

He shrugged nonchalantly before sipping his espresso and eyeing the dwarf behind the counter once more. Satisfied that it didn't have any extra slimy ingredients added, he continued, "I managed to score a global here and a global there, but nothing noteworthy. I did hit the hall of fame once in a group, but because there were so many of us we each only received the equivalent of a small global."

He shrugged again. In realms such as Caly and Ark, the profits he pulled off of hunting or mining fell into three categories. Making enough to cover his portal fee back was typical loot. If he got lucky, he came back with money in his pocket, earning himself a global and the hall of fame... The hall of fame was a distant dream of not having to worry about keeping the lights on in his bachelor's bungalow down on 10th Street.

Worvacs shrugged again as he sipped his heart attack in a cup. "You look good though, Vegas or not. Where are you staying? Here in town? How long have you been here?"

"Thank you. I have a place on Renaud Street for now," Angel looked down at her cup. "It's not much and I wound up having to pay double the rent just to paint the walls red but…" She sighed heavily in defeat that she had to make such a decision.

Discretion was necessary, so was a three-car garage. No windows was mandatory on wherever she chose, as was a jetted whirlpool tub. She had to make sure her clients were fully satisfied when they left her services.

The white walls wouldn't have satisfied the men who were expecting a night of pleasure for their money and her landlord knew what she needed the place for. Everyone knew of her scarlet letter in the little town filled with whispers.

"Will occasionally cuts me a discount above the pub, so I guess the two of us are in the same boat. Making plenty, but it sure doesn't feel like it!" She laughed away her worries, her cheerful personality and optimism helped her to take it in stride.

"It's been…" Angel stopped, lost in thought for a moment, "Four years since I left Mom's in Salem? Being a witch in a town with such darkened history for our kind was too much for me. I needed something… happier."

"I had once heard that happiness was nowhere to be found," she shrugged before smiling. "My dad lived here so I thought why not? At first I stayed at Misfitz, but eventually I had to go out and stretch my wings. This is what I always wanted."

The twenty-one-year-old's smile was one of pride now. "To go west and find a saloon where I could wear fancy dresses and attract rich men." A small snort escaped Angel, causing her to cover her bright red lips.

Worvacs laughed heartily. "I don't know how big your clientele is around here, but I'm sure the amount of money for the few makes up for the lack of many. Will and I have an understanding that if I need to hide for a while then I can come to the tavern and in exchange, I sometimes…" Worvacs gently tossed his head from one side to the other before continuing, "Acquire and deliver things for him. It's a decent trade, I think."

He sipped his espresso again, thinking back to the times Will had provided him a hiding place or a free jump from one realm to another to escape from his many enemies. "I like what he's done with the place though. Not to mention the new staff," he wiggled his eyebrows suggestively at her before smiling. "I'm sure you and this new bartender Legs are just two peas in a pod, aren't you?"

"She's actually starting to grow on me," Angel answered honestly. "I wasn't quite sure in the beginning how a quiet barista would handle serving greasy bar food and breaking up drunk cyclops' fights, but she can handle her own and is nice enough. First girl Will has hired in a long time that can actually hold a conversation of intelligence and value."

Angel eyed the man across from her, gazing over his firm blue muscles and how they contrasted in a very attractive way against his purple and yellow armor and hazel eyes. "I must ask though, why is she sparking your attention? Last I knew you were traveling the realms with the woman of cotton candy hair? What's her name, your sweetheart?"

"Fawn and no, she's not my sweetheart. We..." Worvacs thought back to the many travels and dangers he and Fawn had endured together; the ups and downs, the many perils and regrets. "She's my friend. There were other benefits at one point, but that's all it was. We have an understanding that you shouldn't get in the way of a friend being happy in a relationship."

He sipped his espresso again, looking at her thoughtfully before adding, "I hear though that I'm not the only one with relationship interests here of late. Word does get around you know."

He winked at her playfully in regards to Maxx, the single father of two that had pre-occupied most of her nights with paid pleasures. Downing the rest of his drink, Worvacs set the empty cup on the glass coffee table between them. "How is that going, if you don't mind my asking?"

"Can we get another espresso, Jameson?" Angel waved to the dwarf who was eyeing Worvacs again from behind the counter, ready to start round two of the tiff with the blue alien, "Quadruple espresso, extra caramel love and another of those delicious iced coffee's you make?"

She gave the dwarf her warmest smile when he nodded back, quickly getting to work on them. "I'm paying for both Jameson, so hold the beard hairs."

She knew this conversation was going to come up. "You mean Mister Conner?" her voice dropped to a whisper to keep her client confidential, "It had been a thought, but me and boyfriends... they never end well. Usually with the same response I'm sure you get. 'It's me or your job' and how do you say you'll drop your career in hopes that things will work. Not to mention, Savannah's my best friend. The way that Missus Conner treated him, and then left..." She shrugged as Jameson brought over the fresh drinks.

Angel handed over a few coins. "Keep the change."

She focused her attention back to the blue-skinned man and pushed his drink closer to him. "I just don't know yet. There's so much involved."

“I bet there is. I do understand the difficulties when it comes to maintaining a relationship with someone when you're working." He downed the espresso, hoping the extra spike of caffeine in his system would keep him going for his next run. "Or who knows? Maybe it's us who has the problem. The last woman I dated was not very understanding that my kind of work requires travel."

He sighed, leaning back in the overly plush seat in mock exhaustion. "But what are we supposed to do, ya' know? I mean, I love my job and love what I do. Every day it's a new adventure or a chance at a better payout or an upgrade on equipment that keeps me going. C'est la vie? To hell with it, carpe diem I say!"

Worvacs held up his glass in a mock toast at their bravado towards life. "Legs is good though. She's fun to flirt with and knows I can't be around all the time, whether I'd like to or not. Is he understanding towards your predicament when it comes to working and being in a relationship?"

Angel nodded her head. "He is, or he wants to be at least. He is begging me Worvacs, pleading with me to give this a shot. To let it be more than what it is and the sad thing is... I want to. Aphrodite, I want to!"

Angel froze, not realizing how long she had been searching for someone she could say that to. To speak the truth of what her heart held and it felt good to let it out as she continued confessing to her friend, "For years I have watched as that man cooks in his own kitchen, making meals for me and Savannah, and wanted nothing more than to walk behind him and simply kiss his neck. To know what he smells like after a shower or just be able to bring him a fresh cup of coffee in the morning and now... now it's finally here, looking me in the face and I'm so scared that I'm cursed. That Aphrodite hates me and has cursed me to be damned to live the rest of my life as... as the one thing that I want more than anything else. My career, the job of my dreams. I love what I do and... and dammit! He understands! *Why* does he have to understand?"

Angel covered her face with her hands.

Worvacs nodded sympathetically before realizing that with her face buried she couldn't see his agreement. He patted Angel's shoulder gently. "I understand love."

His mind wandered to distant memories, of a different time, in a foreign realm far past the merciless space pirates of Zerideth.

"Fawn was the same way. She seemed to understand what I needed and that this job, it's my career whether she liked it or not. She completely understood, but I wasn't ready for it. I'm still not sure that I am now, should I be lucky enough to draw Legs' more permanent attention but..."

He shook his head, unable to articulate how the woman attracted him. It wasn't just her looks, he could find beautiful women anywhere. It was who she was.

"Still it could be worse, you know. It could be that they never even noticed us at all. Then where would we be? Probably in bed together, but that's not the point." He puckered his lips at her playfully before sipping his espresso again.

"Have to get a decent global for that," Angel answered with a wink before licking her lips, allowing the option to remain open for the man to take at his discretion.

"Wait!" she blurted out, catching on to what he was saying. "So, you and Fawn... she wanted more? What stopped you? What exactly, I mean?"

He laughed heartily at her vague attempt to make a sale before replying, "I have a feeling it wouldn't matter how big my global was, that I still wouldn't be able to afford your prices."

He winked at her again as if to say 'sorry I can't play today' before finishing his second espresso of the morning. "As far as Fawn is concerned though, it was at a high point in my career. I felt like I didn't have time for any attachments or distractions, other than a business partner and the occasional friend with benefits. Time, it seems, is never on our side."

The alarm on his computer bracer started beeping continuously. "Ah hell! I hate to cut this short sweetheart, but the exosaurius migration just started so I've got to head out of realm again. Can I give you a lift anywhere on my way out?"

He stood swiftly, sliding into his gray trench coat.

"No, I think home is close enough to walk. Thank you though." Her smile was once again warm and welcoming, brightening the room as she stood to hug the man.

"Thank you Worvacs, for everything. It helped put things a little more into perspective. As for Legs..."

She stopped, thinking about the friendship she was starting to develop with the woman who enjoyed bubble baths and thick novels, one who was quiet yet kind. A lot like the blue man before her. "Give it a shot. Worst-case scenario we both lose. If that happens you better hope those dakibants pay out nice for you… and I'll still have to cut ya' a discount."

***

Parliament Neurology and Sleep Clinic is pleased to announce that two of their head doctors, Doctor Larce and Doctor Mink, have made a medical breakthrough in their most recent study.

"We have found that patients with both the YT chromosome and the neprocell deficiency can prolong their sleep patterns to what was once considered unnatural amounts, up to 76 hours at a time." Doctor Larce proclaims, "With this new-found information, we can continue our studies on the brain and sleep patterns of both the Adlet and Tikbalang breeds, possibly extending their wake time to a total of 84 hours. While there have been some minor side effects with our last study group including immense foaming at the mouth, peeling or loosening of the skin, and slowed heart rates, we do believe test group F will show more successful results."

Sir folded his newspaper, placing it on the table before him. The news from the Margonia realm never seemed to carry helpful information as of late and he found it tiring. He sipped his coffee outside the café as he enjoyed one of the few warm days they had left before the chill of the Nebraska autumn air took hold. He embraced mornings like these, when he and Pet could just sit enjoying each other's company and the beauty nature had to offer.

Taking another tentative sip of his coffee, the man instead moved his attention to the woman sitting across the table from him. "What preoccupies your mind, my Pet?"

Though he was a stern man with a voice that rumbled like the depths of an earthquake, his slate gray eyes and light skin warmed beneath the sunlight; nearly making its way to his cold stature. "You've been lost in thought all morning."

Pet's eyes darted up at Sir's words and his notice of her distraction. No, the morning hadn't been an easy one for her. It had been one filled with constant staring back at herself in the mirror. One of deepened meditation, calming thoughts, and white candles of peace and serenity in regards to her current situation.

Her disobedience of withholding information resulted in the natural consequences; anxiety attacks and a weak stomach. That alone was a thought that troubled her. It left her with guilt that she hadn’t followed through with her duties. Perhaps now was as good a time as any to explain her distracted mindset.

"I would rather it be discussed in private if it suits you, Sir." Pet whispered softly, closing her own book and placing it in her lap. Her periwinkle eyes glanced across the street in the direction of the darkened walls of their cohabitant building.

"If not, I will speak of it here, Sir." It wasn't like the patio of the café was crowded enough anyway that Pet would have to worry about anyone overhearing them talk. A well-built man had just walked out of the front door, followed by Angel, the young courtesan of the Misfitz Tavern.

She would much rather discuss it openly than disobey Sir again as her eyes looked down at the glass tabletop. Her black dress, a faded gray through the glass beneath was the exact place where her secret rested, silently enjoying the day in its own safe existence.

Sir's gray eyes follow her gaze across the street to their current habitat before turning back to his Pet and then looking up into the sky of daybreak.

"I think we shall take a walk. There is a new dragon residing in our local park and I wish to make myself known to him." Sir folded his newspaper and tucked it under his arm, finishing his bitter espresso before standing and straightening out his black suit.

"You may speak your mind freely along the way," he

informed her, lifting their typical rule that she must ask permission to voice herself. He agreed that whatever was troubling his Pet was a matter that was best discussed in private.

"Thank you, Sir," Pet replied in a low voice before gulping at the change from her norm and standing up with a small smile, "A walk would be nice."

She took Sir's paper from him as usual after their time at the café. As Sir walked toward the park, Pet followed a half-step behind him. She looked at Sir's back in the dark suit, wondering how she was going to approach him before the park came into view. What was typically a beautiful sight of lined trees and playground equipment instead reminded Pet that it was time for her to speak freely while she had the chance. The park was nearing.

"Sir," Pet began, keeping her head down as she spoke, "You remember how we discussed the terms of our contract prior to agreement? We stated that there would be stipulations that came up that wouldn't be covered by any of the clauses."

"Yes of course, Pet. It's a standard part of most contracts that are… of our particular nature. What is your point? Has such a stipulation arisen?" In his mind, there were few things that his Pet could need that he didn't already provide, yet he was always curious to hear when a new one arose.

"And if so, then why am I just now hearing about it?" He stopped, staring ahead at the children already enjoying their Saturday morning on the swings and waited for her reply. Their laughter filled the silence of Pet's thoughts. Laughter that she knew she must soon grow accustomed to.

Pet looked down at her sandaled feet, her toes pedicured with a precision that pleased Sir, thinking of how to present the situation that had arisen. How to approach it with the proper words as to not have to say exactly what it meant out loud and for Sir to still catch on to her phrasing so that she wasn't confronted with an outburst from the man. She didn't think her raw emotions could handle upsetting him right now.

"It has recently come to me, Sir," she answered before sighing as she tried to pull the words forward. To taste what needed to be said, the sweetened nectar of truth that needed to be stated out loud, "I won't be needing my week of relaxation this month."

"Oh?" Sir, not quite understanding turned around to face his Pet, looking at her bluish eyes, her dark hair, and her full cheeks. What she said made no logical sense. How could she not need a break whenever…

Sir looked the woman up and down before noticing the slightest misfit of her top, the softest glow of her skin. He instantly understood her meaning.

"Ahhh. I understand now, my Pet. You are correct that this was not covered under our original agreement. Considering recent events, it also raises other concerns as well. Hmmm…"

Sir thought to himself on how to handle such a delicate situation before clearing his throat. Turning back around, the man continued towards the park, slowing his pace as to give them a chance to discuss the recent news in more detail. "What an interesting turn of events, my Pet. How are you feeling about the current situation?"

"I am a little unsettled, Sir," Pet answered honestly in a whisper, her voice low, "Though the news has carried less than comforting information of late, I trust you Sir. There is serenity with you."

"Then you both shall remain with me if it's to your liking. We will adjust your training sessions accordingly to your status. This isn't the first time this has happened in arrangements such as ours, Pet. I'm sure with a little research we will all be fine. How soon? We will need to attach a nursery to your room. Also, possibly consider hiring a nanny, but we will see what happens."

Stopping once more, Sir turned back to his Pet and lifted her chin. Bending the one rule he could, raised her gaze to his own. He stared deep into her eyes, meeting her soul. "You are my Pet and it is my job to take care of you. In any fashion required. This is no different, so don't fret so. It's... unbecoming."

The tension in his jaw eased as he smiled. The warm smile reserved only for his Pet, it covered his cheeks as warmth filled his eyes with the surprising news. He was going to be a father.

Pet smiled back, her dimples shined as a weight eased from her shoulders. Never had she felt more appreciative of the collar she bared and everything it symbolized. She looked back down as a blush filled her cheeks as warm as the sunlight itself.

"Thank you, Sir." She used every ounce of the self-control he had taught her not to wrap her arms tightly around the man before her. "And I'm not yet certain. I just found out the news myself yesterday. My apologies for the delay in informing you."

He chuckled, another occurrence that was few and far between, before saying, "It is of no consequence. I find this news... pleasing. Perhaps you will be my final Pet after all. Hmm..." He turned and started walking towards the park once more. Butterflies filled Pet's stomach with a soft flutter at Sir's thoughts out loud. She had surprisingly pleased him with such news. She smiled down at her still flat stomach, placing a hand where she knew their child rested silently, safe from the world.

As silence swept over their morning once more, Sir allowed his mind to wander. As they passed the outside of the many frivolous shops and stores he couldn't help but wonder whether Pet's obedience was still what it had originally been. Though she had grown accustomed to their agreement over the years, slowly becoming more and more obedient and willing to please, he couldn't help but wonder if she too was getting satisfaction out of their contract.

As they approached the black cast iron gates, Sir eyed the park's many waterfalls, ponds, and statues and thought of his Pet's love for nature's beauty. He couldn't allow his mind to linger on it any longer. "Are you still pleased with our current arrangement, my Pet?"

"Very much, Sir," Pet answered quickly, "You take care of me. You provide me with the calm serenity that I need to keep me from lashing out unto others and… and what I was…"

She looked up, willing to accept any consequences that went with her eyes meeting his, staring into them with the anticipation of the lashings it would result in. She could only hope with the present situation, she would remain suitable for the discipline she so desired instead of being looked at with a cautious touch, as if she were as fragile as the vases that lined Sir's mantle. "All of it Sir… making you happy makes me happy."

"I have a few possible amendments I'd like to submit for review in our current contract. One of them I want an answer on before we move any further." He turned to glance inside the park once more, spotting the black and blue dragon lying on a large pile of gold next to a waterfall. "What I want to know is whether you understand that this will bind us more tightly than ever before. Are you prepared for this? You must obey me without question."

He watched her stance before him, not noticing the slightest hesitation. He added quietly, "The coming times will be trying and we cannot afford any… hesitation."

"Understood, Sir!" her response was quick and timely so it would be pleasing to her master, "How... what do you mean by more tightly binding, Sir?"

Her behavior had been lacking lately and needed improvement she agreed, but how much tighter could her collar bind her to him before it choked?

"That, my Pet, is the question. I don't know. Though I stand by my agreement, and understand that you fully trust in me, I will never deliberately lead you astray or put you in harm's way. Do you agree? This must be a choice made willingly as I cannot command you to do it."

CHAPTER THREE

CAN YOU AIM?

A group of ogres sat at an elevated table, each drinking merrily as they discussed the latest battle they had endured. Round, fattened faces spilled booze between over-sized teeth as deep country accents and camouflage pants illusioned them against the locals.

A young woman sat at the bar and chuckled to herself at their boisterous behavior as they spoke of blood-shed and pat one another on the back until the walls rumbled with their glorious victory.

"So big and bad," Sage mocked as she rolled her mossy eyes before downing a shot of thick, heavy whiskey. "Let's all just pull out our cocks and compare sizes."

Cole eyeballed Sage up and down, noticing his younger cousin for the first time since puberty had taken its toll on her now beautiful body. Though a snarl covered her face, it was a playful snarl that was only highlighted by her red hair and sparkling nose ring. The young girl's tattered jeans gave a view of her right butt cheek. A small tattoo peeked out, unrecognizable yet visible none-the-less. Her black bra beneath the white shirt teased any man who dared to sneak a look twice.

"I know snakes that don't have as much bite as she does," he laughed, nudging a blue-skinned man who failed to provide

Sage with the attention she craved. The blue man's eyes fell on the bartender.

Sage turned her attention away from the drunken group of ogres. "You couldn't handle this," she answered, smacking her glossy pink lips. She ran her manicured fingers down the length of the long neck she was using as a chaser.

"Oh I'm sure you could teach me, hot stuff," Cole chimed, allowing the spikes in his gelled hair to turn a bright red with lust. He found himself enticed by a woman not normally his type. She was just so… sassy.

Looking Cole over, her hand finding his knee. "I don't think you could handle this," she said with a pitied sigh as she reached up, rubbing his already hardened member through his designer jeans.

"Besides, what's in it for me?" she added, raising an eyebrow.

"What exactly is it that you want? Do you even know?" Cole replied, truly curious. She might put on a big show, but he had the feeling there was more to Sage than met the eye. As if she hadn't had enough trouble in her life that she needed to make more.

"What?" Sage sassed before rolling her eyes. "I know exactly what I want. I just don't know if it's something you have to offer. A hard cock. One that will leave me falling into an exhausted sleep and hopefully waking up to a morning that most women would regret. If I could get a double, barkeep, that would be great!" she added, yelling to Legs with a drunken cat-call of a whistle.

The bartender hid her urge to growl in disgust, instead merely walking over and serving the young girl.

"Well if that's what you really want I'm sure I can make you regret tonight in the morning. And yet, for some reason I'm doubting that's all, isn't it? Tell me what else it is you want. Money? Glory? A good buzz that won't bring you down for days? I've done it all and am prepared to do it again because, if you haven't realized yet, I have no shame. It's both a blessing and a curse as I'm sure you already know." Cole nodded, knowing that they had more in common than she thought.

Sage looked at her cousin strangely, as if she were seeing him for the first time. She stared into his brown eyes, checking his whitened smile for any chance there might be the slightest lip quiver of doubt. His firm chest, hidden beneath the tight-fitting shirt begged for her hands to trail down it. His goatee begged to tickle her navel. "You have my attention," she answered with an evil grin. "Continue and, please, don't leave out any details."

"Shame is a thing for other people. People who care what others think of them. I've learned that life is too short for regrets, for shame. I live my life to the fullest every moment of every day. I drink, eat, smoke, snort, and fuck whatever I desire because if I die tomorrow, I want to make sure I didn't miss anything."

"I want power!" Sage's request was devious. "And if I want it, it's mine!"

Cole's eyes lit up with excitement. "Why should we not take what we want? We deserve satisfaction the same as everyone else does. More so because we're not idiots and we realize the world is up for the taking if only people would reach out and grab it. We are those people. I do what I want when I want and no one is going to stop me. I'd rather die sinning than live forever as a saint. What about you? Are you willing to take what you want?"

Sage covered his mouth in hers, spinning the barstool around as she climbed into her cousin's lap.

***

Worvacs moved to one of the wooden tables to clean his weapons. He buffed his armor to a polished shine, doing his best to ignore the session of breeding between Cole and Sage. Worvacs had too much on his plate to concern himself with whatever trouble Maxx's daughter was causing. It was an issue he would rather not be a part of.

Wiping with a circular motion, he buffed out his last teleport to Caly. He cringed at the soft ache that Earth's gravity put on his right shoulder blade from the exosaurius that had come charging at him during his last hunt. He rotated the painful joint with caution before forfeiting on the polish job. Instead, with another drink of his frosted mug, the blue-skinned humanoid counted his bullets and probes. That couldn't be right. Frowning, he recounted them in hopes to get a different number.

"Will, let me borrow your gun," Legs whispered, reaching past her boss to the tequila behind the bar.

"What?" Will asked, slightly taken aback by the question as he looked at her. "Why?"

The woman smiled, her green eyes glittering in the light as she looked from Will to the cobalt blue man at a table along the far wall of the bar alone. A handful of plasma rifles, grenades, and armor plates lined the table.

"Please?" she begged, putting her hands together with her most pleading face. She batted her eyelashes for added effect. The girl had lived in the Pub long before becoming an employee. Untouchable and uncharmable by most men, Will knew Legs only had a weak spot for the weapons. Bright, shiny, with a loud bang, and no safety. "I'll work a double?" she offered.

His friend at the table was just as awkward around women as Legs was, to the best of his knowledge, uninterested in men. At the very least, it would add amusement to his already dull night. "Double shift," Will answered with a smirk, "and I get my gun back. You're off for tonight."

"Thank you! Thank you! Thank you!" Legs exclaimed with excitement, hugging him quickly before she realized the awkwardness of her arms around the blonde bachelor, she pulled away. "I mean… ummm—"

"Go," Will told her with a smile, shooing her away with his

hand, "Have fun."

Legs looked over the mostly empty room, straightening her hair as she tried to appear casual before walking over to Worvacs.

"May I?" she looked down at the shiny, golden rifle. She placed Will's Glock on the table as to not leave the man without a weapon. "Full magazine. Safety on," she informed him.

Worvacs glanced down at the pistol on the table, recognizing it immediately. He kept his cool, smiling internally as he looked at his friend's gun and then back at Legs before nodding. He could trust her. "Any lady that knows how to handle a plasma rifle in this realm has my respect enough to look at mine. Maybe even fire off a couple of rounds."

"Oh I have a round or two I wouldn't mind firing off," Legs answered, holding the rifle as though it were natural. She eyed down the scope, the red cross-hairs landing on the caramel-colored Tatianna at the far end of the tavern. There was a bitterness held towards the woman wearing a leather jacket that Legs' couldn't explain. She simply didn't like her.

"At what distance can this make an accurate head shot? I have a few… pests I need to get rid of," Legs smiled, knowing she was loud enough to be heard.

"Will, we're headed downstairs!" Legs' bluntness didn't leave Worvacs space to argue what he had already agreed to. Will simply nodded his head, holding up a single thumb.

Worvacs watched her glide across the bar room. She was beautiful to him. Her straight hair pulled back in a tight ponytail, angelic green eyes that could only compare to the rich emeralds he pulled from the soils of Ark. Her smile reminded him of ancient goddesses from foreign realms. A black pencil skirt hugged tightly to the woman's hips, revealing at the knee what earned her namesake. Fit legs that went on forever with curves in all the right places. Worvacs shrugged, dropping everything back in his inventory and followed Legs down the stairs.

"I know what you mean by pests. We all have them." Worvacs thought back to Christopher upstairs who he'd have been more than happy to make a bloody smear on the tavern wall. But he was a guest in Will's place and everyone knew just how easily that could be revoked, or worse… "A pistol lady, are ya'? I have found joy in some of the pistols myself and not including just my own."

Legs shrugged as she closed the door behind them that exposed the tavern.

"I prefer rifles," she said honestly, simply thankful to be in company of someone who understood her love and respect for the weapons. "Something with a scope and distance. A little more familiar in my hands. Will has this strange 'end of the world' theory though. He's become obsessed with it and insists that pistols are more discrete and less messy. I can't argue it really. Just takes some getting used to, having added weight next to my leg," she spoke the words before realizing they may carry a secondary meaning.

Legs fought back a blush at the possible sexual reference to a man who she couldn't deny, even with blue skin, had hazel eyes that melted her heart and a smile that sent butterflies soaring through her. "I like a .45's weight and precise aim. The way it fits perfectly in your hands." *I can't win for losing!* She shook her head that pistols weren't what was on her mind, or were they?

Worvacs chuckled. He watched as her hips swayed casually down the stairs. Her hair trailed a back he figured he would never have the pleasures of seeing bare. "Longer and heavier is better, eh? I'm sure I've heard that a time or two before."

He followed Legs down the steps before they passed a room full of weapons, locked with a small box beside the door that required retinal screening. Coded with a pin number was the door to the tavern's teleport.

The room made of glass was see-through. Worvacs watched

as a creature from some unknown realm climbed into the teleport chamber. Looking up at the touch screen with the single eye that protruded from her stomach, the heavy bronze door of the chamber closed behind her.

Worvacs knew Will was making thousands off the tavern's teleport. He too had used it occasionally when his own was on the fritz. If you needed discrete travel with a light load, it was often provided to any of the 752 local realms for 20 gold.

Legs paid the teleport no mind as she continued on past rooms filled with plants and technology that Worvacs had never seen before. Once they reached the end of the hallway, Legs flicked on the light with comfortable ease.

Fluorescent bulbs flickered before shining brightly down on the white walls. Nearly long enough to be a hallway, targets sat along the far end in aisles separated by waist-high counters that held safety goggles and ear plugs. Worvacs nodded his head in approval that a range he hadn't seen in months was still in good, working order.

"Have you ever handled a plasma rifle this damaging before?" he asked not realizing until afterwards his own innuendo. *Fight the blush Worvacs,* he demanded of himself not wanting to ruin the moment with a purple tinge filling his cheeks.

"Never," Legs answered, putting on her safety glasses as she looked Worvacs over once more. She tried not to stare at the bulge in his pants that was intimidating to say the least. "I'm assuming since you ask, it's going to leave me with a few bruises. I mean," she furrowed her brow, trying to regain herself. "Show me." Her mind scolded her silently, *Really? What are you trying to do with him, Chara? Shoot or shag?*

Worvacs raised an eyebrow, hesitating just long enough to see her own eyebrows rise as she wondered to which he was going to show her. He finally decided to take the rifle from her, placing it against his own muscular shoulder.

"The kick on this one is a bitch but the rapid fire is a perk." He lined up his shot on the target at the far end of the range and squeezed the trigger, feeling the kick of the powerful gun against his shoulder along with a loud ring. The target had a very precise pen sized hole in it... and so did the wall behind it that ended with a black spot on the bedrock.

"Hopefully Will won't mind the damage too much," he chuckled, handing the rifle back to her, "You sure you're up to handling my weapon?"

"Try me," she answered with a devious grin, excited at the thought of finally having access to such a dangerous firearm. It was enthralling, the thought of being in control of that much power. Of knowing such a delicate movement such as a squeeze of the trigger would leave a hole like that. Legs bit her lip against the flurries that were now traveling from her belly to her core. Taking the rifle from him, she stood in a position where she knew she couldn't hit the broad side of a barn.

Legs focused in on her sights. Looking behind her, she shook her ass a few times casually in hopes he would step up to correct her stance. She looked through the scope, "Check out that hole. How?"

"I could ask you the same question!" he answered in shocked disbelief, "How do you ever hit anything?" Worvacs stepped up behind her and placed his hands on her hips straightening her stance. He wrapped his left arm around her waist, stepping up behind her so their bodies aligned, his firm chest pressing against Legs' back. The butterflies descended lower. Worvacs raised his other hand as he lined the butt of the rifle firmly in her shoulder cup and then whispered into her ear, "Are you ready to feel the power of a real weapon?"

Legs couldn't help the gasp of breath that escaped her at Worvacs' words. Her knees weakened as she closed her eyes, refocusing her thoughts. "Honey, I was born ready," she answered with determination, "Let's see how it handles."

CHAPTER FOUR

ANGEL'S EXPLOSION

The following evening, Will stood behind the bar with Christopher, Worvacs, Cole, Sir, and Maxx all sitting on the other side. "How about a drink after a hard day, boys?" Cheers and catcalls rose in the bar, filling the empty void that had loomed over the tavern's walls.

Legs laughed at Will's comment, quickly jumping over the bar to join him in serving. "A round on the house!" she yelled, pouring the regulars their preferred drinks.

***

Worvacs swallowed half his mug of ale in one gulp. He let out a long sigh and then a belch of satisfaction, "Now, this is the way it's supposed to be!" He unslung his rifle from his back and set it on the empty barstool next to him, patting it gently like his sweetheart. It had been a bad run and he understood the rifle's frustrations. Legs watched, causing him to smile sheepishly, "Well sometimes it has a mind of its own. Doesn't always work out well, but it is what it is."

"Well, with a mind of its own," Legs replied as she poured another drink, placing the other in front of his rifle. "Are you sure it wasn't shooting blanks?" She smiled deviously as she leaned across the bar.

Worvacs grinned and, unable to control it, laughed heartily causing his cobalt body to shake. "Blanks indeed love, blanks indeed. If you don't ever find anything worth shooting. Me however... I think I've found something worth shooting for." He winked at Legs before flipping an ark coin in the air. He allowed it to fall to the bar top and watched as it spun.

Legs smiled back, pouring the man another. "There's always something worth shooting," she whispered to him. She handed him the frosted glass, using her fingers as a pistol before pointing it towards Christopher discretely. "And something to shoot for." She added with a slightly devious smirk.

Worvacs raised his glass in toast. He pulled out a new pistol. Flipping it around, he slid the butt across to Legs. "Picked this up for you today. Saw it in the auction house on Caly and thought you might like it. Low ammo burn for high damage." Winking, he took another drink. "Want to go test it out?"

"I don't know if I can get away with how busy we are." Legs looked back at Will for permission. Her words seemed to fall on deaf ears.

Will downed another drink and looked around the bar. Most of the evening crowd had thinned out. Now, only the occasional goblin or dwarf sat by themselves or in dark corners making deals.

He was confident he could handle the workload. He slowly turned toward her and nodded his head. "Go on, go have fun. I'll have Kritter clean up in the morning. But if you leave a mess like last time I'm pulling the time it takes Kritter to clean up the shells and, everything else, out of your tips." He smiled as he watched her snatch her new pistol from beneath the bar. Grabbing Worvacs by the hand, she pulled him down the steps toward the range.

***

"Sir, may have mine," Pet whispered softly.

"Are… you sure Pet?" Will asked, raising an eyebrow in confusion at the petite woman who had never turned down a free drink.

"Yes," Pet answered to the bar top, her eyes were glued to the wood grain though her round cheeks held a soft rose color. "Sir can have mine," she repeated a little louder, hoping Will wouldn't question her any further. Instead Will simply obliged Pet's request with a nod.

Sir downed his scotch in one gulp and motioned Will for another one. After it was filled, he began to slowly sip the second glass as if it was much needed. Looking over at his Pet sitting next to him, he let out a rare smirk. "You may have one, Pet." When her eyes went wide with shock, he continued with a wink, "Only because your behavior has been exemplary here of late."

"Thank you, Sir," Pet answered with a nod of appreciation. She glanced up momentarily looking over the bottles. "Amaretto sour," she whispered to Will, avoiding eye contact with him as she spoke.

Sir nodded to Pet as she ordered a drink that he would approve of with her pregnancy. He smiled at how well-behaved she had become after such an intricate training. Looking down the bar, he watched as Tatianna stirred her drink and contemplated how much time and effort would be required to gain her compliance.

He found himself impressed by the woman's iron will. *A challenge,* he thought to himself as he took another sip of his brandy. *An iron will that should… no that wasn't right… That needed to be broken. To put her in her place.* The woman was a darkened beauty, one that could only be compared to a wild stallion. She had a tall, muscular build. Her dark, curly hair surrounded her cocoa face and doe-like eyes. He knew there was a reason why wild horses no longer ran free in the fields of Nebraska. Some things were too strong-willed not to be tamed.

"You remember the moment where I broke you, correct Pet?" he asked, knowing it was loud enough to be overheard by the woman he so desired. When Pet opened her mouth to answer, Sir didn't allow the words to leave her lips before replying, "Good. Describe how it felt when I did so."

"It was a relief, Sir," Pet replied quickly, "Knowing I never again had worries or frets because everything was in my master's control. My master would never let me hurt or go without."

"Must be fucking nice!" Angel shouted back at Pet's response as the tavern door slammed shut. A heated fury entered the tavern with Angel's footsteps, not intimidated by even the coldest of Nebraska winds.

"Will, pour me a strong one. Fucking assholes don't even know what they want, then expect me to work Merlin damned miracles."

Will's pace was too slow for the agitated woman. "Drink William!" she shouted.

She looked at Christopher, the attorney with shaggy hair and a smirk of satisfaction beneath his thick mustache. "Don't even try it tonight," she warned the man who was unfazed by her outburst, causing Tatianna to snicker. "Never had a bitch of my own before, but I'm in that kind of mood."

"Angel's legs are officially closed for the night," Sage mumbled to herself, not wanting to turn the girl's fury on herself but unable to bite back her chance to make such a comment.

Maxx's eyes never left the woman as she walked in with fire and brimstone following in her wake. Her brown eyes held a storm that would result in tragedy. The normally sweet, calm woman who always held a smile now had blood boiling as it ran through her veins, her fists clenched. As she sat down next to him, Maxx tried his best not to be caught eyeing her too closely.

An incredibly sexy, dangerous, and driven woman sent something stirring south of the border for him. He motioned for Will to make her a drink and then tipped his glass to her for a clink of respect. "Hell hath no fury than that of a woman pissed off and on a mission."

"It's just such bullshit!" Angel bit back, still livid as she slammed the empty glass back on the bar, causing Pet to jump at the loud sound it produced. "Another William," she ordered, snapping her fingers as she threw three gold coins on the bar.

"Oh, 'I know you, give me a discount'," she mimicked in disgust, "Or 'but we went to school together' and my personal favorite, 'family discount'. No, I'm building an empire. I don't have time for free romps when there is money to be made."

"No discounts!" she screamed, turning the heads of random ghouls and wizards. "I didn't earn my dragon as a cheap whore and don't expect to charge the same prices for fucking added benefits!" she yelled again, catching the attention of a one-eyed rabbit. Her eyes burned into Christopher's back as she screamed the words, fear and pain from the night before was replaced with fiery rage.

"Angel, are you already drunk?" Pet whispered softly, the woman's hands rested in her lap as she kept her head down. The smell of thick alcohol mixed with heavy perfume already answered the submissive's question.

"No!" Angel snapped, "I had a customer ask to blow an eight ball up my ass last night! Fucking idiot! What part of no powders don't these assholes understand?"

Maxx chuckled at Angel, "I've had days like that. Once a bullet hit my helmet and I swore I was dead for a few days. When I woke up the doctor said I had a concussion and was lucky to be alive. Just remember, it could always be worse."

"That's why I do what I do," Angel answered honestly, straightening her red skin-tight dress as she spoke. She found herself slightly calmed by her regular customer's words of comfort.

He was a customer who not only treated her with respect during their sessions, but outside of them as well. He was also the parent of her best friend, Savannah. His voice eased her outbursts into confessions. "Nights like tonight, I think that's the only reason," she admitted to both Maxx and her glass, "I like being my own boss. It's not about the money." She continued, stirring her straw before downing the next drink.

"William!" she shouted again, pushing her empty glass toward him. "Or the respect, Merlin knows there's not enough of either. Or nights off, for that matter." She chuckled, "But to be able to do what I like, when I like. I like sex. So, I work for it. The sweaty, disrespectful men like him..." she pointed down the bar to Christopher in her drunken slurs, "Because in the end, I'm still in control. It's me. My job. My business."

She sighed before lifting another shot, "To fucked up decisions."

Maxx nodded to Angel, "To fucked up decisions. I'm sure this isn't the first and won't be the last time we have this toast. I agree though on owning your own business. I own my business and my little Savannah helps," he said, holding pride for his youngest girl's good behavior.

Will poured another drink. This one was stronger than any other so far of the evening, including his. Stepping down the bar, he placed the glass in front of Angel with the little crooked smile only a bartender can give. "Bad day?"

"Can say that again," Angel sighed, ready for her night to just be over with. "What would I owe you to keep a drink in front of me at all times?"

Will glanced over Angel's shoulder at Christopher, who quickly looked away to avoid guilt. He had a feeling it had been a long, hard earned paycheck with the attorney the night before. That, followed by his own awakening, caused him to not question her demand.

"Just put it under our tab of 'you owe me one'," Will winked as he pulled two bottles out from underneath the bar and handed one to Maxx and the other to her. "Just try not to tear the place up too bad, okay? There's a nice quiet booth in the corner right over there with your names on it." He nodded his head towards the booth behind the red silken sheet in reference to the man beside her. "Have at it."

Angel looked at Maxx, raising an eyebrow of interest. She turned toward the darkened corner, allowing Maxx to lead the way and waited until his back was turned to grab Will's shirt, quickly whispering the prior night's escapades into Will's ear, alerting him of everything that had occurred.

Will's blue eyes flared as he looked at Christopher across the room and gritted his teeth at the sight of the attorney and Tatianna sharing a drink.

"Just because badges aren't allowed, doesn't mean put yourself in handcuffs," she informed him, concerned at Will's response.

Angel was right. Christopher was a bad man, but sometimes being the bartender of a neutral site had its downsides and killing the man in the tavern wasn't allowed. Even for the owner. Not on Karma's watch.

"Kritter!" Will hollered up the back steps hoping she hadn't gone to sleep yet. She'd come if she was awake, but when that pixie snored the apocalypse could happen and she wouldn't know until breakfast.

"Kritter knows when Master Will's jaw is tense," the pixie answered from behind him instantly, already shaking with concern. "Master Will's jaw should never be tense. Master Will's jaw is tense when Master Will is angry. Kritter doesn't like when Master Will is angry. Kritter is sad when Master Will is sad. Kritter is happy when Master Will is happy. Kritter is scared when Master Will is angry. Bad things happen when Master Will is angry. Please don't be angry, Master Will." Kritter shuddered while breathing heavily, her eyes wide with fear.

Will looked back at Christopher. Disgusted with the man and what he had done to Angel, his own blood boiled as he now understood the rage Angel had entered with. If he was going to obey the laws of the tavern, he couldn't be anywhere near the attorney who craved chaos. "I'm going to do inventory," Will told Kritter through gritted teeth, "You're in charge."

***

Maxx sat at the booth and raised an eyebrow at Angel's delay, but decided not to mention it. "It happens sometimes, no?" he nodded towards Christopher. "Still you can choose your customers, but not their desires."

"Isn't that the truth," Angel sighed, looking back at Christopher with disgust, "But then things go south. There is not enough money in all the realms for men like…" She shuddered in remembrance. "Like him. The sun will rise again, Mister Conner, but I'm sure that's not why you seek my company." She smiled, making it obvious as she uncrossed her legs before crossing them again to catch his attention. "Though technically, I'm off the clock. Thank you."

A sincere smile of appreciation crossed her face and she rested her hand high on his thigh. "It helped. You didn't have to."

CHAPTER FIVE

HOPE AMONGST THE RUBBLE

The Quad's dual generators hummed outside as Worvacs' reminder that he would soon be leaving Earth and returning to his own realm with hopes of bringing back rare leathers and ores. His time on this planet was limited only by the currencies that lined his pockets. And with more frequent visits to the Misfitz Tavern, he found his pockets lighter and his trips to Caly more frequent.

Today, like so many before, he sat at the bar and admired Legs. He watched as she effortlessly maneuvered around the bar, grabbing drinks with a knowing ease as if she were just an extension of the tavern itself.

"The way you move darling, is nothing short of a gift from the gods," he admired after a few moments.

"I'm going to take that as a compliment," Legs answered with a bartender's smile, passing a drink to a long-eared elf. "But in all honesty, I have to give the heels half the credit," she added with a wink.

"It was meant as one darling. I've met a god or two in my time. I may have to ask them whether they had a hand in your making."

Leaning across the bar, Legs bent her finger in a come-hither motion. "I got you something," she whispered softly.

Worvacs' hazel eyes lit up as he downed his drink and then

leaned in as if he were only passing his glass to her. "Oh and what's that? Now you've got me excited," he whispered.

"Got it from across the street," Legs whispered back, watching Will on the other side of the bar to make sure she wasn't overheard about the police station that was getting rid of some of their old supplies. "Don't say anything." She tilted her head in Will's direction. "The two of them don't exactly see eye to eye but... it's enough to keep you warm on a winter's night."

Worvacs looked down the bar to see Will preoccupied in what appeared to be a deep conversation with a yard gnome, paying no mind to what his current bartender was doing. "Fair enough. So what exactly is it?" He was puzzled by her secrecy.

"A plasma pistol with an unbelievable ammo burn," Legs replied with a grin, "Two cans of military grade acid spray, and a diamond shrapnel grenade." She laughed silently as his eyes lit up again. "Thought it might help against, well, anything really. Large mobs, punies—"

"Absolutely!" he exclaimed before looking around and quickly lowering his voice to ensure he didn't attract more attention. "Yes it will. Especially that last one. I've got a tenth-generation warlock that I've been meaning to settle a score with and I think that grenade will come in handy. Thank you, love." He leaned across the bar and planted a seemingly innocent kiss on her tender cheek. "I could use another well-oiled gun for this next run. Think you can get off work long enough to help me out?"

***

Cole threw his darts at the dartboard. He did his best to keep focused, despite the fact that Sage was slithering up and down the wall in front of him with pure seduction in an attempt to make him lose. There was something about the girl that was addicting, making him want more and more of the rebel before him.

Her red hair, the bright green eyeshadow that caused those mossy eyes to stand out even more and that smile… The smile that begged for all the trouble she could find. Cole could only plead to know whether her carpet matched the drapes.

"You know," he laughed, "I would call that cheating, but you'd only admit it was and then keep doing it anyways." He tossed the last dart, nailing the red seven on the outer ring before he cursed under his breath.

Her cousin was cute. Sage couldn't deny that. Faded blue jeans and a t-shirt that fit to his chest; muscles that when flexed were firm and toned; brown hair with colored spikes that he could change on a whim. Yes, Cole had more money than brains and was everything the young rebel sought.

Sage pulled the dart from the board and walked towards him. She made sure her hips shook as she circled Cole. "Yup," she answered with a smile, rubbing her breasts across his back before nibbling on his ear. "Tell me you don't like it," she whispered. The smile swept wide across her face as proof that her flirtations were merely a distraction to win the game.

"My turn!" she giggled with youthful glee, moving behind the yellow and black striped firing line on the wooden bar floor.

Cole shrugged and took a step back. Allowing her to take his place in front of the firing line, he admired the shake of her hips the entire way. Standing behind her, he leaned over her shoulder inhaling the familiar scent of her hair mixed with bar smoke. He gently lifted the red hair against the nape of her neck before blowing softly in her ear and whispering, "Don't miss."

"That's not fair!" Sage bit with fury, as the dart missed the board completely and bounced off the brick wall beside it. "I hate you," she growled with dishonesty lining her throat as her mossy eyes pierced through him.

Cole couldn't help but grin at Sage's outburst, finding a strange comfort in her playful demeanor. He wrapped his arms around her waist and pulled her against his body as he whispered into her ear once more, "No, what's not going to be fair is when we start playing for articles of clothing in a few more drinks and you're standing naked in front of me." He kissed her earlobe and let go of her waist. Stepping up to the firing line he released a dart, and hit the white outer ring of the bullseye.

"Oh darn," she mocked with an artificial pout. "Take 'em off big boy. Show the Misfitz Tavern what you're packing," she teased, laughing as she tugged at his belt buckle.

***

Will stood behind the bar, unsurprised by the Sunday night with only a handful of customers. Cool air entered the tavern as the front door opened. A chill slid down his spine as the crisp air overwhelmed the little warmth the fireplace had to offer. Snapping his fingers, the fire sprang up higher and hotter than before.

Savannah peeked her head in as she slipped through the crack of the door. The teenager made her way towards the bar cautiously. "Where's Daddy?" she whispered to Will, pulling the hood of her jacket down from around her round child-like face. A few random snowflakes that had landed in her blonde pigtails melted from the renewed warmth of the room.

Will's eyes landed on the younger of the two sisters as he poured her a drink and slid it in front of a barstool. "Otherwise occupied for the evening. The entire evening. In other words, you're safe for now."

Savannah looked back at Will hesitantly. She then turned to look at her sister tugging at Cole's belt buckle. Sage's flirtatious behavior eased her mind enough that Savannah took her seat in front of the drink.

She glanced around the tavern. Her baby blue eyes scanned

the area and caught sight of a shortened man with a long nose and white, scraggly beard drinking at a far table, before landing on Christopher back in the corner. She couldn't help but want to visit with her recent friend. One she had been warned he was dangerous, but seemed gentle enough with his actions. He was simply misunderstood.

"Daddy's with Angel, isn't he?" she asked Will, already knowing the answer. "Does Sage know?"

"If she does, she doesn't seem to care." Will nodded his head over to the corner where Sage and Cole were playing darts. He finished his drink as Sage playfully punched her older cousin in the arm.

"Which makes me wonder little one, why you do?" Will leaned forward on the bar.

Savannah's blue eyes held a magic to them. Nothing like the magic of Knowhere, but a more innocent magic; the magic of a child at heart. It was a magic that saw good in everyone.

"It's just weird," Savannah answered softly, looking down at her flower print dress. Before, lunch conversations with her best friend were filled with talk of homework and rumors. Today Savannah had quickly gathered her food and books and rushed to the library to enjoy her lunch in silence rather than listen to giggles about her own father. Her bubbly cheeks went pale at the thought of having to avoid her friend. "I mean, he's my daddy and she's my best friend. I don't know. What if Daddy loves her more than me?" she asked, looking down at her drink sadly.

Will knew Savannah was more behaved of the two sisters, daddy's little girl. His princess. Barely eighteen, she did her best to make sure her grades stayed up and her room remained tidy. Unlike her sister Sage, who Maxx oftentimes had to bail out of jail, Savannah was the apple of her daddy's eye. "Do you honestly think anyone could take your place in your daddy's eyes?"

Will raised his eyebrow at her before taking a sip of his drink.

He let it sit on his tongue before swallowing it. "The bond between a man and his daughter is unbreakable. Bendable maybe, but not breakable." He left young Savannah alone with her thoughts as he walked away to refill a drink for a nimble woman with almond shaped eyes before coming back. "You want him to be happy right?"

"Well yes, of course I do," Savannah answered without hesitation, "But it's Angel! And Daddy is so quick to…"

Her mind drifted to years past. When her father had been in love, and then left by her mother, causing him to become the man he was now; a man who found comforts in the arms of a young mistress. He paid money to feel a lust that Savannah knew was only a mild replacement of his love lost.

"He has a weak spot for young women. Angel has an eye for money. What if my best friend hurts him? Where do I stand?" She groaned in fear that she would be stuck in a situation where she was forced to choose between them. Even more she feared what would happen to her daddy if they did fall in love, if Angel did leave him. If his heart let things get serious. "You wouldn't understand Will!" she added quickly with a bite that reminded the bartender that the young girl was still merely a teenager. "The tavern is yours, no matter which or how many girls you decide to take to bed. My daddy doesn't have that luxury. He thinks he's invincible, but I know he's not."

Will shook his head before looking up and down the nearly empty bar, checking for refills out of habit. He couldn't help but pity the delusions her young mind had absorbed about her parents' marriage.

"Come with me. There's something I want to show you." The bachelor with blond hair and a muscular build dipped under the staircase behind the bar. "Kritter, you're in charge."

It didn't take but a moment for the tiny woman, only half the height of Savannah with a button nose to peek her head out from the stairwell between the bar and kitchen. Her sparkling purple eyes went wide as a smile crept across her face. "Master Will is leaving Kritter in charge? Master Will trusts Kritter with the bar too? Kritter will not let Master Will down. Kritter will do everything Kritter must to make sure that Master Will is satisfied. Kritter will clean the kitchen and Kritter will clean the tables, and Kritter will—" The pixie rambled with quick excitement, her words circling around Will with chaos as he closed his eyes.

"Just... watch the bar Kritter," he answered, clenching his eyes shut, "That's all I ask."

"But Kritter wants to make sure that Master Will is pleased. It is Kritter's job. Kritter is to make sure Master Will is happy and Master Will—" The woman continued, wiping her tiny hands off on her apron.

"I have asked you to stop calling me that," Will groaned, rubbing his face in defeat. And yet she would continue with a term that disgustingly reminded him of Sir and Pet's relationship. He looked at the mint-skinned pixie with over-sized ears. Her petite figure was likely attractive to those of her own sorts but with her purple eyes, and her orange wings close to her side. *No, just... no,* Will reminded himself, *Kritter needed to stay away from Pet in her off time. Far away.*

Kritter stood at the bar with her hands on the bar top, her button nose held high to the ceiling with a sense of pride that Master Will had trusted her with such a task. "Come on," he insisted, leading Savannah towards his office.

He opened the door with purple stained glass and led her inside. Walking over to the shelves that lined the back wall, Will pulled down a picture frame, handing it to Savannah. "That's all of us after the last time the gates of hell broke loose in my tavern. Literally. Demons were running around, imps hanging from the ceiling, succubus and incubus as far as the eye could see."

"Those things aren't real," Savannah answered back matter-of-factually.

Will looked down at the photo, pointing out the man who shared Savannah's DNA. It was obvious where she had gotten her rounded cheeks and button nose in the faded photo. "Here is your dad. What do you see?"

Savannah shrugged before taking a closer look at the picture. "I've seen that look somewhere before..." she mumbled in thought as she pulled it close. She tried to place the facial expression that she had seen somewhere so many times. *Where though?* She turned around, glancing out the one-way, see-through wall. Her eyes fell on Sage's pursed lips and furrowed brow when a gasp escaped her.

"Determination," she answered, "That's the 'You're not going to stop me' look but... why?"

Her eyes roamed the framed photo that had never been shown to her. Over the years her parents had shown her old scrapbooks, photo albums, and polaroid pictures. This photo wasn't among them. She looked at a younger version of her parents, Will, Cole, Sir, and Christopher standing in front of a large pile of rock rubble where the bar top now stood. Her finger traced across the smile her parents held for one another, her young father's arm wrapped around her very pregnant mother with love.

Savannah eyed the familiar long hair she had seen in pictures of her mother until her sister was born. *Sage,* she thought to herself, *She would have been pregnant with Sage at this time.* A younger Sir wore a dark collar and kept his head down. Her older cousin, still a mere toddler with blue hair, hid behind her father's leg in a beaten and tattered leather jacket. Christopher held a snarl of disgust towards the splintered wood and falling pillars, and a laugh covered Will's face as he held up a broken beer bottle in toast.

"Did you guys rebuild the tavern yourselves?" she asked the owner of the once destroyed tavern.

"Partially. The power that created this place did the rest. This is an old building filled with old magic. Your father helped keep this place from really going to the dogs." Will gently took the picture from her hands and placed it back on the shelf. "I don't think you need to worry too much about Angel hurting him. He can take care of himself."

Wondering just how much of the man's strength had been transferred to his daughter, Will led her towards the front of his office and sat behind his desk. He motioned to the seat across from him and hoped his old friend was right. That Savannah possessed the gifts Maxx claimed.

"You, on the other hand, may have a bigger problem. With the world you know about now," Will twirled his finger in the air as he spoke, "You have a higher chance of falling in a bad way now that you're allowed in the tavern. It's easy to befriend the wrong people if you don't know what you're doing in this world. So, I have a proposition for you—"

"I already know what you're going to say," she groaned, "You want me to stay away from Christopher because he's bad. Daddy already told me. He doesn't seem very bad though. In fact, what he does is very nice. Daddy put you up to whatever this proposition is so I will leave Christopher alone, didn't he?" she questioned, feeling her first spark of rebellion.

Will chuckled at the innocent girl's outburst. "Actually he didn't, but I'm not surprised he told you that. I'm surprised he waited this long." Will dreaded the thought of parenting, but he had to wonder what made Maxx think he could go this long without telling Savannah the dangers of the world in a town that was surrounded by the Misfitz Tavern's spell. Demons, bogies, and more walked the streets. With her being an adult and not knowing the true nature of Knowhere, that meant dangerous manipulations around every corner. "That spark that you have... You get that from your father. That's actually why I want to hire you." Will leaned back in his chair smiling as he laced his fingers across his stomach, loving the look of shock that covered

Savannah's face with his proposition.

"You... you want to what?" Savannah's eyes were wide with shock. "But, what can I do?"

"Your age is a problem, no doubt. You would be with at least one employee at all times, or with your father. I trust him enough that he won't have too many free drinks." Memories of Will catching Maxx getting himself free drinks in their younger days caused him to smile momentarily. Shaking away the distant memory, he looked back at Savannah.

"The jobs you learn are completely up to you." He opened his desk drawer and looked at his schedule. "My first suggestion would be Legs. She's quick, efficient, and deadly. Angel can teach you etiquette, and you could learn a thing or two from Worvacs about armor and weapons. Fawn is good at hunting and mining and Cole or Sir can train you in manipulation and interrogation."

"Wait!" Savannah interrupted in shock, "Armor? Weapons? Interrogation? I thought this was a tavern? An Inn?" She raised an eyebrow. "Will, what aren't you telling me? What's going to happen?"

Will frowned at how quickly she caught on. Maybe Maxx was right about her having a gift but there were still some things he feared Savannah's fragile mind couldn't handle yet. He sighed and leaned forward across the desk. "The downside is now that you know about all of this," he twirled his finger once more, "So you won't be hidden from it anymore. Now all the big bad monsters can see you too."

Savannah was confused beyond belief but a few of the words Will said made sense. She had enough to piece it together.

"I'm going to take a wild guess here," she used the problem-solving techniques she'd studied in math class, leaning forward and crossing her fingers as she put her small hands on Will's desk. "You are talking about something most people in this town don't know about. I'm also going to assume that since you haven't mentioned Christopher or Tatianna having job titles, it's something dark. Something I probably shouldn't know about. Since you mentioned this," she spun her finger in the air, "Handcuffs and a badge probably aren't going to help with whatever 'they' are."

Will nodded. He was impressed. "You are quick. Definitely get that from your dad. There is magic in Knowhere. Not everything here is as it seems and it's not just here in this little town. It's anywhere you go. There are beings out there, both good and bad. The kind your daddy read to you about in your fairy tales. Dragons, witches, aliens, fae, and more; they are all real. Now you will be able to see it. Everyone who learns about the magic of the world can see it. They can no longer ignore it."

Will looked over at a map tacked to his office wall with push pins all through it. Holes in cities over numerous states that marked spottings, catastrophes. He knew it was just a matter of time before something happened. Something big.

"Think of it this way. You know the short man who works as a crossing guard for the school here in town? He isn't just a midget. He's a gnome. He appears to you as a midget because the power of the tavern protects him. It protects all of Knowhere and allows those with magic to walk among everyone else. It allows them to appear human like you and me as a part of Karma's law that judgment can't be passed. The spell of the tavern makes Knowhere safe for magical beings until you learn about this world. Our world within this world. Once you learn about the spell, you can't go back. Some people don't know about the magic, they are protected for lack of a better term. It has always been there. You just never saw it before this. Now, you do. You have no choice."

"So, if I see the beings, but can't do anything about it because I don't know magic myself, I'm defenseless. I suppose that means I have to take the job now. If I don't, I will spend years in a no-magic padded room while I try to convince the doctors that dragons and faeries are real." With a smile, she added, "I'll take the job, a job. Some job. I'm not really sure at this point."

Savannah scrunched her button nose with a giggle, still slightly confused. Her brain hurt from trying to piece together the puzzle with extra pieces.

"Good," Will answered, picking up a pen. He wrote Savannah's name into the schedule with red ink. "You start tomorrow."

Savannah stood up and looked out of the one-way see-through wall in thought. Blinking her eyes a few times, she rubbed them in shock as she watched Legs walk across the bar. The bartender pulled out a bottle, pouring a drink for the gray skinned being before her. On its circular head sat two upright ears, pointing to the ceiling like antennas.

The shadow-like being reached with its fingerless hand, taking the frosted mug before it turned to face Savannah behind the door. It's bright blue eyes stared ahead without pupils or eyelids.

Sage and Cole had left during Savannah and Will's conversation. The tavern was instead filled with unfamiliar faces. At a side table, a set of larger men made of granite laughed amongst themselves. Beer fell between the cracks of their chiseled lips.

"Is it like this?" Savannah asked as she watched a pair of pointed-eared elves take their shots. An old wizard dressed in starry robes moved towards the bar. "Everywhere now? Or is it... more?"

"It's like this. In Knowhere, it's always been like this," Will answered as he hoped his words comforted the girl.

"I'll see you tomorrow then," Savannah answered quickly, turning back to him, "After school."

Will slid a handbook with crisp and pristine pages across the desk. Savannah ran her fingers across the leather-bound cover. *The Misfitz Tavern Employee Handbook.*

A smile swept across her face. She held the book close to her chest, the words beneath its cover sacred.

"I will read it tonight," Savannah promised as her eyes lit up with joy for her first real job.

"You better," Will glanced up at her. "You may go," he added before looking back down at his inventory reports.

As Savannah walked out of Will's office, she turned back to the man bent over his paperwork. "Thank you," she whispered softly, keeping the handbook to her chest like the schoolgirl she was.

Once Savannah left his office, Will sighed and walked out of the bar. Deep down, he knew that he'd done the right thing hiring her. It was their best way to teach her the ways of the New World.

Still, he couldn't shake the feeling that, somewhere in the recess of his mind, there had been another reason for hiring the young girl. It wasn't just about her learning the ways of their magical world. It was almost as if something was coming and his mind was trying to get as much help as possible for whatever that may be. Will prayed that whatever it was, the Misfitz could handle it.

CHAPTER SIX

THE PERFECT HAND

Pet wiped her hands off as she stood and smiled with pride at her newly planted bushes. The red leaves contrasted beautifully with the yellows and purples of the surrounding flowers. She hoped Sir would be pleased.

Perhaps he would want to go to the Misfitz Tavern this evening. Even more so, perhaps she could suggest it.

She walked over to the sheeted gazebo that Sir sat under, reading silently to himself. "Sir?"

Holding up a finger, Sir indicated that it was not yet time for her to speak. He turned the page of his book again, his slate grey eyes scanning the page before he dogeared the corner and closed the book, looking up at his Pet.

"Yes Pet, what is it? Have you finished your gardening?" he asked as he looked at her dirt covered hands and feet, a soft speck of dirt on the tip of her nose.

"The newest of the group, Sir," she answered, her head bowed with her braid tangled with dirt and mud. Her mid-day collar, a plain black ribbon, stood out prominently against the pale skin of her neck.

Pet stepped aside and revealed to Sir the red bushes that now lined the rock path to where he sat in the small wooden gazebo. Pet waited with silent anticipation, hopeful that he liked what she had done to the outside of their habitat.

"I can add more if you prefer, Sir," she added quickly when at first he didn't respond.

Sir eyed her work, nodding his head with silent approval before saying, "I wish to have moon lilies around the koi pond next week. See to it, Pet." The woman nodded her head in silent understanding of her master's wishes. "You have done excellent so far in upgrading our wonderful little habitat here in Knowhere."

"Thank you, Sir," Pet answered softly, "Adding moon lilies is an excellent idea, Sir. They would look nice around the pond." She added before biting her lip, "Do we have plans for this evening, Sir?"

Sir's eyes darted from the garden up to Pet. His prominent jaw clenched before relaxing once more. Sliding his legs down from the swing, he walked past her to get a better view of the bushes. "Why do you ask, Pet? Was there something that occupied your mind?" he questioned, curious of her motives as he looked over the plants that nearly reached his waist.

"I was thinking, Sir. Tonight is half-off drinks," Pet answered, looking down at her soiled feet as she whispered the words. "That perhaps it might be nice to go visit the tavern, Sir," she whispered softly.

Sir looked at his Pet thoughtfully. "Drinks being half price is of no importance to me, Pet. You know that. Therefore, you must have some other reason for wanting to go." He cocked his head to the side, a wicked grin suddenly crossing his face. "So the question is, my Pet... What is its worth to you? An extra hour in the playroom tonight? Two?" He raised an eyebrow, trying to gauge just how much his Pet wanted what she was after.

"Whatever you feel its value, Sir," Pet answered, avoiding eye contact as she stood with her back perfectly straight. A chilled breeze ran through the air, a reminder that winter was coming soon. "Perhaps an extra hour in the playroom would do me good, Sir. Or we could use the tape again, if you like, Sir." She glanced up at his red tie quickly before looking back down.

Sir leaned his head back and laughed heartily, his Adam's apple rising and falling. "No Pet, it won't come that easily. I shall determine the cost of your want once we return from the tavern this evening. You shall comply with whatever it is, of course, but I want you to think on what new creative training your master will come up with between now and then. Now, clean up and prepare our lunch. I must take a shower." He walked the stone path back to the door, not making his admiration for Pet's green thumb too apparent.

Just before stepping inside Sir turned and, with a thunderous voice that put Pet into submissive anticipation, said, "Oh and Pet, I expect that your attire shall be your submissive garb for our evening trip to the tavern. Completely submissive." With that, he turned and walked into the house.

"Yes, Sir," Pet answered without hesitation, holding her breath. *Complete submissive garb?* The fire deep in her soul, the need to be controlled, burned hot and wild at the thought of what the night would have in store for her once they returned home later on that evening.

***

Fawn dealt out another hand of cards, ready to face the fate of Lady Luck. “Staying in?” she asked Christopher, raising an eyebrow.

Pet sat at the poker table in a black dress lined with multiple straps down the chest and stomach, knee high tights, and a tight black lace collar around her neck.

A single heart shaped lock sat as the charm on the choker as she performed her duties, counting the cards for Sir and tapping his leg when the numbers are high. Pet tapped Sir’s leg softly, watching Christopher’s face.

When the attorney showed tell-tale signs that she had learned to recognize, she slid her hand across Sir's leg in Christopher's direction. Sir twitched his leg under Pet's touch to signal that he understood, cautious of Christopher's intent to cheat. He was ready for such a distasteful playing of the game and would make sure the attorney paid dearly for it.

Pet squeezed Sir's leg again before clenching her jaw.

Christopher paid no mind to the under-the-table messages before him as he watched Fawn deal the cards, making sure that if she were to stack the deck that it would be in his favor.

"Can I play?" Savannah asked, excited to be able to join the others in the tavern. She bounced up to the table with a smile, "I mean, it's like *Yahtzee*, right?"

Her bubbly face matched her chipper personality as her blonde pigtails swung to and fro. She smiled wide, exposing her white teeth straightened by years of braces as her dimples became obvious on either side of her freckled cheeks.

Christopher looked up from his hand, smiling at Savannah with a grin he used to swoon the younger ladies. "Of course my dear. We always have room for one more. We'll even take it easy on you the first few rounds just so you can get used to the game. Anyone have arguments?" He looked around the table to see no objections and slid out the chair next to him. She was a bit too easy for his taste, but he was beginning to get the itch once more; the urge to make a young girl cry.

Savannah's blue eyes lit up with his words. "Thank you," she exclaimed, sitting down next to him.

Fawn looked to Sir who nodded his head solemnly. Her small hands withdrew the stack of cards on the table, shuffling them where all players could see before dealing them out once again.

Sir's face remained emotionless as he lifted the corner of his two cards, placing them back on the table. He knocked his pale knuckles against the green velvet top, signaling that he checked the bet.

Christopher glanced at his cards before he nodded his head in appreciation at Savannah's eagerness to learn.

"You just ask Uncle Christopher if you have any trouble keeping up with the game, sweetheart. I'll take good care of you." He winked at her, glancing down at her breasts before looking back to his own cards. He had a decent hand so there was no need to cheat yet. If his chip stack dropped too low he might have to but, for the time being, he figured he'd bide his time quietly.

"Thank you," Savannah repeated with an innocent smile before she scrunched her nose at her cards. She slid a pair of twos back, straightening up again at the result of her new cards as Fawn eyed Christopher suspiciously.

Christopher looked at his cards once more before looking up at Fawn with a smile that sent a chill of warning down her spine. The look in his eyes was familiar, that of a predator. Fawn didn't trust him with the young woman.

"For now, give me two." He slid his discards over to her and collected two new ones. Smiling at his stroke of luck with a straight, he nodded to Savannah, "You sure you've got it or do you need some help?"

Savannah jumped from her own seat into Christopher's lap to show him her cards. "This one?" she asked, pointing to a card. He snatched a glimpse of her skirted legs peeking out from under the table and caught his breath before letting out a low whistle.

This would be a piece of cake as long as he didn't break her.

He still couldn't afford to indulge his darkest pleasures in this place. Not in the tavern without some other form of protection.

"This one is the one you want. Toss the rest. We'll fix you right up."

Pet took the moment of distraction to eye the attorney. The man's whistle had caught her attention as she watched him lick his lips beneath his thick mustache.

The woman's periwinkle eyes beaded as she clenched her jaw. Watching the man's rounded cheeks, she waited until he did the same. Lifting her arm from under the table, Pet allowed a slight jingle of her charm that warned Sir to fold.

"I fold," Sir growled in disgust with a snarl of his nose. Leaning back, he groaned in frustration. "Pet, go to the bar and ask Kritter for a refill please. I must loosen up if I am to change this rotten luck of mine."

He knew Pet understood his ruse. It was only to loosen up the other players and get them to spend more of their hard earned money. "Would anyone else like anything?"

"Well, what do these mean?" Savannah leaned back against Christopher's rounded stomach to show the man her cards. The smell of cotton candy filled Christopher's nose. She pointed at two jacks amongst the numbers before looking up to Pet. "Vodka and lemonade please," she added with a smile.

Christopher feigned an interest in her cards while sneaking looks down her blouse. "You've got me beat," he lied as he threw back his straight hoping that such a loss would earn him sympathy and make it that much easier to wiggle in, as it were. Had to make the dolls feel special before he stripped off all their clothes and made their legs spread in ways they weren't supposed too.

Sir nodded to Pet in indication that she should get the young girl her request.

"Might as well give it to her. Deal out the next hand, Miss Fawn. If you don't mind, I prefer with something worth playing?" Sir asked as politely as he could, enjoying the lesser of two evils with her instead of Christopher.

Fawn obliged with a nod and a smile, shuffling the cards. "You… you mean I won?" Savannah asked excitedly, "I like this game." She squirmed, wrapping her arms around the brute's neck, hugging him tightly and causing Tatianna's doe-like eyes to dart to the teeny-bopper.

Feeling glares staring into him, Christopher caught Fawn's glances and then looked over at Tatianna. She was eyeballing him as well.

Grinning wickedly at both, he moved his hand behind Savannah's back where she couldn't see him twirl his finger around the room for the other two women to see; the universal sign in the tavern. No judgments, neutral ground.

Fawn let out a huff, dealing the next hand as Christopher slid his hand down Savannah's back. He figured Karma didn't mind a simple ass grab.

Sir eyed his new cards thoughtfully. He could stay and play it, but he knew that Pet would be disappointed that he continued without her. His poor Pet always feigned for his attention, needing his desire, and this time, she had earned it.

He looked over at her huddled before the bar while Kritter filled their drinks. "An extra lashing tonight, my Pet, for the delay," he called out across the bar.

"My apologies, Sir," Pet answered quickly, her periwinkle eyes went wide as Kritter fretted, nearly spilling the drinks as she slid them across the oak wood.

In a rush, Pet placed a glass in front of Savannah, meeting eyes with Tatianna momentarily before placing Sir's drink down as well. "May I sit, Sir?" she asked, holding her head down with her hands behind her back.

"You may kneel until I state otherwise. Your tardiness has offended me, my Pet. Should it happen again, it shall result in double lashings this evening. Understood?" Sir was more than happy to give double lashings and knew his Pet would be more than happy to receive them, but it was all for show. He would lash her yes, as he did every night, but she would have to earn the extra's that she loved so much.

"Yes, Sir," Pet answered quickly, dropping to her knees in shame of what she had done.

Tatianna's attention turned back to Christopher at the jingle of Pet's collar when she dropped to her knees. Sir and Pet had motives, motives that didn't include her roommate coming out ahead.

Standing up, Tatianna walked behind Christopher and placed her hand on his shoulder. A smile covered the woman's face, surrounded by thick curly hair, as her leather jacket sleeve slid across Savannah's shoulder. "Keep these three, get rid of those and," she leaned in to the girl's ear, "Pray for a king."

She turned, looking to Christopher. "May I speak with you a moment? You can return to your training in poker and I'm sure Miss Card Shark won't mind. Your lap will be more comfortable than any wooden chair." She smiled a warm smile, artificial in the fact that she had no concern for Christopher's own plans and goals.

Christopher let out a growl, tapping the girl's bottom.

"Up for a moment love. I'll be back."

Walking behind Tatianna, he waited until they were beyond earshot before asking, "What? Just because you're my cover doesn't mean you can dictate actions to me." The chub in his cheeks grew red with fury as his grey eyes flashed a dangerous warning.

"I am your cover therefore I am saving your ass," Tatianna bit back in a low whisper, her brown eyes glaring at him. "Unless you want to lose every dime you've made over the last three hours at that table and that young piece of ass you were groping because she thinks you're an idiot!" She looked down, rubbing her eyes in annoyance before she let out a sigh to clear her mind.

"This isn't about me earning back what I lost. This is about you. The Pet is a puppet. It reads back to its master every twitch of your nose, every sigh she can pick up on and every nervous glance. I've seen it before with card sharks and when she flicked her hair, it rang that collar. He folded. It wouldn't surprise me if she was counting cards too. To top that off, when she got Savannah's drink, she saw her hand. She was tapping on his leg.

Why do you think he demanded her return?"

Christopher silently cursed himself for having been so easily distracted by a young piece of ass. He turned, looking back to the table as he watched the petite woman of submission kneeling before her master. As she knelt before the man her dress covered her sandaled feet. Her bowed head left the single braid trailing down her spine. Her hands rested on her knees in defined obedience. Such behavior both enticed and disgusted him as he ran his hand through his slicked back hair in thought.

Christopher straightened his pin-stripe suit, resuming his professional appearance as his suit coat fit snug to his rounded stomach. His sandy blonde mustache twitched in thought, knowing Tatianna was right. *Time for a change in strategy.*

Nodding his honest appreciation of her, he smiled and tapped his plump finger to his temple before turning and walking back to the table. Upon sitting back down, Savannah immediately jumped back in his lap showing him her cards.

"Play it out sweetheart and don't let anyone tell you otherwise. I'll deal the next few rounds if it's all the same to you, Miss Fawn. Not that I don't trust you of course," he added with a Cheshire grin. He knew folding out the first few hands would let them become complacent with his dealing.

Sir ignored Pet kneeling at his side. With Christopher taking over the dealings, he had other issues to worry about at the moment.

In a display of power over his Pet, everyone understood she belonged to him. However with her kneeling, she was unable to assist him with his game play for the time being. He'd have to wait an appropriate amount of time before allowing her to rise and join him once more.

"Then I request a new deck, Mister Christopher. I would also like first cut. Not that I don't trust *you* of course," Sir added without the same smile extended to Fawn. He'd insure that if he couldn't cheat then neither could anyone else.

Fawn obliged, handing Christopher the deck of cards with no argument before looking down at Pet. "Will you at least get her off this floor?" she bit finally, "She is human."

Her words fell upon deaf ears as Sir ignored the alien's request.

***

Will finished the last of his orders and shut down the computer. Turning in his chair, he looked out the see-through wall spotting the poker game played near the bar.

Pet rested on her knees and Tatianna's dark eyes watched the table like a hawk. Her hands shoved into her leather jacket as her body stood tensed. Suddenly Fawn yelled out in exasperation.

"Ugh. Better get out there before they get stupid again," Will muttered. Standing, he left the office and locked the door behind him. Walking by Tatianna, he tried to defuse some of the situation as quickly as possible. "How about a drink? He's a big boy. He can take care of himself."

Tatianna held up a single finger to Will, as if to say 'Give me a second' before joining the poker table.

"How about both of you take a break for the night?" Tatianna asked as she stepped up behind Sir and gently massaged the man's shoulders. "Not just running one life, but two. It must be so… tense," she whispered seductively into his ear, her doe-like eyes meeting Christopher's as she said the word. Christopher eyed Tatianna with a slow burning heat, but eventually let it fade.

Her teeth gently grazed Sir's ear as her eyes begged Christopher to take a neighboring room, to listen for her cries of help if necessary. "It's only one night," she added, allowing her breasts to gently graze Sir's back.

"C'mon dear, let's go see if I can teach you how to play poker more effectively." Christopher picked Savannah up in his arms, heading towards the staircase behind the bar. Stopping at the base, he turned around.

"We'll be back in a while. Don't worry about us I'm sure we can take care of each other." His words were easy, but his glare dared anyone to oppose him. He had been without for too long that everyone in the bar knew better than to mess with him or it could just as easily be their throats crushed in the night.

Savannah giggled in Christopher's arms with no idea as to what awaited her behind closed doors. She batted her eyes as she wrapped her arms around his neck.

Sir shuddered at the feel of Tatianna's breasts grazing against his back. "Very well then. My Pet, you are officially relieved of your duties until morning. The night is yours. However, I do expect for you to be up and ready for your morning lesson. Are we clear?"

At Pet's nod of understanding, he quickly grabbed Tatianna's tanned hand, pulling her into his lap. "So, you have finally figured out what it is that you desire?"

"Perhaps for a night," Tatianna answered with a smile, running her lanky fingers through Sir's thinning hair, "and only the night." She watched as Christopher disappeared.

Fucking asshole, her eyes glared at the man's back. *I do this with him, for you. I beg you for safety and you take it! Your excuse for young ass to literally leave with streams of eyeliner down her cheeks.*

"And perhaps for one night, I would like to get to know the man that Pet thinks so highly of."

Pet stood up, looking back at Sir with confusion of what to do as she stood, watching him with his new companion. *Off? Relieved?* Her attention was then grabbed by the familiar, comfortable voice of a man she had rarely spoken to, never really had much but an occasional glance to look at and never once made eye contact with.

"Pet, why don't you come here and have a drink?" Knowing Tatianna no longer needed the beer, Will gently slid it to the end of the bar waiting for Pet to come and claim it. "For you, nights off are few and far between so you might want to enjoy it while you've got it."

"Thank you," she whispered to the floor, walking up to the bar and sitting before the drink. Taking a tentative sip, she awaited order she wouldn't receive from Sir.

Instead, she twirled her straw silently. "It's delicious Si... Mister Pearson."

Fawn realized that Lady Luck had shown her no favors tonight as she walked over to the bar. Picking up her new drink and taking a sip, she feared for poor Savannah and watched the doorway for her return.

"How? How does Karma not bite all of our asses for allowing him to do such a thing?" Fawn commented in disbelief, "How does she not blast him for doing such a thing? If any one of us were to do half of what he does, the tavern would step in and take matters into its own hands."

Pet looked down at her lap, her mind wandering at the thoughts of what was occurring upstairs, what would soon occur between Sir and Tatianna.

Her periwinkle eyes glanced up, looking at the three individual signs on the stairwell that read out BAR before she spoke up. "It's hard for even the Misfitz Tavern to judge a man who has danced with the devil."

***

"I won't tell you the details of what Lucifer had told me, only trust when I say that there is a reason they tell you never make a deal with the Devil."

The cavacour was dark, mysteriously dark as Christopher waited for something to appear, anything. Something to prepare him for the man he would see. The eyes were those of a woman, their icy white color pierced into his soul. They held everything he had ever wanted, everything he had been told was bad for him.

Lust, the lust that no matter how many nights of bedding, he knew he wouldn't fulfill. They held gluttony, only wanting more of what he had to offer and then some of what he couldn't. They held greed. A selfish masking desire for everything Christopher had once possessed, his soul included.

The eyes carried envy, a dark fury of jealousy for what he had done, what he had seen and experienced. What she never had. The privilege of walking the Earth with free will. Never before had a stare sent chills down his spine the way hers could. She envied his life, his family, his wealth. The very fact that Christopher had ever breathed, she wanted that for herself and he could see it in her eyes. She didn't just want to own what he had, but to possess his every fiber. To put it all under her lustful power.

Her eyes held pride, pride for all the pain she had caused. For the sorrow she had forced and the blood she had shed. It was a satisfying pride in her eyes for the famine, the disease; the battles that had reigned of the holy lands as she sat back in…

Sloth, laziness. Sitting back allowing others to do her dirty work, to take her prisoners captive, to shed the blood she desired.

Finally, Christopher saw the last of what made this being in front of him. Wrath, a furious wrath capable of torturing victims more than he had ever fathomed with any of his. The man couldn't help it, seeing such dangerous things in her eyes. He asked the woman her name as she stepped out of the darkness and answered.

"Lucifer," she whispered, her voice cold, "My name is Lucifer." Her eyes left him, looking on to Omen. "My dear," she said to the goatman as he brought Christopher forward, "What fresh meat have you brought for me?"

Her red dress clung to child-bearing hips, the large breasts of something not even possible to describe as a woman, as the truth behind the Garden of Eden was exposed to him.

Was it truly forbidden fruit that the serpent had told Eve to deliver to Adam or was fruit simply a metaphor for this seductive body in front of him, venom dripping from her ruby lips that promised not only lust, but a blood lust. Her eyes were dark, cold as the frozen embers used to keep Hell in its righteous state. It was no wonder she had once been an angel, cast down from the Heavens for the ill-use of her beauties and needless to say, it was a beauty even he didn't want to partake in.

Christopher fought against the bindings holding back his bruised and bloodied wrists as Omen yanked him forward. "Another potential bidder," he answered with a smile that told him the last bidder hadn't won the auction they were placing in, "Wants to earn his way out of our humble abode."

"Does he now?" she asked, looking as if she were going to eat him alive. "And tell me Christopher…" He didn't like her knowing his name. Sure, he did some things others may call cruel, heartless even, but for Lucifer, him… herself… to know his name?

"I know your name because this is where you belong. You are worthless to the world, set out to do crimes unimaginable to most. You belong here," she growled, her voice no longer human, darker and more demented than anything Christopher had ever heard before as he fought the urge not to break down and cry. Knowing if he did, Omen's pointed teeth would quickly find his flesh as their meal. The bones in the corner told him his fate if he broke down now. "You belong with us. Your soul is mine now."

Christopher nodded his head softly, any masculinity he had when entering the room now sitting at the door as his mind pleaded to just be able to leave.

"Ahhh…" she answered, leaning her head back with a moan as he knew she had read his mind, "Isn't that what everyone wants, Omen?" She said with a grin. "It's all fun and games, living on the edge of the deadly sins until they realize that everything has a price. It may be good, with volunteering and flowers and puppies. Then you get to go up north but no…" Her eyes turned blood red as she glared at him. "It's so much more fun to wrap your hands around the neck of a beautiful woman," she said as if the words excited her more, "That is why you are here, isn't it Christopher? Such a dark price for such a fun

task."

***

Christopher jerked awake. Sweat dripped down his face from the memory. He could still feel the icy air against his skin as he opened his eyes more.

"Ugh," he groaned into the darkness, rubbing his face in disbelief that, after so many years, such a horrid memory would come back to haunt him.

Christopher looked next to him to see the young girl in pigtails curled up to her pillow with pursed lips. Any thoughts he had of strangling that delicate neck before were gone now. The sight of her pure innocence could only be matched with that of the goatman, Omen's, teeth. Or Lucifer's glares.

"Sleep little one," he whispered, pulling the blanket closer to the girl's neck, "I promise, tonight you are safe. Tomorrow, you may not be so lucky."

CHAPTER SEVEN

SYMBIOTIC RELATIONSHIPS

Tatianna climbed the stairs and walked into her tiny apartment, kicking off her tennis shoes. Today was a disaster. Not only did she have to deal with the idiocrasy of Double-Coupon Tuesday, but having to endure it after hearing Christopher's boasting about his night with a paid hooker, a teenage girl, and now, of all times, the rent was due.

She knew better than to even ask Christopher for his half. It wouldn't be there so she would have to come up with it on her own with a "pay you back" promise that the man wouldn't keep. She swore if it wasn't for the fact that this was better than death, she would kick the man out into the cold.

Tatianna's chair, though battered and torn, beckoned her warmly only a few feet from the door. She felt pleasant relief as she fell into the faded green fabric before a door in front of her opened, exposing her built roommate and his ash blonde hair slicked back from his day in the office.

"So here we are again," she groaned as she leaned her head back, closing her eyes.

Christopher couldn't help but smile as he sat down in his over-sized leather recliner, unbuttoning the top buttons of his white shirt to expose the curly hairs of his chest.

"Here we are; two lonely sinners on a long road. Where it

leads, no one knows." He smiled, downing his brandy before refilling both their glasses from his bottle. "As long as Will stays behind the bar tonight, we'll be alright. If he comes out and it's not to go upstairs with someone, it'll be a long night. Some people."

Tatianna hadn't been planning on going out drinking, but with the day she had a beer in a smoky room sounded really nice right now. "What do you mean? What does Will have against you, as of late?" She figured she should ask as she raised a darkened eyebrow in suspicion.

"Will and I… we are of the same make, but not the same model. I consider myself an upgrade, if you will, from his limited perspective."

Tatianna chuckled to herself, unable to believe her roommate's delusions, as Christopher continued, "He considers me a downgrade from the same. So we don't often see eye to eye and get along even less. What's your beef with Angel? And don't think that I didn't see it. Or that I haven't noticed that the enemy of my enemy is my friend. You and I may not always see eye to eye, but tell me that you see more potential in him than you do in me?"

"My beef with Angel," Tatianna leaned in closer to Christopher with her own wicked smile. "Is that she is foolish! How close were you to getting off last night before you changed your mind? And she allowed herself into the same predicament with full nudity and no weapons. My beef with her is that she is an idiot. A whore asking for someone like you to do what you do best," she answered, rolling her eyes.

"And Christopher," she sighed as she got up and tossed a snack cake at him with artificial love. Distaste filled her own mouth as she watched him eat it. Crumbs covered his mustache as icing fell into his shirt, his hair disheveled. "I see more potential in a barstool than you. You are heartless. You are cold and gruesome and disgusting."

Christopher looked up at her. Crumbs still filled his mustache as his grey eyes, suffering from withdrawal to the drug of murder, stared back at her. She scrunched her caramel colored nose before adding, "In all the wrong ways. And yet, I have something worth earning. I have to behave myself. So, I choose an over-sized pit bull such as yourself to join me in travels. Why? Because if someone like him," she whispered, pointing a finger in the direction of the tavern, "Decides to do anything stupid, I know you will go for the throat. And you won't let go until the job is done." Straightening up, she refilled Christopher's drink, "This one's on me."

"Pit bull eh?" Christopher nodded with understanding, contemplating the term pit bull before deciding to take it as the best of compliments as he clinked his glass to hers. "I can handle pit bull. And we both know what I'm getting out of this, don't we?"

Christopher looked at Tatianna's curves, her casual appearance and curly hair before looking back at the door to their apartment that, based on appearance of size, couldn't be more than a one bedroom and smiled wickedly. "I need your cover. You make me look semi-human as far as everyone else is concerned which is just enough to leave me off the grid from getting into trouble. To symbiotic relationships, love!" He raised his glass again before downing the beverage and holding it out to her once more.

***

The door to the tavern opened, exposing a siren with hair of green. A black sequin dress clung to the woman's succulent body. The bottom of it draped down past her feet to cover her scaly, bird-like legs and the top clung to her chest to expose milky white breasts. She walked up to the bar, her hips shaking with a seductive grace, and when the woman ordered her drink, her voice rang out in a harmonic tone that left many of the bar's male patrons weak in the knees.

Sage watched Cole staring at the vixen. He was nearly drooling at the sight.

"What is your problem?" she bit with envious jealousy before she took another shot of whiskey and crossed her arms.

Cole sat, staring back at his cousin for a moment. "I don't have one. Envy is a good color on you though. The rosy red in your cheeks is, well, hot. As far as it goes though, I'll be honest. I don't think I could handle you and another woman, beautiful. I think you're more than enough woman for me." He smiled as he poured himself another drink.

"What?" Sage snapped back in shock, "No! I'm mad at you dammit! That means you don't get to say things like hot and beautiful and… and compliment me and shit! Just… ugh!" she groaned, smacking his chest as she glared through furious eyes.

Her chest rose and fell with heavy breaths before she covered his mouth with her own, kissing him passionately.

As their lips parted, he felt the need to add, "A threesome is only a man's fantasy. Think nothing of it, lover. If you want to be more permanent co-conspirators, you only have to say so. As long as our needs align, I am more than happy to share some of the more marvelous and devious pleasures of this world with you… and you alone."

"You mean, you're willing to be mine? To make this sincere?" she asked as fear and excitement rose into her chest. Her heart raced. Fight or flight kicked in.

She hated them both for what they told her to do. She was speechless to his words. Her throat tensed up, unable to say anything.

"For now. I can't say that with the life we live that it will continue indefinitely, but for now I am content with you and only you satisfying my needs… and satisfying yours. That is if you need a Clyde, Miss Bonnie."

"Yes!" she squealed, hugging him tightly. Her mouth met his in passion. "Be my Clyde," she begged, "be bad with me."

Sage needed some form of release. She needed a way to be bad, to misbehave. Not just the orgasmic groping of love, but the racing heartbeat of life.

Her attention turned away from Cole as she searched the bar, looking for another fight to start. She had to get out of her cage, and soon. This nearly-bad thing wasn't cutting it. She was getting soft. She was caring about him and… *No, Sage don't feel butterflies! Where was the slut in the dress?! She could use an ass-kicking!*

Savannah, who was sitting in a nearby booth, consistently looked over her shoulder at her older sister. She knew that look.

It was the one Sage got when someone caught her off guard with a compliment; the one where her eyes would soften slightly before she punched Savannah. *Remember what Daddy told you*, the teen reminded herself, *keep her out of trouble.* When Cole was around though, that was easier said than done.

A devilish smile covered Cole's face as he watched Sage's green eyes scan the room.

He couldn't explain why, but tonight he wanted power; strong power that filled him to the brim with unbridled warmth, electricity that danced and played under his skin. To feel others bow before him.

That's it!

"Wanna' go take down a government?"

"Can we?" Sage asked as she clenched and unclenched her fists. The indescribable energy surged through her veins with no reason for the pulsating vibrancy. It left her anticipating adrenaline. She had been too good lately. Something had to change. "I have been waiting for you to ask all evening. Please?"

"You bet we can, sweet cheeks. I know a little south-western African nation that needs a new deity. Sound like anything you'd be good at?" He raised an eyebrow with a smile and rubbed his fingers together; the universal sign for cash.

"We'll have to do some shopping before we leave, but it'll be worth it," he added as he grabbed her hand and headed toward the Tavern exit. "Savannah," he called out to his younger cousin, pulling Sage toward the door, "I'm sure you can take care of yourself… make sure your daddy is happy this evening in case we need bail money."

"Wait!" the young girl exclaimed as she jumped up from the booth. "Bail money?! No! You guys can't just go and take over a country!" Her wide eyes and rounded face made it difficult for them to take her seriously, "Daddy will kill you! I'll… I'll tell him!"

Sage froze in place, holding up a finger to Cole, "One second."

Danger following in her wake, Sage turned on her heels. She stormed back to her trembling sister. Her green eyes held a deadly glare.

"You're not going to tell Daddy shit. You know why? Because you don't want Daddy knowing his precious little Savannah let big, bad Christopher take her upstairs. You don't want Daddy knowing why you weren't home when he called last night! Do you? Back off!" She turned back around, emotionless to the tears that welled in Savannah's eyes.

"Let's go sexy," Sage laughed, wrapping her arm in Cole's as she guided him out the door.

Savannah waited until the tavern door closed before she blinked, allowing the first tear to fall.

***

Sir watched the scene before him from one of the bar's high tables. As Savannah wiped the tear away, he turned his attention back to Pet and continued quietly discussing her night off.

"I don't understand, Sir," Pet whispered softly into her lap.

Her pale skin turned whiter with the discomfort of the conversation as she picked at the cuticles of her nails.

"I hadn't meant to upset you with my tardiness, but understand that the proper punishment was relief of my duties. It won't happen again," she added.

Sir smiled silently at his Pet, stroking the woman's braid that fell down her spine. "My Pet, do not be confused. Never for a moment were you out of my control or 'relieved of your duties'. It was a point I was forced to make. You are to obey all my commands all the time. Do you understand?" He sipped his scotch and scanned her over, waiting for her nod of approval.

"Yes, Sir," Pet answered quickly with a nod of her head, "I never broke any of your rules nor removed your collar, Sir. I knew eventually you would come back for me, as you had promised." She kept her head bowed, despite the motion that occurred throughout the bar room. "Did you have a pleasant night, Sir?"

"It was a... progressive one, I do believe. You may have a playmate soon enough, my Pet." He smiled at his submissive lovingly, allowing his white teeth to be exposed. The crow's feet of age surrounded the corners of his gray eyes.

Oh yes. I love Pet. Don't let that ever be confused, he thought to himself. *But it was still and always would be a game of control.*

"Would you like that, Pet?"

"Of course, Sir," Pet answered as she glanced up for a moment. Her voice raised slightly with excitement. "I would love to have someone to play with, someone to talk with who... understands my eagerness to please you, Sir. I had a good night as well, Sir. It was... relaxing to simply sit at the bar and talk with William," she confessed.

"And your talk with William? What was discussed?" Sir asked, interested as to what the two of them would have to speak of. He was tempted to see just how deep he could push his Pet when it came to Will, but decided for now he would listen to her story of the night's activities.

"My day," Pet replied honestly, "What I think of our agreement as sub and dom. I told William I was very satisfied in pleasing you. That it was one of the happiest decisions I had ever made. He seemed doubtful, yet his opinion of our arrangement is no concern of mine. We discussed what I do when I am not taking care of you, Sir. My hobbies. His hobbies. It was pleasant." She smiled as she cocked her head to the side. Her chipmunk-like cheeks were full and her eyes glistened.

Sir nodded. He was happy that Pet could spend time in the company of another man without being dominated.

That was his job to provide. It was hers was to receive and yet, it didn't mean she couldn't have a life outside of being his pet. Though it was a 24/7 job, he tried to be understanding that some of that time she was merely on call.

"I will continue to try and ensure our new pet's agreement. In the meantime, I am pleased with your conversation skills with other males. You gleaned something from your conversation with William that is worth sharing, I expect?"

He anticipated her telling him something about how the bar operated or where money was coming from but was surprised when Pet answered with, "He is sleeping with Miss Angel. Regularly, sometimes without pay.

"Hmmm, I cannot say I find it surprising. William and Miss Angel once had a business relationship. Never you mind, Pet. Excellent collection of information on your time off. I am impressed. Half lashings this evening and a glass of wine before we begin tonight's training."

He was pleased that she was still on que for her duties when he gave her room to stretch her legs. *Not too much room though,* he reminded himself. The timid woman before him in a collar and black dress had to remember who was in control, for everyone's sake.

"Thank you, Sir," Pet answered, happy with herself for

pleasing her dominant. "It was very difficult to find out," she continued to explain, "Ma... William doesn't give up information quickly."

Sir raised an aging eyebrow at her almost misuse of terms as the quiet woman caught herself. Her body tensed up as she felt the name so easily leave her lips. *An error from speaking with Kritter.*

It was worth the lashings she would get to make eye contact. To speak of the truth that surged beneath her skin. And yet the words, they danced upon her tongue, spinning to the music conducted by a deaf orchestra. How to explain how she felt, what her words truly meant. No longer was she merely a submissive signed with a contract. No, now she was with child.

How could she explain the words of how she felt, wanting them to be perfect. Beautiful.

Pet closed her eyes. The storm raced beneath her skin. The thunder crashed as her heart pounded.

You are one with the storm. Ride it. Embrace its center for that's where you are most calm.

You control nothing. Your control is a mere perception of the troubles at hand. You merely control one leaf.

I shall not try to exert my control. If the storm rolls, I cannot stop the winds. I cannot stop the rain.

The only thing I control is my response to a situation.

Pet opened her eyes, her thoughts replenished and refocused.

"I promise you Sir, my collar remains. That doesn't change simply because I am relieved for the evening," Pet reassured, breaking her final rule for the evening as her hand lifted from beneath the table. Her fingertips shook with fear, uncertain of the response he would carry, what he would say as she set it down. Her fingers covered his. "I am always under contract as your Pet, Sir."

CHAPTER EIGHT

THE COURTESAN

It's Tuesday night. There is no reason to sit here on a Tuesday night, Maxx reminded himself. Tuesday night was lasagna night. Tuesday night was Spanish homework and softball practice. Tuesday night was… whiskey night.

Maxx sat in the same red leather booth that he had shared with Angel. He hoped to see her again. He also hoped she wouldn't be as despaired as last time.

He took another sip off his whiskey, praying she had a better evening at work as the foul liquor burnt down his throat.

Angel rushed into the tavern only a few moments later. Comfort shined in her eyes as she smiled at the married man in the corner before continuing her mission towards Will's office.

Angel looked up at the purple stained-glass that lined the top of the door before pressing the buzzer on the wall.

She straightened her tight-fitting burgundy dress, pulling the top down to expose the full curvature of her breasts. A large slit rose up the back to tease men with the nearly visible contour of her bottom.

"See you in a few," Maxx called, glowing with warmth as he was returned with a smile over Angel's shoulder. Her bright brown eyes forced a matching smile to cover his face.

Maxx silently wished that she would join him for another

drink. He could already taste the sweetened honey of her skin. He could smell her perfume.

***

Will looked up from his paperwork as the zip of the buzzer pulled him from the dreaded stacks before him. He looked through his see-through wall to see Angel standing there, waiting to be let in.

"Come on in Angel, it's unlocked." Quickly finishing his paperwork, Will signed one last payroll check as the girl entered the room. Shuffling the papers aside to be filed later, he held an open hand out to the chair across from him.

"How was work?" the bar owner asked, curious to the glow emanating from her skin.

Angel enjoyed the men who came to her; men of all professions that came from not only different countries, but different realms to Knowhere, Nebraska for her. For a night's worth of company with guaranteed satisfaction of whatever their desires might entail.

Angel loved that she was her own boss, in charge of her own schedule and who she chose as clients. Unlike many of her friends in New York, whose pimps demanded they not return until they had made enough; being forced to accept any men available just to beat the competition of the other whores lining the same dark streets.

She didn't want to be one of those women who was picked up by a badge or strangled and left for dead; another forgotten face whose life and death were summed up with the blame of an unsettling childhood.

Instead, Angel had dreams; dreams of being a saloon girl. One men swooned over with an ache in their loins. She wanted to be known for having class and grace. With a bosom as soft and succulent that any man would pay double to be able to enjoy.

She had aspirations. The goal was to be respected for having one of the oldest careers in women's history. Her dreams were that one day whenever she called her mother, she could ease the woman's mind instead of hearing fret in her voice. Angel would tell her that she could finally retire from the life of worry she held onto for so long.

"My tab," Angel answered, dropping a bag of gold worth well more than her outstanding balance onto Will's desk. Sitting down in the clear chair across from him, she crossed her legs and watched as Will's eyebrows shot up at the coins that spilled onto his desk.

"A good day at work then I take it?" Will didn't look up at her as he reached into his desk drawer and pulled out his black leather binder. "Mind if I ask their occupation? I know the rules. No names but occupations aren't off limits, are they?" He flipped through the first few tabs as he searched for Angel's name.

Angel could only laugh at Will's persistence that he know something of her clients. Occasionally the question changed over the years, none of which gave away identities, merely demographics.

"A pastor, two judges, and a badge… retired of course," she answered as she leaned back in her chair, "The pastor told me something interesting. He asked me if I judged him. I asked him what for? Because he sinned differently than the rest of us? Then he told me 'No, that we all sin the same'. I wound up entertaining him for the next three hours coated in coconut oil that he licked off my body." She leaned forward, looking in the binder between them, "That puts me ahead, right?"

Will ran his finger down the list until he found Angel's name and then ran it across the page to find her total due. "Yep. You officially have a credit. Not a huge one, mind you, but if you use it right, you're covered for at least a month. Try to keep it above the redline this time if you can, please? Liquor from foreign realms doesn't come cheap. Especially not the shit you people drink." Will gave her a teasing wink before he pointed his thumb toward the see-through wall.

"What are you going to do about Maxx? He seems to fancy you a bit." He held up his hands in a non-threatening manner, knowing Angel's wishes of discretion, "If you don't mind me asking, that is."

Angel sighed, looking out the one-way window, "I don't know yet. I nearly asked him upstairs… free of charge, I mean." She looked down at her lap, nearly ashamed, "Just to be respected in bed, for once in my life, and be able to have a say about what happened with someone who… oh, never mind... How is inventory?"

Will eyed her thoughtfully for a moment. He knew there was more going on between her and Maxx, but if she didn't want to talk about it, he wouldn't pry. "Not good. Stock is running low everywhere right now. It's getting to be that time of year again. I'm asking around and you feel free to do the same. I will pay accordingly for any profitable material that is found," he nodded, knowing she understood what he wanted and that liquor stock wasn't the only hard thing to come by.

Angel covered her mouth as a snort left her nose with the sincerity of a real laugh. "That wasn't what I meant, Mister Pearson," she chuckled, "Though I will ask around for your stock of preference. I was in fact referencing to the alcohol supply. I was hoping, if you weren't in too dire need of a reorder since I was in the red before, that I could make a request with the extra funds." Her tone suddenly turned more formal, businesslike.

Will raised an eyebrow at Angel's request before hesitantly asking, "And what exactly is it you're asking for? You know I usually carry two bottles of just about everything so what is it you want? And don't play coy with me. I know you too well. When your demeanor changes that much that quickly, you want something."

"Well, you see. Our sales go hand-in-hand. Men know they can come here and request my services without fear of badges. They can drink your liquor without fear of judgement. They drink and I get customers, then we drink together. I get them drunk, they request one of your rooms. It's the same one you assign nightly, the red dragon scale door. They pay me, they pay you, we return upstairs. I am merely suggesting with the added service I bring to the tavern I would like my room looking a little more appealing to my clients, as well as one of the voice-coms for my own protection after the ordeal a few nights ago." Angel had put a great deal of thought into how she was going to approach Will with such a proposition, knowing that it was a lot to be asking for. She also knew she needed to show him it was profitable on his end, not just her own.

Will strummed his fingers on the desk as he tossed the idea around in his head for a few moments. "So what you're really wanting to do is upgrade then. You want to become a courtesan instead of a, well, you know."

"A whore, Mister Pearson," Angel answered. Her head remained high despite the degrading term that had, over the centuries, come with her job title. It was a career she held with pride; one that carried self-respect that she had pleased congressmen and saved marriages, even if it did raise a stir amongst other women. "No need for discretion when we have worked alongside one another for this long."

Will nodded nonchalantly, "Okay, but I have stipulations first. One: I take ten percent off of every client."

"Ten percent? Will, I don't get nearly enough for what I do now. Not when half the girls you let in hand it out for free."

"My tavern, my rules. Two: I can advertise you to customers when I so desire, however I still relinquish the final decision to you. Fair?" Angel nodded her head in agreement, willing to listen to what more he had to say. "Good. Three: We can end this contract upon either's discretion. Agreed?" he asked holding out his hand.

Angel looked Will over, attempting to judge the man's sincerity. "I would prefer you only advertise me to safe, higher income buyers for both of us. Use your better judgement against..." She looked out towards the poker table. Her eyes fell on Christopher. She felt the attorney should to be behind bars himself after having taken him as a customer. She shuddered in remembrance, "Ill-willed candidates please."

Will nodded his head in understanding, "I'll also throw in the upgraded room and talk box for free."

"You have yourself a deal, Mister Pearson." She stood up, shaking his hand in acceptance of his offer.

Will took her outstretched hand. He held it for moment, looking her in the eyes, "There are benefits to being a courtesan over a, well, you know. Now you can charge them what you should have been asking to begin with. The money will come and I'll float your rent for the first month or two until you get a solid customer base." He let go of her hand and turned to his computer to end the conversation.

As Angel stood up and opened the door, Will added without looking up from the computer screen, "Be careful what you wish for. It's hard to handle business of our natures and still maintain normal relationships." He waved her away and continued to type away at the computer, putting in the upgrade order to her suite.

***

Angel stepped out and looked across the tavern, only seeing a handful of customers. A yard gnome played darts by the front door while a yeti warmed his hands in front of the fireplace that heated the room. An elf stood and left for the evening, leaving behind an empty mug and a few gold coins for Legs to clean up. Her gaze fell on the man whose demeanor had concerned her since noticing it from inside the office.

Angel sighed, taking in what Will had said as she closed the office door. She watched as Maxx relaxed, his shoulders easing slightly as she walked towards him.

What am I going to do about my recent predicament with the man I desire? Not as a client, but as a partner. One who is content with simply my company. How would anyone handle that?

"Sorry," she whispered as she slid into the booth next to him, "Business. How was your day?"

"Not bad. Better than the last few days for sure," he slid a full glass across the table to her with a smile, "I made some decent money. It's been a long week but there is food in my belly and a drink in hand so I can't complain. How are you? How was your week?" Maxx reached behind him and pulled out the 9mm that had been holstered on his back for the last couple days. Once ensuring the safety was on, he unloaded it and placed it on the table.

Angel looked down at the 9mm, concerned about what his week may have entailed, but knowing he would need more alcohol to talk about it.

Will was right. If she wanted to be with Maxx, she would have to be honest and explain why it was so hard to love someone like herself before anyone… no everyone, got hurt.

"Maxx, I'm a whore," she confessed blatantly.

Maxx let out a hearty laugh that shook his stomach, "You're not a whore Angel. Trust me. I've met whores, my wife being one of them. Currently I'd say with your line of work that you're an escort. Escorts have standards, class. Whores… Well, they don't." He swallowed back his shot before putting it down and pouring another. "I know what you do for a living. I'm not saying I'm thrilled at the idea, but I know it makes you happy. I have no judgements. As long as you can keep work and whatever this is," he pointed to her and then back at himself, "separate then we have no issues. Can you? Keep them separate,

I mean?"

"How?" Angel asked. Tears formed in her mascara-lined eyes as she looked at him. "How do I keep them separate when every night I am in another man's bed? Whenever you see me flirting with any of these guys here? All of them? Telling each of them that I am willing to do anything they desire? Or whenever nights like..." Her eyes dashed in Christopher's direction before returning to Maxx. "You would kill him right now if you knew," she whispered.

"I'm sure I probably would. That's why it's probably not best to tell me. You're going to have clients that I don't approve of. So, how about we just agree not to talk about it unless we have to? If we go about it that way, I'm sure that we can work something out as to whatever this is. Please? I don't want to miss out on something that could be great just because you have a career."

"It's not that easy," Angel answered quickly. She couldn't believe the man was so willing to ignore the situation. He put a single finger up to her bright red lips.

Angel gazed into Maxx's blue eyes, wanting nothing more than to believe him.

There was more to their relationship than the client he once was. He was Maxx Conner, father of her best friend. He had watched as she and Savannah made cookies in the kitchen and studied for tests. He oftentimes would ask her how work was treating her, who her recent clients had been. She would answer with warm smiles, leaving Savannah clueless to their own occasional warm embrace paid out of her daddy's wallet.

Angel opened her mouth, attempting to argue his logic before his lips covered hers. Pulling away, both their hearts pattered with something more than lust.

"Shhh," he answered, his eyes warming her own scared, freezing heart. "We're not talking about it," he reminded her, nodding across the bar to Legs who smiled back and prepared him another drink.

A smile crept onto Angel's face as she toyed with the hem of her dress before looking up. "I have a new abode," she informed him.

"Oh? Made a deal with Will? It's about time! I was wondering how much longer it would take you to upgrade. Being a courtesan is a serious step up from being an escort. It's a more reputable title. Not to mention the pay increase and considerably more control over the clientele you take."

Maxx worried as to what the stipulations were. Will was fair, a bit on the high side at times depending on what he was selling, and real estate was a difficult thing for Will to part with, especially with his bindings to the tavern.

"Raise your prices beautiful. Otherwise, it's not worth the change of location." He stopped, trying to think how to put into words what he wanted to say, "When you're with a client, they are always a client and nothing more, correct? And I don't mean them asking you to be their high school crush. I mean, it's a business deal right?"

"Precisely," Angel answered, her tone matter-of-fact, "It is a business deal where they pay me for my services and I provide what they pay for. A career where demand is high and supply is less than legal, though it has been around since biblical times. And yet strangely, it was even frowned upon then. But it's hard on anyone to know I work nights. To understand that even on holidays, particularly Valentine's Day, I am in the arms of another man. Week nights are no exception; with men 'being held up in the office' or asked to work overtime." She took a swig from her glass of Firebreath. "I do have a couch up there, you know? We could talk where it's more private," she couldn't believe the words as she spoke them, offering her body to her best client for nothing. Was she mad?

"Yes. This is a discussion best held in private anyways. Every wall in this tavern has ears." He stood, grabbing the 9mm off the table. He quickly reloaded the magazine, locked one into the chamber, and holstered it behind his back. He felt Angel watching him. "Just in case."

Angel raised her voice slightly. Just enough to know that she wouldn't be heard by anyone other than her intended target of conversation. "Tell Master Will I need a refill."

***

From beneath the grease-covered fryers, Kritter's pointed ears twitched when she heard Angel's order. With urgency, she crawled out of the hiding place where she had been listening in. Her fingers slimed with splatters of oil as she balanced herself, standing up from the tiled kitchen floor. Her wings spread wide as she scurried beneath the stairs to the bar and stood at Will's side.

"Seductress Angel requests a refill, Master Will. Seductress Angel specifically asked for Master Will to deliver said drink. Kritter apologizes, Master Will."

"You may be a pixie, Kritter, and you may be sneaky, but even you have to be careful getting caught when you eavesdrop, little one. Watch the bar. I'll go take care of it." Will shook his head with a *tsk* as he grabbed another bottle of Firebreath.

Stepping out from behind the bar, Will walked toward the booth, the bottle swinging lazily in his hand. With a bow, he placed the bottle on the table between the couple.

"Thank you," Angel said with a warm smile, taking the liquor from the young bartender, "Take it off my tab please. Mister Conner and I are headed up to my quarters. I will be off the clock this evening, if anyone comes asking."

"Yes, ma'am," turning, he gave Maxx a look of caution before returning to the neon-lit bar.

***

Legs waited, tapping her fingers anxiously at the end of the bar. Her lips were pursed with frustration as her green eyes held a dangerous glare. Will saw the apparent look of distaste as he returned, wishing someone could have granted him the same warning.

"You're not taking the night off too, are you? Not that I really need you or anything." The bachelor looked around at the nearly empty pub. Most of the evening's customers had already dispersed, minus a sorrowful gnome sitting at one of the high tables. An elf sat at the far end of the bar, a frosted mug in his hand. The rest of the night would go smoothly, last call presenting itself around midnight.

Legs let out a sarcastic scoff of a laugh. "Would be nice if I could," she answered, feeling a twinge of jealousy toward her friend as she returned to wiping down a dry glass. She turned her back, prominently leaving Will with the cold shoulder, "Ahh, to be able to stay here rent-free. To make my own schedule," she mocked. "The elf with the beer told me."

Will wasn't surprised how fast word had spread through the tavern. "What do you need, Legs? A month off the rent? You know I'll extend all the same courtesies to you. The same as I do for all my employees. Isn't that right, Kritter?" Will asked, not expecting a response from Kritter.

Legs stopped wiping the glass. She glared at Will, placing her hand on her hip in frustration. The damp rag hung at her side. "I deserve to know why she has a right to say 'hey, I'm taking off' while I'm working overtime to pay my rent!" The tone in her voice was heavy and spiteful.

Before giving Will a chance to reply, the bartender rolled her eyes. "Forget it. Table two needs another beer. I'm going to get the order forms done for next week's supply. What do you want me to tell the construction crew this week? Tavern girl need a

Jacuzzi?"

Will's royal blue eyes flared. His blood boiled beneath his skin. "Kritter, you're in charge for the rest of the evening. Mistress Legs and I need to have a private business discussion in my office."

Without waiting for Kritter's acknowledgement, he swiftly turned back to Legs, "My office. Now!" He jumped over the bar, walking towards his office door. Popping his knuckles along the way, he fought the urge to make a scene in the tavern.

Legs bit her lip as she saw Will's fury. She walked behind him quietly, hoping her jealousy and attitude hadn't cost her both her job and home.

Maybe she had taken it too far. Even in the back of her mind though, part of her said it was unfair treatment. She waited until they were in the office and the door closed behind her before she spoke.

"Will—"

"Shut it!" Will snapped. Legs wondered whether he was referring to her talking or the door as he walked around his desk, plopping down in his chair before looking her up and down.

"Take off your clothes. Now!" He wasn't worried about anybody overhearing him. The walls of his office were soundproof.

The tone in his voice was only partially due to his annoyance. Something else was the cause of this outburst. Was it pride? Was it his own? Was he proud of her?

"What?" Legs looked at him with utter confusion. She laughed with disbelief that Will would even make such a request. "Will, what are you talking about? I… I'm not taking my clothes off."

"Do you still want a job come morning?!" his voice thundered off the walls as he slammed his fist down on the desk causing Legs to jump back. Her heart pounded against her chest as she attempted to look anywhere but at the man before her.

Not waiting for her response, Will continued, "You will do as I say or you can pack your shit and go. Now do it!" Red heat shined in his eyes as his patience wore thinner by the moment.

Legs shivered, silently unbuttoning her white shirt before allowing it to fall off her shoulders. The black bra that covered her breasts came into view. With a heavy sigh, she unzipped her skirt and allowed it to fall from her waist, exposing a matching lacy thong. She lifted her right leg, pulling off a heel before doing the same with the other.

"There," she whispered, barely raising her eyes to see Will staring back at her as she stood in front of his desk.

"Now stand in front of the glass," he demanded.

Her knees trembled beneath her, her pulse racing within her ears as her mouth went dry. Legs did as Will asked, wanting nothing more than to cover her bare skin.

A faint scar sat directly above her black panties. A rose tattoo trailed down her spine, reminding her of younger, more selfish days. All her insecurities exposed for her boss to see. For her to feel as if the entire tavern could see. She held her head with shame and disgrace as tears welled in her eyes.

Will made her wait a full minute before his voice sheeted the awkward silence between them once more, "Feeling exposed? How about now?"

With a tap of his finger, Will flipped the switch under the desk. The one-way wall turned two-way so the only occupant left in the bar, the lone elf, saw her standing before him. He allowed Legs to watch as the elf began to drool over her exposed body. A stream of light pink saliva left the humanoid's mouth and formed a puddle on the bar top. The elf had the look of a predator; his gaze holding an utter want to take her, to eat her alive, shining in his eyes.

Will quickly flipped the switch once more, turning it back into a one way see-through wall. "Feel like Angel yet? That's the kinds of looks that she deals with daily. That's the kind of feelings she is faced with all the time. Before you even say it, yes I know it's her job. It's her choice, but do think she likes it?"

He didn't give her a chance to answer as he poured out his frustrations, "Do you want that elf to flop around on top of you? To feel his spit fall on you instead of my bar? I don't think so. I cut Angel slack because I understand just how hard her job is. First-hand knowledge can be a bitch sometimes. Just because she chooses a rough career path doesn't mean I have to make it any harder on her. Now put your damn clothes on!"

As Legs obeyed, Will turned away to grant her decency. He reached over, keying into the microphone to the speaker behind the bar.

"Kritter, kick that sorry elf's ass out of my bar and tell him he's banned. Make sure that he knows to keep his mouth shut. If he don't... cut out his tongue."

He turned back to a fully-clothed Legs standing before him. "In the meantime," Will opened the black leather-bound ledger he kept on his desk. He flipped it to Leg's employment page, "You are hereby promoted to Bar Manager. This comes with double the pay and guaranteed one weekend off a month. You now have authority over Kritter and everyone else in the bar, excluding me. Now, get out of my office before I change my mind."

Returning to his ledger, Will made changes to the pay calendar and schedule. "If you're having a hard time, you come to me. But don't ever do it in front of my customers again. Are we clear?"

"Yes," Legs answered as she looked at Will. Tears still filled her emerald eyes, waiting along her eyelid for a single blink, enough to send them over the edge. To expose her delicate emotions beneath the solid wall she projected.

She hated Will for what he had just done, yet understood exactly what he was saying. She didn't want to ever see the man again and couldn't help but respect him for showing her the truth. She hadn't seen Angel's career in that light before, having only seen the favoritism she thought he had shown.

Guilt fled over her for her ill-feelings toward Angel. She had a new respect for her friend.

"It may be too much to ask…" Legs whispered softly, her hand still on the doorknob as her throat tensed up with the tears she fought against shedding, "But may I have the evening off… please?" Will glanced up from his ledger and his expression immediately softened.

Maybe he'd been just a tad hard on his bartender. He wanted her to understand so he did what he had to do knowing what would work. But still a bit rough, he thought to himself.

However he couldn't show weakness in front of her, not now. Not after what he'd just done or it would completely undo all of it. Leaning back in his chair, he looked out of the see-through wall into the tavern and saw everything it stood for.

The curse it held, for him and for all the tavern's patrons. The law that rose up, that took hold beneath the bar's wooden planked ceilings and glass chandeliers. The promise that what one did unto others would come forth unto them.

It was a binding that had forcibly formed a bond between Will and Karma, causing him to sometimes carry out both her curses and blessings. He shook his head, reminding himself that this was the law of the tavern, and his duty as the owner.

A heavy sigh left the man's chest as he tapped his pen against the wooden desk in thought, "You know what, it's a slow night anyway. Come in early tomorrow to take care of inventory. Say ten am?" he asked, making Legs' shift an hour earlier than usual but still allowing her a good sleep-in after tonight's circumstances.

"Okay," Legs answered with a deep inhale, composing herself long enough to pass by Kritter before she opened the door and whispered a soft, "Thank you."

Will watched Legs leave the office and smiled, glad he still had all his limbs attached. He watched as Kritter attempted to hide her stares at Legs, who quickly rushed past the bar to the stairwell.

Despite her attempts at containing herself, Legs flushed cheeks and red eyes told all. Kritter held her head down as the woman disappeared upstairs before briskly walking into Will's office.

"Any problems with Joe? You did tell him I said thank you, right?" Will had been friends with the elf since the last Realm Black Ops Convention in '93. He was the gayest elf on this side of the Dark Stratosphere and knew what to do the minute Will flipped the two way glass.

He was to appear as the biggest pervert on the planet; the wider his eyes and more obnoxious his stares, the better. It had gotten Will out of Kritter's blind dates on multiple occasions.

Joe would come back in the next time he was passing through town and charm Legs so she couldn't kick him out.

"Did you send him with a bottle of that cherry vodka his husband likes?"

Kritter nodded her head, "Yes Master Will. Kritter did precisely as Master Will asked. Kritter told Mister Joe thank you, Master Will. Kritter gave Mister Joe the bottle and told Mister Joe to enjoy with Mister-Miss-Mister Jack. Kritter also told Mister Joe safe returns in Mister Joe's travels, Master Will. Kritter must ask if Miss Chara is okay, Master Will? Miss Chara appeared rather shaken up."

"She'll be alright. If she's late in the morning, start the inventory without her. Thank you for being courteous with Mister Joe. He's a unique friend. Will you be able to handle the bar this evening? I have some paperwork to catch up on. I promoted Mistress Legs to Bar Manager. Other than me, her word is law. Understood?"

"Yes Master Will," Kritter answered with a fierce nod of her head, "Miss Chara is Bar Manager. Kritter is to listen to Miss Chara as Kritter listens to Master Will. Kritter is to start on inventory at ten. Kritter will handle the tavern the rest of tonight. Kritter will not bother Master Will."

CHAPTER NINE

WHEN ENGINES ROAR

The empty street rang out with a heavy rumble as Sage slammed on the accelerator. Windows shook as she drove past, filling the homes of elderly couples with her chaos. As the motor revved one last time, the rebel granted the neighborhood peace once more, parking her motorcycle next to a pair of hover-bikes outside an odd-shaped cerulean tiled home. She knocked on the home's front door with a loud, thunderous bang.

"Come on!" she groaned, looking up the road to make sure Daddy didn't see her and spoil the plan she and Cole had devised.

As Worvacs heard the knock at his front door, he stood and headed toward the front foyer from the armory he kept behind his bedroom. Pulling out his black Beretta, he checked the magazine and flipped off the safety before looking through the peephole of his door.

A young woman in tattered jeans and a halter top stood with an impatient look on her face. He groaned and clicked the safety back into place, tucking the pistol back into his thigh holster. Though Sage was mouthy and annoying, she was harmless enough. He didn't need to be armed.

"What are you doing here, Sage?" he asked as he swung open the door. Light rolled through into the darkened interior of his under-furnished living room.

"Girl Scout cookies," Sage answered with gleeful sarcasm. "Want to buy some?" she asked as she poked her head into the condensed home. A grey couch sat before a coffee table that was covered with an empty bowl and coffee mug. This morning's breakfast, she assumed as a television sat on the floor, merely providing background noise to the dark room.

"Nice," she said, fighting disgust at the sight of the blue carpet covered in stains of mud and whatever else the hunter had drug across his floor. The green and red plaid walls held similar stains. "Can I come in?"

"I haven't seen a Girl Scout around here since the day I showed up. Come on in. Get out of the street before someone sees you at my house." He swung the door open the rest of the way, allowing her to step through. Once Sage was inside, Worvacs poked his head out and ensured the street was still empty before he shut and locked the door. "So, to what do I owe this unexpected visit? Fawn carries the stuff you want."

"Well," Sage looked around the room in hopes of finding something of value while she was here before being discouraged, "Ya' see, Cole and I have this little African country. We like took them in and introduced them to band-aids and stuff. Anyways they love us. We rule over them now. So I was talking with Cole when we were tripping balls and was like 'Hey, if our country loves us, why not some other realm', right? I mean, you travel." She added, looking to the man as if she had just dreamed out loud.

"You're asking me?" Worvacs raised an orange eyebrow in suspicion. "Why? There are plenty of other people who can tell you where to look for an indigenous population. Unless..." Worvacs eyed the young troublemaker up and down before continuing with his own verbal thoughts, "Unless you can't get there on your own without anyone knowing. Ah now I see." He crossed his arms and leaned back against the door with a chuckle.

The girl was asking for his Quad Dimension Hopper. A marvelous machine that sported dual generators, a large cabin fit for two, and bright blue controls that matched his skin in color. It was his only personal means of dimensional travel. His only way to pull an income living in a realm with endangered species and hunting permits. She had to be on something now to be approaching him with such a request.

"Please, Worvacs?" Sage begged, batting her eyelashes, "You make the trip all the time! I mean, I can drive Chrome. How hard can using your Quad be? It's not like traffic's bad or anything."

She rolled her eyes, "I mean, it would only be a tiny little jump." Worvacs' arms remained folded across his chest as he stared down at her. "You could navigate? I mean," she spread her arms wide helplessly.

"Worvacs, blue god of..." her nose scrunched in defeat as her hands fell to her sides, "whatever it is you do."

"Vanity will get you almost anywhere. Almost. But not when someone doesn't trust you, and I don't trust you. I'll let you and Cole borrow her, but I want collateral first. Something valuable. That way if she's broken when I get her back, I won't have to kill and skin you both."

He watched as she folded her arms across her chest with a huff before adding, "Human hide sells for twenty-nine gold on Jarvadine, but is difficult to extract in one piece. It'd be much easier if I just sell your collateral and buy me a new Quad."

He's too good at this. "Fine," she bit back as she pursed her lips. "You can have Cole's Jacuzzi and a pound of green."

"Two pounds of green and you guys have to move the Jacuzzi. You can have it back as soon as you get back and not a minute sooner. You can use it as soon as the tub is hooked up and I have the green in hand. Do we have a deal?" he asked gleefully.

"Have you seen that thing?! It's going to be a bitch to get off of that patio. I don't even know how Cole got it there!" Sage exclaimed, raising her voice, "We can't get it off *and* get it hooked up! Not in any realistic amount of time. Not before someone notices. Not before you go back. Then, who would be getting fucked? No. The hot tub, two pounds, and..." She held her breath as she closed her eyes.

Sage didn't want it to resort to this. She couldn't see parting with her pride and joy. Her baby, a steel blue bike with 67 horsepower and a speed that topped out at 150 miles an hour. Chrome had earned his name with the elite deep roar that came from his polished underside, shined regularly by her followers. He had a mind of his own, one that was sensitive.

"Chrome," she sighed as she opened her eyes to meet his. Her cold heart broke as she offered the one thing that was irreplaceable.

Worvacs whistled softly, pushing himself off the door as he paused for a moment in thought before nodding respectively. "If you're willing to put Chrome on the line, keep the Jacuzzi. Just give me two pounds and the keys, an even deal. You promise to bring my girl back in the same shape as you take it out then I'll do the same with your boy out there." He pointed a thumb over his shoulder toward the thick chopper that sat in his front yard, "Sound fair?"

Sage watched as Worvacs moved to his plush couch. Her mouth dropped open as rage filled her mossy green eyes.

"Chrome is a man, thank you very much!" she bit, offended. "A boy can't vibrate like that! A boy don't give other men chubbies. Priests, maybe, but not men. Treat Chrome with respect. The hot tub and Chrome, the keys are mine!" she snapped, disgusted that Worvacs could say such a thing about her baby, "And the two pounds, for fuel costs."

"Fuck that!" Worvacs snapped back, having enough of her negotiating mind-games. His blue face turned purple as the blood rushed to his cheeks, "You want to use my baby for something more than tourism. You want to take it and go make some stone-age aliens believe you're a goddess! Keys for keys and two pounds to cover the fuel. Final offer!" He crossed his arms again, eyeing her inch for inch across the darkened room.

Sage inspected Worvacs, impressed by the normally quiet man who drooled over his prude girlfriend. Here he was standing up for himself. Making deals he was willing to stand by and not taking any less from her. He pulled a pipe from the leg pouch of his pants.

"Smoke on it?"

"Fine, we'll smoke on it." She grabbed a vase that he surely didn't buy himself and looked inside. Empty. Pulling the keys to Chrome out of her pocket, she kissed the keychain shaped like a pot leaf before dropping them in the vase.

"The Quad," she demanded, her eyes stern as she held the vase out.

Digging into his pocket, Worvacs pulled out his keys and sat them on the table, packing the pipe for them to share. "You have to understand, for me it's more than just a machine. She's my only way to make a decent living. Normal modes of transportation don't work for me because of my nature." He shrugged as Sage thought of her roaring motor outside, her only way in or out of this damned town.

***

Sage let herself into Cole's house, not concerned with knocking as she peeked in the oversized windows that lined the front of his bachelor pad.

"Oh Cole!" she called out flirtatiously, "I have something for you!" The sweetened smell of garlic and oregano swept over her as she walked into the spacious living room.

Cole was in the kitchen making manicotti when he heard the door open behind him, followed by his young love's voice.

"In here love," he answered, his hands and elbows covered in flour as he continued to knead the pasta dough. Sage's stomach rumbled as she jumped up to sit on the counter. Red sauce boiled in the pot beside her. "Stir that please. So, what'd you bring me?"

"I went and talked to space man…" she held up the keys with a jingle of satisfaction, "We got the Quad."

Cole let out a whistle, shocked by his girlfriend's negotiations. "Impressive. I honestly didn't think he would give them up." He flattened the dough, cutting out slices for wrapping without looking up. "What did you have to do? Pry it from his cold hands? Or maybe they were warm hands, hmm?" he asked teasingly.

"I operate the controls," she answered firmly, not allowing time for Cole's sexual references. Typically carefree in nature, she was ready to get this done with. Holding the keys to the dimensional shifter was nice. She couldn't deny it was a beautiful vehicle, but she was already homesick for her own leather seat.

"I let him borrow the keys to Chrome," she whispered to the countertop beneath her.

"Ouch! Chrome? Really?" Cole feigned a painful cringe, "I'm amazed he didn't have to pry the keys from your hand."

"Chrome will understand when he gets a new exhaust pipe from these ancient people. They do give gods and goddesses stuff, right?" she asked again for confirmation, nervous about the keys that rested in Worvacs' pocket.

"It'll be worth it. Yes they do and it's usually in large amounts of gold. Transporting it can be a pain sometimes," he shrugged as he scooped a spoonful of filling into the pasta, wrapping it closed.

"If we earned it, which we did working hard as god and goddess, then it is simply transporting our own earnings. The same as other people do."

"Not transporting it through customs. I meant actually moving it. Gold is actually quite heavy, especially if it hasn't been refined." He wrapped the last of the manicotti and laid it with the rest in the bottom of a glass baking dish. "I just hope the Quad can transport it all."

"I'm sure if blue-man can do it with some of the weirdo stuff he brings back, we can with a little bit of gold. It will be a cinch," she reached over and stuck her finger in the red sauce then sucked it off, "Make enough for both of us?"

Cole wiped his hands. He grabbed the cooking dish, placing it delicately in the oven. "A little bit of gold wouldn't be a problem. But what if not just a little? What if it's two tons? Three?" He raised an eyebrow questioningly as he stirred the sauce she had neglected.

"Don't add a thing!" She reached over his shoulder to dip her finger again, tasting the acidic tomato, a hint of garlic, the green of the parsley, and something sweet.

"I take that back," she retorted as she reached into his cabinets and pulled out a white seasoning, "Onion powder. And what if it is? Then we make more than one trip. No big deal," she shrugged, "We already agreed on the cost of fuel. We can run that baby dry, the same as blue-man will probably do with Chrome."

CHAPTER TEN

THE BALANCE

The Misfitz Tavern carried both a blessing and a curse as only Karma carried her law within its stone walls. This was based solely on a person's character; their outcome came from both demeanor and actions.

Christopher knew this as he sat in the back of the pub, drinking a beer as he waited for the mayhem to start. With no trouble going on, he had quickly gotten bored. And for a man such as himself, bored was never a good thing.

He could only hope that word would get back to Maxx of what he had done with precious little Savannah. That the father of his latest conquest would barge through the doors and, typically good-natured, do something completely out of character.

The darkened corner worked well for Christopher; both his face and those on the other side blurred by the curves and edges of the silk sheet curtain.

A cool breeze rushed into the tavern's walls as a hooded figure walked in. The dark hood looked around the bar before walking back to the booth. "Would you like some company?"

Christopher looked up at the hidden figure, raising an eyebrow. Surely if Lucifer had come back for him, she wouldn't have sent the reaper. That would be too easy for Miss Evil personified.

He kicked out the seat across from him and held out an open hand, "To what do I owe this visit?" He remained calm as he nonchalantly reached down to his leg and unbuckled the Glock on his thigh.

The figure was too short to be the married man he had been expecting. However, Christopher had faced beings from multiple realms over the years. One could never be too safe.

"A drink." The answer came from under the hood, not revealing the occupant, "And sworn secrecy that I was never ever here. To anyone."

Christopher tilted his head to the side, trying to get a look under the hood. Its voice that was stern, yet petite and feminine, "A lemon drop please, extra vodka."

"You'd better be worth the effort of me getting up to get you a drink. I've killed people for less." He stood and walked to the bar, glancing back towards the sheered booth regularly.

The person under the hood was familiar, though he couldn't place whether it was for a good or a bad reason.

Ordering the drink, he walked back and sat the glass before the hooded stranger. "Now answer my question. Who are you and what do you want?"

The figure reached up, pulling off the darkened hood to expose blonde pigtails and rounded cheeks. Christopher smiled wickedly at the sight of Savannah exposing herself. Her pigtails flopped into place on either side of her head as a giggle escaped her pink lips.

"Daddy said I should keep my distance. Please don't tell him I was here," she said, her green eyes pleading. The man's smile grew as wrinkles formed around his eyes. How many times he had heard young things tell him the same thing.

He leaned in with soothing words full of false promise, "Not a word, on my honor as a scoundrel. What did daddy dearest tell you about me, anyways? I'm just dying to know. Don't worry it'll be our little secret sweetheart." Christopher winked at her as he took a tentative sip.

"I can see you in public, but he doesn't want me alone with you," Savannah answered, confessing everything to the man she couldn't help but trust.

She looked around the tavern outside the curtain, able to see the figures of Fawn talking to Will. Her sister moved and socialized with others, unaware of her presence in the tavern. Their faces were blurred from the satin sheet. *This is still public, right? So I'm not disobeying Daddy.*

"Daddy said you were dangerous and Will agreed. I don't know why they are so worried about me. Sage is probably already pregnant with Cole's child and planning on robbing the bank on the way to their courthouse wedding. It's not fair," she pouted, crossing her arms as she looked down with innocent defeat.

"Well then I guess we just can't tell anybody what we're up to then, can we?" Christopher clinked the ice in his glass and took another sip, feeling the warming liquor gather droplets on his mustache. "So I hear you got a job working for Will. What made you decide on that?"

"He really didn't leave me with many options," Savannah answered, "He pulled the whole 'Well now that you know, you can see them and they can see you' spiel on me." She mocked the uptight voice of her now employer, sticking out her chest as she did, "Umm okay. So, I guess I'll take the job then. I still don't understand what intero—" She froze, realizing what she was about to say to someone who wasn't an employee.

A deer-in-the-headlights look quickly covered her face. Her eyes grew wide as her lips puckered into silence. Christopher's large body leaned closer to hear what the girl had to say. "Intercropping. I don't understand why he needs two employees for intercropping but perhaps he does truly have that many plants," she corrected quickly with a nip of her words, hoping he hadn't noticed.

"Yes, Will's plants… so when do you start? I might have you look into grabbing something for me while you're down there one day." He smiled at her mischievously.

"You mean stealing?" Savannah asked, her eyes growing wide. "I couldn't do that. Will might fire me. At the very least he would tell Daddy. She shivered at the thought of the special treatment Sage got from their father, the bars on her windows; disappointment showing in his eyes. "I'm sorry, I can't."

"It's not really stealing when it's in such a vast supply. It's like eating a grape at the grocery store while shopping. You still pay for the grapes, they are just a bit lighter when they weigh them. It's only pennies on the dollar. I'm just talking about one leaf off of one plant." Christopher smiled his most innocent smile at her, adding emphasis to the tiny little leaflet.

"I suppose you're right," Savannah answered, "I mean, you do buy the plants from him so really I suppose that makes sense.

Savannah nervously bit her lip as she tried to come up with a plan. "Maybe I can sneak it out, but that means even more so that we have to keep our friendship a secret."

"Excellent!" He smiled, pulling out a pen and his business card from the law office. Drawing a sketch of the three-cornered, long stemmed leaf he was after, he slid it across the table to Savannah.

His right eyebrow, blonde yet faded with a light gray, dipped with a wink as she looked at the picture. "It will have a gold stem and leaves that flash multiple colors. Almost like a chameleon." He smiled inwardly as he thought of the destruction he could cause now that this little minion was willing to help.

***

The following afternoon, Savannah quietly knocked on the purple stained glass door.

"Come on in Savannah," Will's voice vibrated through the intercom, thankful for the break from the blueprints he was having to make up for Angel's new abode as he pushed them away in frustrated disgust.

Walking in, Savannah closed the door behind her. She looked around the room, taking time to see the rows of books that surrounded Will's fireplace.

She couldn't help but wonder with hopeful glee that maybe once she was more comfortable with the job, he might let her borrow one to read. Walking over to the clear chair, she sat in front of Will's desk.

"So, I thought about what you said," she whispered, refusing to make direct eye contact with her employer as she fiddled with the hem of her flower print dress. "About how I need to, like, work different jobs. That it's more than just bartending."

Will sat upright in his office chair, raising a silent eyebrow with curiosity. "Really?" he asked, feigning shock. Will knew Savannah had come in the night before, secretively in fact. That she sat in the back with the attorney her father had warned her about. Little happened within the tavern's walls without Will's knowledge.

"Uh huh," Savannah answered thoughtfully, "I know Kritter is training me tonight in the kitchen, and then tomorrow before school with housekeeping, but Cole does interrogation and… and I can too." Her voice was firm with a childlike desire to do what her older cousin was doing.

Will fought back a chuckle when she crossed her arms with determination, insistent that she could handle the more difficult task. One that he laid upon the backs of men with faces of stone.

Could it be possible little Savannah believed she could question one of the most wanted and untouchable men in the realms? That she could pull information? Will's interest peaked.

"Oh?" he asked, intrigued by the girl's sudden interest in Cole's skill set.

"Actually, I have already interrogated, but it's a secret. I'm not supposed to tell," she answered, looking down at her lap.

Will rubbed his eyes. Now he understood how the child would get information. He also realized that he would have to interrogate her as well to figure out what she learned.

"Savannah," he answered, glancing over at the stack of papers on his desk. He missed the simplicity the blueprints now held in comparison. "The whole point of interrogation is *to* tell me what you found out. You're supposed to promise them that you won't tell, and then you do. That's what Sir and Cole do. Now, what did Christopher say?"

Savannah looked down at the pink and yellow flowers on her dress in thought. She didn't want to betray her friend, but knew Will was right.

"He wanted me to steal," she whispered softly, "But I had to let you know."

"I'm glad you did," Will answered, walking over to the bookshelf.

His mind processed what she told him as he searched the books for an answer. Sometimes it was as easy as the magic holding the tavern together, calling out to him and offering its silent advice.

A dark blue binding stood out among the rest. *Brave New World.*

The tavern knew what was best. Perhaps interrogation was the reason he had hired Savannah. Will sighed once more and turned back around. He had learned a long time ago not to question the tavern's judgment.

"Do it," he told the innocent schoolgirl, "I'll provide you with whatever it is that Christopher wants, but you are *not* to tell him I know. If you do, you will be fired on the spot and be banned from my bar. Permanently. Do I make myself clear?" He looked sternly at Savannah, who nodded quickly.

"I agree with your dad. It's not safe for you to be alone with

Christopher, but I can't control what you do off the clock. However, while you are working, you won't be alone with him. He is dangerous."

"But how—" Savannah started in confusion.

"Savannah," Will cut her off as he walked back to his desk. Leaning forward, his blue eyes met hers. She could tell the man was serious.

He wrote her name in his schedule book. "Saturday, you will be working with Sir. I don't want you practicing any interrogation techniques on your own until then. I also want a report on my desk before you clock in."

Will handed Savannah a piece of paper from his printer. She quickly wrote down the due date before looking up.

"It will be on Sidney Reilly. Two pages; front and back. Handwritten," he continued, pulling the blueprints closer once more.

"Okay boss," Savannah answered quickly with a nod that shook her pigtails.

CHAPTER ELEVEN

THE "PROPER" PLACE

A fire blazed in the white cobblestone fireplace. Sir sat on the plush leather couch with his legs crossed as he read his latest book of choice. Meanwhile, Pet scampered about the kitchen preparing their dinner with swift, precise movements. The couple remained silent, minus the occasional turn of a page.

"What is on your mind today, my Pet? You've been unusually quiet."

Pet's focus remained on the potatoes before her. "I have found myself lonely." She turned her attention to the carrots she wished to add to Sir's favorite dish.

"Oh yes, that reminds me," Sir answered as he turned the page to continue his reading. He left the room in silence just long enough to make Pet's heart skip a beat, "I know you match, but is it the proper set?"

"No, Sir." Her heart pounded.

He looked up from his book. His eyes burned hotter than the fire before him as he held up a single finger, "That is one, my Pet." His tone was colder than the rock floor beneath their feet. His firm palm itched for its first strike. "I believe you should change. In front of me. NOW!"

How had I been so foolish? "Yes, Sir!" Pet answered quickly. She put down the knife and urgently rushed behind the stairs that led up to their playroom. Relishing the punishment to come, her eyes darted up the red velvet stairs to the thick double doors.

She quickly entered her white bedroom. If there was one thing Sir didn't stand for, it was disobedience and her under garments not matching was one of her most punishable offenses. Turning, she quickly knelt before her antique dresser.

"I'm waiting!" his cold voice called out impatiently. Pet dug, searching for a bra and thong set in black. It was the one color that might make up for her infraction

"Shit!" she cursed. She searched deeper through drawer after drawer, flustered and yet secretly enjoying the idea of being able to add another lashing onto their evening session.

Pet heard her dominant's voice call out "two" adding to her evening's lashings. She smiled at the thought as her fingers closed around a lace set. Closing the drawer, she knew to be prompt in her rush back to Sir's side.

Pet stood in front of Sir at the couch, patiently awaiting his acknowledgment. Her eyes wandered up to where he sat, continuing to read.

Without allowing herself to be noticed, she took his silence as a moment to try and read the man. To prepare for what was to come.

The man was typically tense and his body language was more difficult for the woman to pick up on. However, he appeared slightly more somber tonight.

Sir's gray eyes scanned the page as Pet watched to see if he clenched his jaw. His legs were relaxed as they rested on the couch. His narrow chest was taut and shoulders held back, keeping him in an upright position. Perhaps he needed this session just as badly as she did. Pet was enthralled by such an adventure.

Sir continued to read for a few minutes before finishing the chapter. He silently dog-eared the page and closed his book. Swinging his legs down from the couch, he sat with his eyes level at her toned waist. "That's two now, Pet. You earned the second one when you made me wait. Now, show me what you've brought."

He watched as she pulled the red bra and thong from behind her back and held them out in her hands for viewing, looking down at him for approval that she already knew she wouldn't receive.

"Red? *Tsk tsk*, Pet. You didn't make sure that your black set was clean, did you?" He shook his head in disappointment as he held up three fingers, "That's three now, Pet. You may have been missing your collar before, but you won't be after I'm through with you this evening. Now change."

"Yes, Sir." Swiftly turning around, she placed the red set on the coffee table before her. She then knelt in front of Sir, keeping her eyes locked on the floor.

She couldn't deny that the cold marble stone of the living room felt better on her knees than the hardwood floor of the playroom. She swept the dark braid that signified her submissive position over her shoulder to expose the zipper on the back of her dress.

This was a routine that Sir enjoyed immensely as if he were removing the only armor between them.

His fingers traced the back of her neck. Pet couldn't help but crave more of her dominant's touch. As Sir slowly unzipped the barrier her skin crawled with a want for more.

Pet waited until the man stopped moving and sat back in his seat before she turned around. She slipped one sleeve and then the other off her petite shoulders. She delicately peeled the dress down her body past her knees and stepped out of it. Folding the fabric neatly, she placed it on the marble coffee table behind her.

Standing before him, Pet recited the rules of their contract. "As Pet, I will obey all of my Sir's requests without hesitation or fear. With hesitation, I am subject to the consequences of my actions." She reached behind her back and unhooked her bra, folded it neatly, and then placed it on top of the deep blue dress.

"As Pet, I will always remember to address Sir by his proper title unless told otherwise. Failing to do so will result in punishment befitting my forgetfulness." Hooking her thumbs in the waistband of the thong, she slowly slid it off her hips and down her sculpted thighs. Folding it neatly, it joined the other clothes on top of the pile.

"As Pet, I will always strive to please Sir in all that I do. I will be a good Pet for my Sir. For if I am not, I will suffer the results of him being displeased." She stood silently with her vows, waiting for his acknowledgment or correction on her responses.

"In result, my Sir will provide me with safety and serenity. He shall make certain that all of my needs are met. Physically, emotionally, spiritually, sexually, and financially. He shall guide me towards self-control and perseverance."

"Excellent, Pet. You have pleased me by reciting our rules perfectly. You may continue." Sir waved his hand toward the other undergarments on the table waiting to be put on.

"Yes, Sir, of course." She quickly turned and picked up the new clothes off the coffee table.

Nothing was to be folded over or crisscrossed. It was to fit her delicate body neatly, as if she were a mannequin on display. Making certain it was straight on her waistline she applied the same rules to the red bra.

Sir inspected Pet's attire thoroughly, making note of her attention to fine-detail, her eagerness to please.

"Your behavior has been lacking of late, my Pet." The woman stood up straighter, as if to make up for her poor performance. "I have been too lax on your training if it is so easy for you to forget the most simple of tasks that I set for you. This isn't the only mistake you have made in the last week, is it? Are you deliberately trying my patience, Pet?"

"I have been trying to behave myself, Sir!" Pet answered as her mind quickly raced through the days since their last session.

Sir stood, closing the distance between the two of them in one swift motion. He reached over, his finger trailing her shoulder blade, and then down her neck.

Pet knew better than to let a shiver escape her as she felt her pulse quicken. Beneath the gentle graze of his fingertip, her blood began to race through her veins. Her breathing heightened with anticipation of what was to come.

Punish me! I have been bad. Please! Her mind begged as her body ached. Or perhaps this was her punishment; anticipation leading nowhere. She could only hope her master was more merciful than that.

He leaned forward, breathing in the smell of her hair. Excitement didn't describe the feeling that surged through his own body. The flowery smell of the woman before him, dressed only in the barest of clothing. Seeing her heavenly skin and knowing it was best not to touch it, not yet. He didn't just want her, Sir needed to punish the girl before him.

Keeping his composure, he whispered in her ear, "And what do you think your punishment should be?"

A shiver raced up Pet's spine with Sir's words, knowing this was a trick question that was to be answered properly without hesitation. "You can have my hide Sir," she answered without allowing herself to put thought into her answer.

Sir's jaw clenched as Pet felt the tension radiate off him, filling her. Her muscles tensed with his own, knowing that she had displeased him. She felt the insufficient answer already tinging her left buttocks.

"You *will not* tell me what I can and can't have!" he barked back, causing Pet to squeeze her eyes shut against the urge to jump at his scolding, "I will take what I please, when I please! Do you understand, Pet?" he growled as she silently nodded, "That's four."

Hearing the two words she had been hoping to avoid and yet craving to hear, she answered, "Yes, Sir! My apologies."

"Ready position," Sir answered, pleased with the immediate look that filled Pet's periwinkle eyes as she stood without hesitation, ready to wait upon her knees.

"When I say…" he added, "We'll see what kind of mood I'm in. For now, I could use a cold drink." Her heart sunk with his words as she trudged to the kitchen, the shining light of submission dimming slightly in her eyes.

Sir silently opened his book, returning to where he had last left off as he heard Pet rummaging around. She was eager to do whatever it took to please him. A smile that was rarely exposed crept across his lips as he continued his reading.

CHAPTER TWELVE

DAY SEVEN

The familiar smell of old wood and heavy smoke filled her senses as Angel opened the door to the tavern. Her dark brown eyes shined with joy.

"And on the seventh day, he rested!" she called out as she walked up to the bar and grabbed the drink Legs had waiting for her.

"I never rest and there's a reason for that, you know?" Will answered, smiling at Angel as she sat at the bar, "You know it's too bad some angels aren't in here. I would have loved to see the looks on their faces." He smiled bemusedly as he put down the glass he'd been polishing with his bar towel.

He ignored the glare of warning he received from Tatianna from across the tavern. *I must have hit a sore spot on that one,* he thought.

"Speaking of which, has our resident courtesan ever had an angel for a customer?"

"Hmm..." she murmured in thought, tapping the side of her chin before a smile crossed her ruby red lips, "If you'll tell the tale of the tavern, I'll confess." Her smile widened as Will sighed, knowing it was one of her favorites.

Looking around the barely occupied bar, Will snapped his fingers. The lock on the front door swung into place as the neon

'OPEN' sign flickered out.

"Kritter, go down to the hydro bays and bring me some purple genie. If I'm going tell it again, then I'm going to tell it right. Gather around misfits, it's story time." He watched as the few regulars who remained in the bar filtered closer, filling the empty bar stools.

Savannah quickly rushed over to the nearest bar stool, patting the seat beside her for Christopher to join her. Sage leaned back against Cole, who wrapped his arm around her waist. Tatianna laughed, placing her empty glass on the bar top as she sat next to her best friend, Sage.

"Barista!" she yelled to Legs, snapping her fingers before pointing to the cup, "Show us your mediocre bartending skills!"

Legs poured Tatianna's drink ignoring the woman's offensive words. She leaned against the bar, ready to first hear word of how the Pub, her job and home, had been created.

"Come on Worvacs!" Fawn chuckled as she socked the brute's cobalt colored arm.

"Ugh, again old man? Don't you ever tell any other stories?" Worvacs asked half-heartedly, moving toward the bar top.

"No," Will answered simply as Kritter rushed back up the stairs and gently handed him the purple leaf. Pulling a Zippo from his pocket, Will lit the end of the leaf. He watched the flame crest for a moment before blowing it out and placing the still smoldering leaflet into a glass ashtray.

Pet glanced in the direction of the bar before looking back to Sir. He sat straight; his black suit only added emphasis to the stern man's mysterious demeanor.

"May we, Sir?" her low voice asked with hope as she eyed the front of the bar lined with happy-go-lucky patrons and the employees who served them.

"Yes Pet, I believe we shall. It has been too long since I heard this tale. Even I must admit there is something about the way young William tells it." Sir slid his chair back smoothly and stood.

Holding out his hand for Pet, he escorted her across the room with elegance, guiding his queen from one throne to another. Sir nodded to William as he and Pet took the last two seats at the far end of the bar.

"Everybody got a drink?" Will asked as he smiled at his most loyal patrons. They came from every walk of life, from every corner in the realms. "You all have different theories on how creation began. That's fine. Keep them to yourselves for the time being. In the beginning—"

"C'mon, c'mon. Get to it old man," Christopher interjected. Will glared at him mercilessly before replacing the glare with a warm smile.

"And you, Christopher, will most certainly shut the hell up while I'm telling this story or afterwards I'll tell everyone how you came to be here."

Christopher's eyes flared for a moment. What appeared to be both fear and excitement covered his rugged face. It quickly diminished as Tatianna's doe-like eyes flashed in warning from across the bar.

Should he speak another word, she would surely cut out his tongue herself. "Carry on then," Christopher answered, averting his eyes from his comrade. He waved his fingers towards Will in an attempt at nonchalance.

"He told you," Sage laughed as she propped her feet into Tatianna's lap. "Story time! Story time! Come on Will, how did 'Fuckered Up' come into our lives?" she asked, her voice echoing a hearty roar of amusement.

"Hush!" Pet bit back. The warning that escaped the usually mouse-like woman rang throughout the bar not with threat, but with promise following in its wake. She glared at the woman, daring her to tempt her wrath. Her voice lowered once more as her eyes dropped back to the bar top, "Let William speak."

Will nodded in appreciation before he cleared his throat and started again, "In the beginning, God made the heavens. He created the Earth and the stars—"

"And blah, blah, blah. Day seven!" Sage piped in, already forgetful of Pet's threat only moments before.

She was met with a deathly glare from the submissive woman. As Tatianna nudged her, she was reminded that there was no chain on the other end of Pet's collar. A bright smile covered Sage's face as she quickly added, "Please."

"We all know that on the seventh day God rested. Well not exactly..." For added effect, Will lowered the lighting in the room to a soft glow by rubbing the tips of his fingers together.

***

The Creator and Adam sat on the bank of a slow trickling stream that flowed down the grassy plains they had walked the night before. The Creator was pleased with the world he had crafted over the past six days. All was good.

As the birds chirped their beautiful melody, Adam asked The Creator questions about the world, which he would answer. Finally, Adam asked a question that had been weighing on his mind.

"Where will we live?" Adam asked as he scratched the tops of his feet before placing them into the cold, running stream one at a time. He instinctively knew that man required three basic necessities: Food, air, and shelter. Adam couldn't explain why, but deep in his soul, he required a place of shelter.

"Where do you wish to live?" The Creator asked, looking to the first of man for input on his own needs.

"Near here I think. I like taking this walk with you and want to do it more often. If Eve will allow it, of course," Adam replied. He smiled at his creator and tossed some hops into the water.

"Very well, then. Through those woods, on the other side of the stream, there is a clear field that will do nicely I think. Build a house there. It shall be two floors, built of rock and wood. We will walk

together every seven days. Sound like a plan?" The Creator asked, grinning at Adam. He then pulled some barley from the ground, rubbed it back and forth between his palms, and threw it into the water. A lily pad grew where the barley had fallen and a frog jumped on it.

"I have no tools," Adam answered thinking of the woman he wanted to provide for; the one that had come from his rib.

"With me, all is possible," The Creator answered. It left Adam silent for a moment before nodding his head. He listened to the music of the angels cascading gently around them, flowing beautiful from the sounds of heaven to the sounds of Earth and back again. The birds joined in with their high soprano chirps, as the frog on the lily pad added bass with its deep voice.

"Okay. So will it always be like this?" Adam asked.

"Like what?" The Creator answered with a smile, amused at the curiosity he had instilled in man. It was much like his own fascination with everything he created.

"You know... this," Adam waved his arms out dramatically at everything around them, insinuating the peaceful bliss of the world's seventh day.

"I think we're going to need a drink for this," The Creator's voice was full of sadness. Reaching down into the mud of the stream, he pulled out two handfuls of clay and began fashioning cups out of them.

"What's a drink?" Adam quizzically watched his deity fashioning two rounded shapes out of clay.

"It's what you take when you're thirsty," looking over he noticed Adam's still incomprehensible look and smiled, "Don't worry about it, you'll figure it out soon enough."

When satisfied that the shapes were correct, he set them on a rock next to him to bake in the sunlight. "No," The Creator answered with a saddened sigh, "It won't always be like this. Good and bad will happen because you and everyone after you are going to do things. Those things are going to shape this world and the creatures in it. Some are going to be good people with the best of heart. Others are going to be bad. They are going to hurt their fellow man, for the sake of hurting. It is the balance that I put into everything, starting with the first morning and night. I created balance so everything in the universe would stay right side up." Shrugging, he checked the tackiness of the clay before looking over to the woods on the far side of the river.

A deer and her fawn slowly walked out of the woods and down to the creek to lick hesitantly at the water while watching their reflections.

"Am I good or bad?" Adam asked hesitantly, not sure if he wanted to invoke his creator's wrath so soon after creation.

"You? You are like every man that will come from your seed. The same as this plant," The Creator leaned down and gently touched a yellow flower, causing it to bloom. "You carry both, in here," He pointed to Adam's bare chest. Adam looked down with only slight understanding. "There will be others after you, some that will be either completely good or all bad, but you... You're the in-between. The really neat thing is you get to decide which one you'll do more of as I have granted you free will."

The Creator sighed as he saw the days that would follow. He shook his head when he thought of how soon Eve would be picking from the Tree of Forbidden Fruit and offering it to the young man before him. "But you will do both, whether you mean to or not."

Adam nodded silently in agreement with his maker before asking, "So there will be others too? Some good, some bad?"

"Yep. But in the end everyone gets to come home," The Creator answered smiling up at the sky as he closed his eyes and felt the warmth of the sun on his face.

"Everyone? Good and bad?" Adam sounded unsure.

"Everyone," the deity whispered, embracing the fact that for now it could be spoken as such, "Now since everyone gets to make the choice to believe in something bigger than themselves, it's up to them to decide to do it. Man has no fate but the one he makes. Whether I know what's going to happen or not is irrelevant."

The Creator felt the cups of clay again. Satisfied they would hold, he dipped them into the water of the stream before pulling them out again. He set the two clay cups back on the rock and returned to his seat next to Adam.

"Can the good help others become good?" Adam asked quietly. He needed to know there was still hope for all of his future brethren.

"Of course," The Creator answered, "And the other way around too. But they'll need a place to meet. Somewhere that both sides can come to and the in-between can keep the balance." Picking up the two cups he handed one to Adam, who took it gingerly between his hands. Lifting the cup to his lips, the deity drank the cool amber liquid and let it roll gently across his tongue.

Adam watched in fascination as his creator… drank? He understood the term instantly as he watched The Creator's throat move with each gulp. Looking down at the clay holder of golden liquid, he shrugged before lifting it to his lips and mimicked his motions.

As it crossed his tongue, he felt a flood of emotions hit him: Satisfaction, hopefulness, sadness, and everything in between.

"Not bad. We'll call it 'beer'," The Creator said with a nod as he looked into his clay cup.

"Beer?" Adam asked questioningly before looking back down at his own. Shrugging, he took another sip of the heavenly liquid.

Emotions cascaded over him once more like the rays of the sun and he understood. The sun and the moon, the heavens and the earth, the light and the darkness. He could see it all and, for a moment through the divine spark that was deep in his soul, he knew in the end everything would be alright. "Beer."

"Second sip is always better."

The Creator watched as Adam continued to draw off his mug. He smiled before clearing his throat to pull Adam from his contemplations with the drink.

Adam finished the muddy container and dropped it to the ground before his whole body shook from head to toe with a very vocal, "Brrrrrrrlllllpppp."

"You're a misfit Adam, a misfit among nature, but I think I kind of like you. You'll need some place for them to meet, you know…"

"Who?" Adam cocked his head to face his creator, momentarily

drawn away from the conversation.

"The good and the bad, focus dear boy."

"Oh, right. Ummm... here's good. I can serve them this and everyone will be happy! Right?" Adam asked gleefully. He dipped his cup back into the river and refilled it.

"You are a misfit, Adam."

The Creator smiled as he sipped his beer and thought of all the things to come.

***

Tatianna handed Will a twenty as he cashed out her tab for the evening. "Consider us square then. So, you're not a no-mag?" She climbed back into the barstool beside her, leaning towards Will in the dim lights of the closed tavern. "What's in your blood, may I ask?"

She already knew the answer. Anyone who had been past the pearly gates knew the answer. He was a son of Adam, both blessed with a solid foundation of land to live on and cursed to stay where their head lay. Generations of father and son, forced to stay on the precious property touched by the hand of The Creator.

Money and a well-built establishment were guaranteed, success flowing through the brick and mortar, but it came with a cost. Once a man was bound to the building, his time away was limited. She had to know for herself if the rumors amongst angels were true.

Will smirked, shaking his head before answering, "No, I'm not a no-mag. I just choose not to use it as frequently as everyone else. It's always seemed a bit like cheating to me. Like people who abuse it because they're too lazy to work. There is a place for magic, just in moderation. As far is what's in my blood… are you sure you really want to know?" His blue eyes glistened in the empty tavern as he raised an eyebrow. Catching a glimpse at the afterglow where her wings once rested, he questioned whether or not he had truly seen the purple feathers or if the neon lights were fooling him.

"I've heard worse, so nothing surprises me. What's in your blood?" Tatianna asked again, this time a smirk peeking across her lips.

Will exhaled. He closed his eyes, letting down the wards that had concealed his nature for years. As his forefather's blood coursed through Will's veins, a blinding white light radiated from his skin, the gold blood in his veins shined through as the darkened room lit up from where he stood behind the oak bar.

Tatianna's gasp informed him that she could see his true nature, his lineage. For a moment Will exposed his direct link, all the way back to Adam and everything it entailed. When he was satisfied she had seen enough, he replaced his wards to hide what he considered a curse. When he felt they were securely in place and the light had faded, he opened his eyes.

Tatianna nodded her head softly. Her heart ached at the sight of such divinity, remembering her own falling from grace. "So, the bloodline traces you to him. The story of Adam was true?" She looked away, avoiding eye contact.

"He was my great-great-great-blah-blah-blah-grandfather. The only reason I told you is because I know what you once were and I know you hate divine intervention just as much as I do," he sighed again, pulling his nubbed cigarette from the ashtray and relighting it.

"Divine intervention took my wings from me," she confessed with disgust towards herself. Towards the decisions she and Christopher had made.

She missed the wings that she had once held with so much pride. Their dark, purple beauty where she could find comfort in their warmth by surrounding herself in feathers as though it were a blanket pulled straight from the dryer. There was an ache that still filled her, wrenching through her chest and out her spine as her wings were pulled, taken from her forever.

"Apparently God is not without a sense of irony?" Will laughed heartily, his face glowing with a warm smile before shaking his head. "All my life I've been on the road. I never had a place to call my home, never needed one. Now I'm stuck in my home and can't get out."

"At least it's a guaranteed roof over your head," she answered, her brown eyes meeting his.

CHAPTER THIRTEEN

AND PSYCHEDELIC SHROOMS

There was no proper way to measure time within the capsule of the Quad. Yet Cole waited impatiently as his structural system was scanned, organized, and reprogrammed all at a slow, encumbering pace. He leaned back against his seat in the teleport pad, attempting to comfort his aching ass from the wait.

The auto-nav of the Quad scanned though realm names and distances on a holographic screen. Cole watched as the teleport sent them past planets smaller than the moon in realms that had never before been seen by Earthly humans. Realms that carried stars twenty times larger than the Earth's sun in both size and grandeur tugged, causing a soft turbulence in the sphere that still sat within Worvacs' home.

A starry nebula of greens and purples appeared on the screen. A white dwarf star winked back playfully as Cole stared at the diversity of foreign realms the Quad had to offer. The feeling of just how small he truly was had yet to wear off.

"There! That's it! We need to make a pit stop!" Sage gasped, yanking Cole from his thoughts. She jumped forward in her reclining leather seat, immediately pushing buttons and turning dials on the equipment. The screen rotated as meters read with statistical numbers of the realm in focus. The Quad jerked viciously, causing Cole's stomach to jump into his rib-cage as the auto-pilot stopped scanning and Sage regained control.

"Whadda' ya' mean make a pit stop? What kind of pit stop?" Cole leaned over her shoulder from his own seat, glancing at the dials with concern. "Do we have enough juice for a pit stop?"

"Look!" she spouted using her free hand to point at a tiny sphere on the left of the enlarged touch screen before them.

The entire realm was a psychedelic trip. Florescent pinks rose and fell like waves, splashed with the dark, heavy foams of navy and magenta. Shades of bright yellow burned into fiery reds before dying back down to a soft peach. Blues, greens, and purple flowed beautifully as the gases radiated in a tie-dyed fog.

"We have to check it out, I don't care!" she demanded, giving the command word causing the computer to activate the automatic countdown for transport that quickly turned the miniature Quad on the screen to face the foreign realm.

"Easy there love! I don't want to imagine what Worvacs will do to us if we tear up his precious toy."

"Well!" Sage huffed, "Worvacs will understand. Whatever kind of balls they're tripping for the whole realm to look like this, I want some." She bit her lip in concentration before calling out the activation code.

As they entered the realm's atmosphere a ripple shook the sphere surrounding them. A red laser ran over both of them, collecting their composite data as their knees went weak beneath them.

Cole released the breath he had been holding in, suddenly understanding why DNA molecules twisted as they did. He could feel his organs forming in the same braided tie. The Quad's artificial gravity dampeners kicked in as the turbine generator roared behind both their heads. Almost instantly Sage's mossy eyes went wide. "Dude, look!"

The window before them showed the outside of the receiving teleport pad. Mushrooms of every shape and size greeted the pair of aliens to the foreign realm. Neon pink and orange stood out with temptation against the darkened colors of wine and ruby. Electric blue shined among the mushrooms' rounded covers. The tinted glass did little to dampen the new realm's excitement.

A red and yellow landscape seemed to go on for miles. The colors mixed like oil and water, lying next to one another but never joining as they zig-zagged into a distant mirage. Cole eyed the breathtaking landscape, finally conceding.

"Now can we take a pit stop?" Sage asked with a knowing grin.

"Okay, you win." Eyeing the display in front of him, Cole scanned the surrounding area. Before him was a flashing button. Pushing it, he activated the sphere release.

As the sphere began to dissolve around them, Cole and Sage quickly felt the new realm's gravity take effect on them. They moved clumsily at first as they realized that it was less than the Earth norm. Their physical movements happened a second or two faster than back home. Eyeing the teleport sphere around them, older model screens filled the room giving various readouts on the local habitat.

"There are life form readings. Possibly a small populace."

"Really?" Sage asked with hope, "Anything else? Power sources? Vehicles?"

"None. There's a small, and I mean small, clearing near the center of a few huts. The infrared is picking up warm interiors on some of the mushrooms. I'm assuming they have homes built inside?" The thought of living in a mushroom appealed to Cole in a strange way, almost a teasing idea of retirement. "Baby, I think I'm in love. Let's go see if they're friendly. Is the air safe to breathe?" He hoped to be able to interact with these hippie locals.

Sage looked at the air composition meters. The needles bounced within the safety zone on the oxygen and carbon dioxide odometers. Gazing over methane and carbon monoxide, both indicated safe. Her lips curled in one of the most dangerous smiles to ever cover the girl's face.

Cole failed to notice Sage's devious grin. He was too enamored with the view of the landscape, pointing first at one spot and then another. He searched for a local inhabitant of this new realm as his excitement grew.

"There! There! Aww look! The natives are coming out to meet us!"

"We're good," Sage snickered. She wouldn't tell Cole of the foreign chromoxide and neurotropogen gases. It would be more fun watching as the man became light headed and started hallucinating. "Can I drop the sunroof?" she offered.

"Go for it. I've been breathing this stale air since we entered the Quad at Worvacs'. The oxygen scrubbers only work so much on longer teleports. Ooh, look at that one!" He laughed at the sight of the small populace that gathered near the clearing they had spotted on the display monitors.

"They look like wrinkly smurfs! And they're green! Want to give these guys a shot? I know it's a little closer to home than we had planned, but it's the only inhabited sphere for twenty or thirty realms in any direction."

Sage paid no attention to Cole's excited rantings as she pushed the down button on her right. A loud clank sounded as the dome-like windshield built into the ceiling slowly began to retract.

"Cole!" she hushed, inhaling deeply. She embraced the fresh air, allowing it to fill her lungs as she closed her eyes. She felt the grooves of her fingertips, each individual canyon touching the skin of her palms. Opening her dilated eyes, the psychedelic purples circled the man's now-orange face.

"Just…" she inhaled deeply once more. Her mind rushed to a light-headed oblivion as her skin tingled. The fibers of her hair stood on end, each one straightened, unique. "Breathe…" she exhaled, meditating alongside the heightened air.

Cole inhaled the air deep into his lungs. A smile curled at his lips as a shiver ran down his spine. The air alone was a miracle cure after being stuck in an inter-realm teleport sphere for twelve hours straight. A child-like giggle escaped him.

"Oh thank the gods we are about to become," he exhaled, inhaling again as his head lightened. Soft voices twittered in angelic tones from below causing Cole to open his eyes.

"Are they... are they singing?" He peeked his head through the exit hatch of the building. "This is great!"

Sage looked in a mirror, applying a fresh layer of pink lip-gloss. She pulled the ponytail from her hair and flattened out the frizz, making sure to look nice for her future followers.

The tiny beings before the doorway continued to sing as Cole stepped out. Sage joined him, doing her best to fight back a giggle. The creatures' skin was sea-foam in color. Wrinkly and prune-like, it folded over in layers. Their rounded ears had floppy skin that drooped as they fell to their knobby knees in worship. As the natives threw their heads up toward the clouded sky, their glazed-over eyes looked up at the teleport's glass dome.

"All hail!" they squeaked out in mouse-like unison. Sage snorted and her face turned red, fighting back the urge to burst out in laughter. The petite wrinkled hands of the followers flailed forward as they faced the ground once more in a bow. Their ears flew over their heads, hitting the trippy rock surface with a *querplack.*

Sage finally lost it. Grabbing her stomach with a roar of laughter, she fought back tears at the sight before her.

CHAPTER FOURTEEN

THE LAWS OF INTERROGATION

The last house on the corner of Ricky Road was two-stories tall with no windows on the top floor. In the backyard a small pond rested where koi swam peacefully. Flowers surrounding the pond bloomed with a beauty that, other than the owners of the home, only bees and hummingbirds got the pleasure of enjoying.

A black cat sat outside, an omen to the young girl as she knocked on the door softly. Through the large door with red stained windows, Savannah could see into the glass terrarium of a front porch.

More flowers, some foreign and unrecognizable, climbed the walls with deep green vines. Rocks and sand covered the floor and a glassed-in tunnel went down the middle of the room. It protected the delicate foreign plants from mankind. Savannah waited on her heels, ready to turn around if someone didn't answer immediately.

Sir heard the knock from the living room couch and nodded at Pet, who had quickly looked to him for confirmation. "See who it is, Pet. I may not be in the mood for visitors yet, but we shall see." He licked his finger, turning another page in his current novel.

Pet nodded. Standing up quickly, she moved to the opening

in the front of the room that exposed the glass walkway. Blonde pigtails ruffled in the window as Savannah moved her face closer in curiosity.

"It's Savannah Connor, Sir," the petite woman in black informed her master, her eyes never parting from the door. Her voice was barely audible over the cackle of the fireplace.

Sir held up a finger as he finished his page, making Pet wait a few moments. When Sir finished the page he dog-eared the corner. Setting the book on his end table, he sat up and turned to Pet, nodding for her to open the door. The young school girl stepped through the entryway timidly.

"Ah young Savannah. William told me I'd be seeing you sooner or later. To what do I owe this pleasure?"

"I was told to come here for training," Savannah answered cautiously. Her blue eyes darted about the spacious, darkened interior of the co-habitation.

The entire room was decorated in shades of gray and black. Rock walls and marble floor left the vast space feeling cold, clammy even. A large fireplace provided the room's only warmth and was surrounded by bookshelves, couches, and a large oriental rug.

The young girl wrapped her arms around herself as she looked at the grand staircase in the center of the room. It led up to a red set of double doors. A shiver ran down Savannah's spine as to what might sit on the other side.

Savannah turned to the stern man. "The boss said you were going to train me in interrogation?" she asked, holding herself against the chill that seemed to creep into her bones.

Her arms are crossed. Uncertainty perhaps? Sir's mind reeled with the possibilities. "Did he now?" Sir asked with a devious smile creeping across his lips. He closed his book and placed it on the coffee table before motioning to the seat across from him. "Pet, please bring me a whiskey sour and a..." He looked at Savannah questioningly. A person's drink order could often tell a considerable amount about their personality and attitude.

"A Sprite, please," Savannah answered, smiling to Pet.

Pet nodded and obediently walked to the far corner of the room, silently making the drinks requested and leaving Savannah and Sir alone.

Savannah moved, sitting across from Sir. She kept her knees close together, her ankles crossed, and her posture straight and ladylike. The man's smile, rarely seen by anyone, grew as he noticed the girl's feet were pointed towards the door, making Savannah feel like his attention was one she didn't want.

"Christopher has been asking me to do things. And, I liked them," her voice was chipper with naive excitement. It then dropped, carrying a more serious tone, "Then he asked me to steal from Misfitz. I wasn't going to and..." She looked down at her lap, ashamed, "I told the boss what Christopher wanted me to do. Mister Pearson told me to do it though."

She cocked her head to the side. Her right pigtail rested on her shoulder as her eyes held confusion. "After today, of course. Right now, I'm not even allowed to talk to Christopher. But he's nice. He's my friend," she insisted.

Guilt while lacking the rehearsal-strategy, a re-collective glance. She's honest. Sir took the drink Pet handed him. "Christopher can be a bit instrumental at times. I will not dissuade you from speaking to the man," he sipped off the top before continuing, "However I would offer a word of caution. Sometimes his amorality gets the better of him. Not everyone that is nice is a friend you wish to keep. But we have other business to attend too."

Placing his glass on the table, he stood. Savannah watched as he walked to the tall wooden bookshelves that nearly encompassed the whole wall of the living room. Sir ran his hand over multiple titles, some in languages long since forgotten and barely legible, before finally landing on the one he wanted.

He pulled the book from its nestled home between two other

dusty tombs and walked back to the comfortable gray couch he'd occupied only moments before. Leaning over the coffee table, Sir placed the brown leather book between them. She gazed at the book while he picked up his glass, taking another sip.

Sir waited, watching as she looked at the book. Had she been lying, the girl would reach out. She would hold the book and hide behind it. "The book before you is *The Art of War* by Sun Tzu. He was a famous strategist from China, fifth century BC. In order for you to use interrogation properly, you must first understand what it is used for. What do you know about war Savannah? And please don't insult my intelligence with what those silly history books from school tell you."

Years of endless studying, memorizing names and dates of the most important events in both US and World History flooded her mind. Moments that shaped society with rebellions and bloodshed and left only written documents to hold their ghostly shadows invaded her thoughts.

And yet, Sir wanted more than King George III, Hitler, and Christopher Columbus. Did he want to know the darkened corners of what the internet held on the Revolutionary War? Stomach churning photos of nuclear bombs and the rumors that followed Christopher Columbus?

"I know that it isn't negotiations and phone calls," she answered, "Every story has two sides and the winner is the one that gets in the history books. War has never been pretty, Sir."

She continued, "In 1775, it was traitors standing up in a rebellion against the British parliament. Men fought alongside children younger than me. They died from everything: disease and infection to battle wounds, freezing and starvation."

"It continued with the Civil War. A war fought upon the same need for independence, not slavery. Fathers died fighting their sons. You could trust no one to be on one side or the other. They were all farmers and blacksmiths," she read off her mental report as to what war truly was, "World War I was known for secret spies. World War II for nuclear weapons and mass casualties. History repeats itself, just with bigger and stronger weapons."

"Though that was an excellent explanation of those wars, it is not what I wanted to know. Why do we fight wars? Why do *you* think we fight wars?" He finished his drink and held up the empty glass. "Pet, I need you." Pet rushed to the man's side with urgency and stood over his shoulder in silence.

Savannah thought his question over before answering, "It's human nature, to have opinions. To disagree. And then when others disagree, you must prove why your point of view is correct?"

Sir smiled, hiding a chuckle at the young girl's answer. While not incorrect, it was a slightly over-complicated interpretation of the question. She was nervous.

"Pet, please acquire me a refill and the chessboard from my study. Since you have been so well behaved today, you may then go put on something more comfortable for this evening. Your standard rules of attire still apply."

"Yes Sir," Pet answered with a nod. Silently she walked through a black entryway in the back of the room, eager to obey his wishes.

"My daddy taught me how to play chess," Savannah said with a proud smile as Pet prepared the gold and black chess set.

"Yes I'm sure. Maxximillian favors brute force when playing. However, his technique is not the issue when he plays," Sir digressed as he thought back to all the games he and her father had shared many years ago, "I enjoyed playing against your father many times. Eventually I had to stop when the challenge was no longer present."

He shook his head with a sigh, "In response to your answer, I do believe you have the concept correct. However, it can be summed up much more simply. We fight wars because we want something that belongs to someone else. No matter what appears to be the cause of conflict on the surface, the true nature is that man is greedy. He wants what doesn't belong to him." Sir shrugged at the growing look of shock that covered Savannah's face as she heard his bitter truth.

The girl shook her head in denial. She searched through her mind, examining mental time lines and facts. She merely needed one that could prove the man wrong, but fell short. He was right. It was man's greed that caused war.

"Here is your drink, Sir," Pet whispered as she placed the sweat-covered glass on a coaster before him, "May I be relieved to change, Sir?"

Without looking at Pet, Sir picked up the drink and brought it to his lips. He let the sweetened sour liquid wash over his tongue, satisfied with its consistency and mixture.

"Yes you may Pet. Thank you for your swiftness. Now Miss Savannah," Sir picked up the board and slid it to the center of the coffee table between them, "Much like chess, interrogation is asymmetrical, which means though both of us are playing the same game, we have different goals and methods to achieve those goals. Please place your pieces and I will explain why interrogation is a useful, but potentially dangerous tool to use. I don't enjoy being interrupted during a lesson, so do you have any questions before we go to war?" He started to place his pieces in their proper places on the board. The blue marble was cold and strong beneath his deft fingers as he quickly lined his pawns across his front line.

The young teen shook her head, her pigtails swinging from side to side as she set up her side of the board. A gleeful giggle escaped her, "Actually just one, Sir. What is your favorite piece?"

Pet's ears perked up at the girl's question as she froze before returning to a silent walk. Her smirk remained hidden to both Sir and Savannah.

"The queen, my dear, she is the most dangerous piece on the entire board. Yet, her sole job is to protect her king," he cleared his throat at the obvious relation to Pet as he lined his back row, "And yours, Savannah? Who do you consider the most powerful piece?"

"My favorite is the knight," she cocked her head to the side as if it were obvious before adding with a giggle, "It's a horsey."

***

Pet listened in on every word of the conversation that filled the usually-silent house. Quickly moving to her armoire, she pulled out a black dress with a single leather strap going up and around the neck. That would do nicely. She pulled it from its dedicated place and walked across the room. Setting it on her bed, Pet made sure not to leave any wrinkles in the soft cloth.

***

"A wise choice; the knight always comes at you from the side. That says a lot about your personality and how I'll need to train you," Sir remarked thoughtfully. He was pleased that the Reid Technique would be most effective. It was mostly detection of body language and would leave Savannah little room to slip and say something she shouldn't.

Sir eyed the board before he made his first move, pushing his far-left pawn forward. "Interrogation is only one useful tool of a much bigger game. What is one spy in a war of espionage? When you get to training with Worvacs, I'm sure he'll teach you how to fight five grown men unarmed. I'm going to teach you how to command thousands—"

"Mister Pearson hasn't said anything about Worvacs training me, Sir."

"Less than ten percent of what we say is verbal," Sir answered irritated, nodding towards the board. "It is your turn."

Savannah looked at her pieces, biting her lip. She moved the single, tiny pawn into the center of the war zone before smiling, "Your turn, Sir."

***

Pet stood before her full-length mirror and shook out her braid. The tight crimp flowed down her shoulders and landed in the dip in her spine. Humming to herself, she brushed out the minute tangles the braid had left and added a soft blush to her cheeks. She didn't have to see the table to know the move the naive girl had made.

***

Sir hid his smirk at Savannah's choice of moves to start with. "Tell me about you and Pet." He watched the breathing in her throat, looking for change in quickness or depth. She still had so much to learn. Her innocence would only get her so far in the magical world, right before it stopped her dead in her tracks and got her killed. Sir slid his second pawn into place and waited silently for her answer.

"She's really nice," Savannah answered, her eyes never left the board as she thought out her next move. Though it may be a simple move of a pawn, a single move could likely forfeit the game.

She moved the pawn on her far right forward. "She is always polite and is a really good friend." Savannah tilted her head as she wondered what Sir might be asking before she shrugged off the thought. "She keeps my secrets. She tells me what I should do to stay a good girl."

***

Pet's movements froze in the bedroom at the sound of her

name. She awaited Sir's answer as she reached into her dresser drawers, pulling out the black and gray panties Sir had bought for her. Paw prints on the rear end, though normally playful teen panties, symbolized her as his pet.

Her heart raced at the excitement such a pair would send surging through her master. She peeked around the corner to see the stern man's back towards her. Returning to her room, she put on the dress and sprayed herself down with a light perfume.

***

Her shrug was symmetrical, complete. She questioned the response before brushing it off, he smiled inwardly at the thought. Sir watched Savannah move another pawn, leaving her bishop exposed. He quickly took the piece.

"Check. She is your friend and you trust her. That's good. It's good to have friends to keep you safe. Would you trust her with your life?" His black suit and gray eyes held intimidation.

Savannah stopped at the question. She looked up at Sir as she tried to read into what he was saying. His jaw remained tense as he stared at the young teen before him. His face was as cold as the walls that surrounded them. He was keen to hear her answer and nothing gave to whether he was joking. Could it be a trick question?

"Umm... why do you ask, Sir?" Savannah answered nervously as her thoughts went back to the door at the top of the stairwell. What secrets did it hide about the strange couple?

Pet waited behind the wall, allowing Sir his moment. She pursed her lips in thought of the proper collar for such an evening.

"Just curious. Of the many times you and my Pet have associated, you and I have rarely spoken. I am curious as to why she holds you in high enough regard to be considered one of her very, very, few select friends," he shrugged, as though hearing her answer didn't really matter that much to him to begin with.

"Oh! Okay," Savannah nodded her head in acceptance of his answer and returned to her bubbly self, "Yeah, Pet is really quiet, but I think she's just shy. She's smart too. She helps me with algebra and chemistry. I wouldn't have passed last week's test if she hadn't helped. I really like her." A smile covered the girl's rounded cheeks as she moved her king out of Sir's range.

Avoidance of the answer with detection of a lie. Excellent! Sir nodded in silent approval.

As she spoke the words about Pet, the petite woman entered the room with graceful ease. Nearly unrecognizable to Savannah as her friend, Pet was dressed in a black, knee length dress that wrapped around her shoulders, a matching collar covered her pale neck. Her periwinkle eyes shined against her skin, white as ivory, as her dark hair flowed down her back in shallow waves.

Savannah gasped at the beauty the woman, normally unseen and unheard, could carry. She felt a twinge of something, jealousy perhaps? Arousal?

Ah there it is! Just what he had been looking for, a way into Savannah's mind to show her the lesson at hand. Moving his rook forward, he quickly put Savannah back on defense in their chess match.

He turned to see Pet standing stunningly before him. She still made the air catch in his throat as he could only stare at his beloved.

His eyes warmed with Pet's appearance, fighting the urge to reach out and touch her; to feel her delicate skin beneath his hands.

Patience, there is a lesson to be taught, his proper voice rang out in his head as he cleared his throat, finding his voice once more.

"A most adequate choice, my Pet. Please go and fetch me the velvet restraints," his voice remained calm as he spoke the words.

Restraints? Savannah gulped heavily as Pet nodded her head, leaving to go up the stairwell to the room behind the double doors.

Turning back to the young girl, Sir nodded for her to make her move. "Interrogation is why you came to me today. We shall begin in a few moments."

"I… I have to be home in time for dinner," Savannah stuttered out softly, rubbing the back of her neck.

Lie. "Fear not, young Savannah. You will be home in time for dinner. Please let us finish our game before the lesson begins," he held out his hand, motioning for her to continue while he sipped his highball. "Do you know what the point of interrogation is? It's not just torture for fun, you know. That's what sadists are for," he chuckled at his own jest.

"It's to gather information, Sir. Information that the person believes they are confiding in secrecy." She tilted her head in confusion, her innocent eyes wide, "What's a sadist?"

"Never mind, I'll explain it some other time. Your move, please." His quick frustrations with the young girl's easily distracted mind would be a difficult obstacle to overcome.

Savannah looked down at the board. Her feet swayed beneath the table as she thought out her move. "Check," she said with a grin as her knight stood just squares away from the cornered king.

Quickly eyeing the board, Sir slid his queen in from the left, taking her knight and trapping her king in place. "Check and mate my dear Savannah. I have to give you credit, you made it two moves further than your father did during our first game."

He waved his hand in the air as if to brush off a passing memory before returning his attention to Savannah. "You are correct. Interrogation is used to acquire information and any piece, *any*, can be acquired."

"How?" Savannah asked as she scrunched her brow. "Mister Pearson, I… I don't think the boss intended for me to break fingers," she added, causing Pet to break out a squeak of a laugh as she walked down the stairs with restraints in hand.

Sir let out a chuckle, "That is only one way to collect information. There are many others that usually only takes a small amount of persuasion. Let me show you what I mean."

He snapped his fingers and pointed at Savannah. The girl's eyes went wide.

***

Will walked down the length of the bar and smiled at Tatianna before raising his eyebrows in concern.

"Long night?" He poured a shot and slid it across to her. A long-neck apparently wasn't going to be enough.

Tatianna sighed heavily and leaned across the bar so no one else could hear her confessions to the barkeep.

"Christopher," she answered softly, "He's cruel, but... do you think he would turn? On me?"

Deep down, Tatianna already knew Will's answer. Maybe as she spoke the words, she hoped he would tell her otherwise. That he would lie. She pushed the shot back across the bar in rejection. "Just this." Raising her beer, she took another swig.

Will sighed, "In a heartbeat." He downed both shots and refilled his shot glass. Raising the tiny glass, he held her eyes, "He did on me." The young bachelor took his shot and grimaced as the hard liquor and hard memory burned his soul once more.

Tatianna cringed as she rotated her right shoulder blade in pain. Never make a deal with the devil, the ache in her upper spine reminded her. She fought back the tension that built in her throat. "How?"

"It was a long time ago," Will refilled the shot, not looking at Tatianna as he told the painful truth, "When my father died, the bond of the bar was passed to the only other living male of our lineage, me. I found out I was stuck here the rest of my life. It gets to you after a while. I was used to traveling, seeing the world. One time I was desperate to get away and I went to Christopher for help. He agreed, but—"

"He helped you?" Tatianna's eyes went wide in shock.

Will ignored her, tossing back another shot. "The bond that holds me here is very old and very strong. Shit hit the fan. Christopher bailed and I was left for dead," he sighed, rolling the shot glass around in his palm. "Worvacs and Maxx carried me back. They kept me alive, but I paid for it dearly." He closed his royal blue eyes for a moment. Taking a deep breath, he allowed the memory to fade. "I've managed to extend the bond on my own, with some magical tweaking of course. I can leave now, but only for a few hours at a time so I never go very far."

Tatianna thought back to the selfish man-child that still sat in her living room. She remembered when her shit had hit the fan.

Christopher was there.

He had been there when she had lost everything: her dignity, her wings. They had bled for one another. Nearly died for one another, but why?

Because it was at his convenience to still have her around? Because she made him appear normal? She couldn't argue the times they had fought side by side with their backs to the wall. Nor could she argue every time she had nursed his wounds. But, there was always more darkness ahead. What would she mean to Christopher when there wasn't?

Tatianna looked at the empty bottle, wishing it offered something more than just liquid comfort. "Keep them coming."

"How did it go with Sir the other night? That is, if you don't mind me asking of course?" Will handed her a drink and took a seat next to her.

"The evening was very nice. I suppose if Sir put his mind to it, he could be a car salesman. He makes a strong, very manipulative point. One that makes me question everything survival has taught me."

She allowed her mind a moment to fade back into distant memories.

"Of course, I want to survive," she answered as if it were obvious. Her heart pounded against her chest with an ache unlike any she had felt before. Her hands were sweaty as they gripped her knees, her knuckles white. "What kind of a dim-witted question—"

"Then shut up and stop playing the victim. This is Earth. No one cares," Christopher bit back, dropping the car into drive as he slammed on the accelerator, squealing the tires. He turned a corner and pulled out of the garage.

Tatianna shook the memory from her head. She knew what Christopher had told her in the darkest of moments was true. It was the first time she had seen evil for what it truly was, when her life was nearly pulled from her again with a final gasp.

"The sex wasn't half bad either honestly, but I don't think you want to hear about that." She leaned back into the bar stool. A smirk covered her face.

Will let out a chuckle, downing another shot. "Sir is the only man I have seen you take to bed, but he doesn't really seem like your type. Why, if you don't mind my asking?"

Tatianna looked down at her drink in thought of Will's question. She furrowed her brow, twisting her lips in thought. "Maturity?" she asked herself out loud, "Decency? Self-Respect? No… disgust!" she finalized with a laugh. "I don't know. I just was never one of those to need a different man in my bed every night. Or the same man for that matter. Sometimes it's just nice sleeping alone; less chance of getting killed in your sleep." She played off the statement with a chuckle. It was her attempt to pretend she was joking.

***

Sir entered the room with an eeriness darker than his suit. His face was stern like the brick walls that surrounded the bar room and his jaw was as tense as Tatianna's own entry had been.

Pet quickly followed her master, sore from their recent visit to the play room. Though her face remained pale and peaceful, her discomforted walk was a reminder to the couple's secluded lifestyle.

A soft smile crossed Pet's delicate lips as Will gave them both a curt nod. Turning back to Tatianna, he said two words that sent a chill up her spine, "Times up."

Sir sat at his usual table and watched Tatianna's every move. He could see as her spine grew tense. She peeled once more at her label. Was it out of fear? Discomfort?

He waited patiently as he knew she would come to him. Even if it was just out of curiosity, she would come.

Tatianna felt Sir's grey eyes stare with interest. No, interest wasn't the word. He stared at her as if he were a predator. A stare she knew too well from the darkened experiences of her life. A stare that left the hair on the back of her neck raised. It sent her heart racing, her blood boiling, but that wasn't what raced her beating heart.

It was the fact that for once, in the history of everything, Tatianna questioned whether she wanted the predator to catch her. She looked down at her bare left hand wrapped around the long neck bottle. *It's bare for a reason,* she reminded herself.

***

"What if she doesn't, Sir?" Pet whispered softly to make sure they weren't overheard. Sir raised an eyebrow at his Pet before smiling. "She's strong willed. Stronger than most, Sir."

"Do you doubt my ability, Pet? I thought you, of all people, would have known better by now. She will come." He sipped his drink and, without looking, reached behind Pet. He ran his fingers down the length of her dark braid.

His eyes were trained on Tatianna. He imagined her doe-like

eyes staring back at him as she waited on her knees. The chaos of her dark curly hair wouldn't do for his intentions. It would have to be neat and pristine.

He would even let the fallen angel keep her leather jacket. He already had a collar in mind that would match. "Perhaps you'd care to have a chat with her, Pet? When I succeed, she will be your new playmate."

"Yes Sir," Pet answered, hiding her distaste towards Sir's request. She reminded herself that it was to please her master as she got up and moved towards Tatianna.

***

The woman quickly raised her scarred hand. "Drop it. You're speaking with his tongue," she said firmly.

Pet turned around, giving her master a confused, questioning glance. He neither moved nor changed his demeanor in any way, merely raising his hand. He waved it forward.

Tatianna couldn't help but chuckle at Pet, her timid responses and jumpy behavior. The pathetic being was always on edge.

"You know the difference between me and you? Your 'Sir' allows you to thrive on his promise of a safety net," Tatianna growled before beading her eyes towards Christopher as he walked into the bar, straightening his own suit.

"I live with... that!" she snarled in disgust as he searched the room for his next victim. "That is what Sir is keeping you safe from. Me, I sleep with one eye open."

"But you don't have to," Pet whispered softly, looking up into Tatianna's brown eyes, "Sir can keep you safe too. He can make sure that Mister Christopher never hurts you again. He can grant you a serene, peaceful place. One where we could both stay."

Tatianna laughed, filling the tavern with her sinister humor. "Yeah, so could a battered woman's shelter. Or a jail house," she chuckled, nudging Pet closer to her. The petite woman obliged.

"But you know why I stay?" Tatianna whispered as Pet shook her head, "I stay because I am just as dangerous as he is. I am something else Sir keeps you safe from. I'm the thing that goes bump in the night."

Pet quickly darted back to the table. She leapt into a chair to sit up straight next to Sir, her safety. Her eyes faced forward as mantras raced through her mind. Despite the calming words of reminder, Pet's jaw remained tense.

CHAPTER FIFTEEN

BRASS HONEY BALLS

"Look Sage," Legs growled in frustration, trying to remain calm, "I'm not going to argue with you. One more time and you won't be allowed to rent the bedrooms."

Sage rolled her eyes with a huff as Legs guided her from the rest of the crowd at the bar. "Whatever," she snapped, "You are not my mother!"

"I don't have to be! There's a powder trail from the table to the bed!" Legs scolded. She slammed her calculator on the bar, finally having enough of the attitude Sage was serving. "You rented the room. If Kritter has to keep cleaning up—"

"Kritter don't mind cleaning Miss Chara. Kritter enjoys cleaning. Kritter believes that—" her squeaky voice rang opinions from the serving window nearby.

"Shut up Kritter! You're not helping!" Legs answered without even blinking an eye. She met the rebellious woman glare for glare.

"We were celebrating. I'm a goddess. You can't judge me. Neutral ground, remember?" Sage bit back, sticking out her pierced tongue.

"Neutral ground only applies to the tavern itself," Tatianna sighed from a nearby bar stool, adding her two cents as she leaned back. She propped her legs up on the bar only to have them quickly knocked off by Legs.

Worvacs nodded to Legs, making sure that she noticed as he reached over the bar and grabbed a bottle. Pouring her a drink, he set it in front of the bar stool next to him.

"Goddess or not, don't do it again!" Legs warned, pointing a finger at Sage before she walked around and sat next to Worvacs. She lit a cigarette, knowing it was a battle she hadn't won. "Young freaking brat!"

"I heard that bitch!" Sage yelled back, helping herself to a shot. She stretched, leaning back against Tatianna's side.

Cole was disappointed that the fight between Sage and Legs was over. He was even more disappointed that it didn't end with a make-up kiss. Grabbing his bottle, he walked over to the table that Sage and Tatianna occupied.

"You ladies look like you could use a drink," he smiled at them both. Pulling out a chair, he sat across from the two still flustered women. Once comfortable, he took a swig from the bottle and then slid it across the table to them. "And a stiff one at that—"

"I could use something stiff," Sage answered with a snarl. Her green eyes glared at Legs. She tilted the bottle and took a heavy swig. "You know, Tatianna, Worvacs has a few battle scars. You two could trade war stories!"

The sudden glare on Tatianna's face told Sage to drop it. Shrugging, she handed the darkened bottle back to Cole.

He brought the bottle to his lips. With slow drinks and heavy gulps, he absorbed it as if that were the last bottle of booze on the planet. After finishing his drought, he slid it back across the table to the ladies with a heavy belch.

"As much as I've had to drink today, I'm sure I've got something stiff for anyone who wants it," he smiled. Though slightly drunk, he hoped to keep the blood in his veins flowing everywhere that mattered. His eyes drifted around the room. As he looked over every woman in the pub, he found his odds with

Tatianna who sat across from him.

She wasn't typically his type but he had heard rumors lately; rumors of a dark-skinned angel's talent when she was on her knees. He wanted to find out for himself if they were true.

"Whadda' say Tat? Wanna' join me and Sage upstairs for some fun?"

Sage rolled her eyes. "Really?" she asked, a slight tinge of jealousy washing over her. "And what makes you think you could handle two?"

"I'm a god now. I've got enough stiff to satisfy a realm," he shrugged nonchalantly, "Don't judge. I'm sure it wouldn't be the first time you were involved in such a three-way companionship."

"Involved?" Sage raised an eyebrow at his discretion. "You mean the first time I fucked a guy while another woman licked his balls as if they were coated in honey? Hell, why stop at two?"

"Hey you!" she called out to a brown, hairy creature across the bar. It sniffed its mosquito-like nose back in silent response. "Ever done an Eiffel Tower? I wouldn't mind a good stuffing. You can have ass!"

Tatianna dropped her head, stifling a chuckle with the back of her hand.

Cole shrugged, "I'm down. If he can't help, I'm sure we can find someone who can. Hell!" He shrugged again, "I'm willing to give an old friend a courtesy jerk. Drink up. Whatever happens, happens. That's the best part here at the Misfitz Tavern. There is no written future or unwritten past so it doesn't matter anyways."

"To no sense of direction!" Sage hooted, raising her bottle. She handed it to Tatianna and smiled at Cole, "I fucking love fucking you." She laughed as the furry mosquito-faced creature walked up to the table.

***

The sound of the door opening was nearly too much for the tavern owner. His head throbbed in agonizing pain, threatening to burst beneath his aching skull. He clenched his eyes shut, rubbing his temples in attempts to relieve some, any of the tension that grew with the slightest of sounds.

How did this happen? How did this always happen?! The burning scent of tequila filled his nose causing his stomach to clench. It seized into his throat, demanding to rid itself of contents he had already expelled. He gulped back the remnants of last night's alcohol mixed with the sour bile that quickly filled his mouth.

It had been a night well worth the hangover. Boasts had been made, liquor been consumed, and guns were fired. But as Will stood behind the bar with his head in his hands, he tried to stop the misery he had earned the previous night.

"Whatcha' doing Will?" Sage bellowed, leaning over his shoulder with a smile. She couldn't help but have a little fun. Watching the man who typically held his head high with pride behind the bar with his comic book hero t-shirts and smooth smile hold his head in torture. It was priceless. "Got a headache? Drink too much in your room last night? You know what causes that right?" she exclaimed boisterously. Her laugh echoed off the tavern's brick walls.

"Sage," Will whispered quietly into his hands, a groan in his voice from the ache that filled every muscle in his body, "You are here only by the strictest of my graces. Take it down about twenty decibels or I will ban your ass for life." He poured himself a shot and hoped the hair of the dog would clear his head a bit. "Besides, don't you have some indigenous population somewhere that needs a new goddess or something?"

"I wish," Sage rolled her eyes, "They haven't summoned us back yet."

"You know, there is a lot of responsibility that comes with

being a deity. You have to take care of your followers. It's not all fun and games." Will warned, his head resting against the bar. The young woman didn't hear as he whispered, "Take it from someone who knows."

"Yeah, whatever!" Sage sassed back, blowing off the man's warning. "Look, they feed me grapes. They bring me wine. It's like this place, minus the tips."

"It don't work that way..." Will warned again before sighing, giving up on the cause.

"Anyway, I can help ya'. Just let me behind the bar. Just this once and I'll fix Willy's wittle' headache," her pink lips puckered with the words as she pinched his cheek playfully before shrugging, "Or kick me out. I'll kick and scream. I will make as much noise as possible on my way out. Just to make your last time seeing me worth remembering. May I? Please Uncle Willy?" Her Cheshire grin grew as she batted her lashes playfully.

Will sighed. At this point his head hurt bad enough to welcome any relief, even if it was from such a vixen succubus. "Fine, but I'm not in the mood for games tonight. I swear to every god and demi-god, yourself included, that has ever stepped foot in this tavern, if you make a mess you will clean every drop of it up." Will motioned her to walk around the bar and join him.

Instead Sage stood up on the bar and jumped over. Quickly glancing around, she grabbed a large glass next to the touch screen registers. Going to the back and grabbing a handful of ice, she tossed it in. An orange liquid, a green one, and then a red one followed.

"Where's the cocktail shaker?" she asked.

Still resting his head on the bar, Will pointed in response without looking up. His hands covering his face provided a darkness that helped against the migraine pulsating beneath his skull. Now more than ever, he understood how the tavern was run by Karma after she peeked her evil little head out from the glass chandeliers this morning. Her presence shined brightly in the florescent lighting.

Sage hurried this way and that. Adding a blue drink and then a brown one, she poured them in the glass and placed it in front of him.

Will eyed the drink warily as he picked it up and looked more closely. The fruity smell some contents held mixed with the bitter spice of others. Only more concerning to him was the sight as his stomach clenched once more.

"Oh," she giggled, "and for memory sake, here's my cherry." With a wink, she topped the drink with a red cherry. It sank just beneath the liquid. "Drink it up and choke it down," she added with an evil grin.

"Do I want to know what's in this? Never mind, I'm almost certain I don't. Ugh!" He shook the glass in a circular motion softly, mixing the heavy drink and instantly regretted doing so.

Orange pulp and banana slivers float among the ice. A chunk of pink gurgled within the glass before bubbling to the top of the now vomit-colored drink.

Taking one last wary look at Sage, Will held his nose and downed the liquid as quickly as possible. He kept his eyes squeezed shut until the last of the drink, tasting of mango and lime, finally passed his tongue. The pressure against his temples eased and his stomach calmed once more.

"Well my headache is gone." He let out a pleased, thunderous belch and looked at Sage, "Not bad vixen. What do you call that concoction?"

"Regrets," Sage answered with a proud smile, "Now my work is done." She jumped back over the bar top and returned to being a patron.

"Bartender! Refill!" she screeched at the top of her lungs and pointed to her glass. "This time make it a double!" She laughed and placed Will's recently stolen gold on his bar.

"I like it. I think we could improve the taste though," with deft precision, he pulled bottles from the shelf and placed them in front of her. "I expect all of that gold back in my bar by the end of the night," he informed her, nodding towards the coins on the bar top. He knew before letting Sage behind the bar that her kleptomaniac tendencies would get the best of her. They always did.

"Doesn't it usually?" Sage answered with the most innocent smile she could manage. She popped the cork on one of the bottles and poured an equal amount into two glasses.

"Where's the tequila?" Sage asked with a grin.

"Here," Will pulled a green bottle from beneath the bar and handed it to her. "Try that. You've lost a dollar or three in my place before missy, so don't think that you're sneaky." He folded his arms and waited for her to finish mixing the glasses. "My new hangover drink, Don't forget it's my liquor. One of these two is going to be mine every time try you mixing them." Will tossed back his new drink and scrunched up his face at the bitter flavor. "Something sweeter on top."

"Anything else?" Sage bit back, reaching for the red syrup and remaking the drink once more. She splashed the red liquid in the top and added an orange slice. "Enjoy," she growled, smiling a cheeky grin.

Will took the glass, admiring how much better she had made this one compared to the last. He slowly took a sip off the top. "Now that's a drink I can serve to customers. You're not half-bad at bartending. I think I'll change the name though. I think I like 'No Regrets' better, don't you?"

When he saw a smile creep across her lips after she'd downed a quarter of the glass, he added, "See what I mean? Anyways, it has me thinking… What would you say to bartending for me?"

CHAPTER SIXTEEN

SQUIDLINGS AND SHOWERS

The tables were full as two gnomes walked into the Misfitz Tavern, searching for a place to sit. A group of golems lined the wall next to the fireplace while a couple of centaurs placed their bets at the dart board.

"Another one over here!" the tallest of the centaurs, Jerome, yelled as he put his empty beer bottle on the green pool table.

A handful of pixies in a corner booth giggled. They pointed to the tanned centaur with large muscles flirtatiously.

Will shuffled through the ticket orders for the lunch rush. It was one busy Thursday afternoon. He had heard Jerome's request, but paid him no mind. He had bigger things to worry about.

"I need four giant squid specials, a fried griffon cheek, and two more unicorn rump roast sandwiches. These are for the construction crew, priority."

"Refills!" Legs informed Will as she placed the bucket of empty long neck bottles on the bar top. Turning around, she started on a mixed drink ordered by a fairy that sat at the bar. "Where are those falcon wings, Kritter?"

Kritter's mint green hands shook. Her eyes were wide as her wings flapped vigorously. Standing before the grills, she looked frazzled back and forth between the hot coals and the deep fryer.

The tickets gathered, lining and overflowing the window.

"Kritter is trying, Miss Chara. Kritter had to grab a new bag of—"

"I don't want excuses Kritter, I want falcon wings!" Legs called back in frustration. Lunch rush was always a busy time for them, but more-so today when Sage never showed up for her shift.

Will deftly refilled the bucket of long necks and then put it back on the tray. As an order of fried pickles appeared in the serving window, he added it as well. "Take this. Tell them it's on the house. That should buy Kritter enough time to get the wings out." He handed the tray to Legs and smiled his most charming smile, "There's no business like our business."

"Yea, well our business is about to have the entire back patio walk out!" Legs looked out the glass window in concern. Six bogies with dark gray hair and pointed noses glared back in disgust. Their red eyes burned, frustrated with their wait.

"I'm going to tell them we had to warm up the fryer," she explained to Will. Cotton candy hair caught her eye behind him. "Fawn's trying to get your attention," she said, nodding towards the back booth.

Will placed a drink in front of the green skinned goblin sitting at the bar. Looking over at the corner booth, he saw Fawn's attempts to wave him over.

"Call Sage. See if she's busy with her disciples. If she's eating grapes and getting her feet rubbed, tell her to come in and get her ass to work." Legs bit her tongue against the argument before walking back to the kitchen.

Maybe she would get lucky and the bogies would think Sage was a child. If she was really lucky, they would eat her. The bogies usually left a hefty tip when their lunch was served live.

She tapped her foot as the phone rang in her ear.

"Hey you sexy bitch!" Sage's voice answered on the other end.

"What?" Legs exclaimed in disbelief, shaking her head. She

was just going to ignore the comment. "Sage, we need you to—"

"Just fucking with ya'. This is my voicemail. Leave a message at the beep. If your cock's big, make it hot!"

"Ugh!" Legs groaned, repulsed with the rebel. The beep of recording went off in her ear. "Sage, it's Legs. Call me back. We could really use you here for your *scheduled* shift." She knew Sage wasn't going to call back. Looking around the corner at Will talking with Fawn, she dialed another number.

"Hello?" A more innocent voice answered softly.

"Hey Savannah, are you busy?" Legs asked. Two more trolls entered the tavern and sat at the tall tables, waiting for drinks.

"Ummm... I'm working on an extra credit report for Psychology. Yeah, Psychology! Daddy was upset when I got a B last week. I have to make sure I get it up. I can't break Daddy's heart again."

Legs rubbed her eyes. *Why did this always happen to me?* "I need you in here Savannah," she said firmly.

"But the report—"

"I'll do the report for you tonight if we need you late. Just get in here. Sage didn't show up this morning... again."

***

"If you're not too busy," Fawn said, smiling at Will, "I would love that crab leg salad you make." She winked, sliding a few extra silver coins across. She pouted, hoping he would make an exception since it was typically only served on Wednesdays.

"I've still got some made up from yesterday that's chilled in the fridge. It's all yours, but I can't make any promises next Thursday." He picked up the stack of coins from the booth's heavy wooden table. "This is more than the leftovers are worth. You have a good run or something?" he nodded to the blood that crusted on her armor plating.

"Good enough," she peeled back the shoulder guard to

expose the large lashing with pride, "Stung a little and," she looked down at the gash, bright red against the white of tendons, "I think there might be nerve damage." She shrugged and replaced the arm guard. "Was worth it for what I harvested from the lamisaur once I skinned him. Fifty-five ped worth of wool. Can't wait to brag to Worvacs." A smirk of friendly rivalry covered her face. She could still see the ostrich-like bird, its body and legs covered in thick wool, fall to the ground in defeat.

"I heard he didn't do so badly himself on his last run. Said that the dakibants are hitting decent right now," Will informed her leaning against the table.

Fawn snarled her nose. "Of course he went for the dakibants. Sure, they drop like a dream but a level nine has tusks the size of your head. I mean, imagine taking down a buffalo with drool, snot…" she groaned, "I can't ever get bragging rights over him."

"Are you done for the day? Or are you going back out after lunch?" Will asked, curious of her plans for the day.

"I suppose I'm off for today. Lady Luck won't be nice enough to bless me twice," she laughed, "The odds are no longer in my favor so, Earth it is."

Will nodded in understanding. Fawn always seemed to know when to fold and walk away.

"I'll get your lunch. Hang out after the lunch rush leaves and maybe we'll go for a walk. It's been a while since I got some fresh air." He turned and headed back to the kitchen.

Savannah rushed into the tavern. Legs pointed to the window opening that went to the kitchen. "Your hair needs to be up before you walk in this door, Savannah. Always assume when you are working, it's with food."

Will stepped into the kitchen and saw Savannah pulling her blonde hair into tight pigtails. "Thanks for coming in. I assume your sister was otherwise occupied?"

He looked at the pot on the stove that Kritter was stirring, occasionally smacking purple tentacles back with a wooden spoon. "Good luck with the squid special," he laughed, "They can get a bit grabby."

Opening the fridge, he pulled out a large bowl containing the leftover salad from the day before. Adding additional dressing to freshen it up, Will scooped a generous portion onto a plate and walked back out to the booth.

"Here you go love. The dressing is the secret, I tell you."

"Oh, the dressing is what makes it," Fawn agreed with a pleased smile. The bowl of salad held carrots, peas, and bits of fresh crab. She took a bite, closing her eyes to savor the taste. "I think I could stay for a walk. But… could I use the shower upstairs? I still can't convince George that I need a bathroom in my own place." She mimicked her half-giant landlord's dim voice, "Use George store."

"Yeah, use the shower in my room. It's a bit more comfortable than the shared bathroom for guests." He pulled a small scrap of paper from his wallet. Writing 0222 on it, he slipped the paper across the table to her. "Here's the security code. I'll have to come up and change, but make yourself at home." He would need a shower too, but figured he'd best wait until he got upstairs to mention it.

Fawn looked down at the paper in shock. "Ummm… thank you," she replied with a blushing smile. Folding up the paper, she stuck it in a hidden pocket of her armor. "But I must say, you don't have to."

"Oh, don't think you're too special getting that code. It changes every twelve hours. So, you only get my shower 'til midnight."

"No Kritter! Smack it! Smack it! Don't stab it, smack it!" a squeaky teenage voice screamed from the kitchen. The attention of the full tavern turned to the serving window to see a purple tentacle begin to slither out.

Will covered his eyes, chuckling at the sounds. Looking up at Fawn, he could tell she was doing her absolute best not to burst out into a fit of giggles.

"Never in my life have those words come out of that kitchen. Not even when my father was running the place," he laughed and headed toward the commotion.

"Miss Savannah!" Kritter shrilled back, "Squidling is out! Put Squidling in! If Master Will sees—"

"I know Kritter, I'm trying!" Savannah's voice called back.

Legs sighed, putting down her tray she stormed into the kitchen.

"Don't kill the food on the floor! Kill it in the sink or you'll get blood everywhere," Will's voice echoed through the kitchen.

Legs' voice followed with, "Contamination! Watch for contamination!"

Fawn no longer held back her urge to laugh. Tears of laughter streamed down her face as she finished her crab salad. Walking up the stairs, she caught a glimpse in the kitchen.

Legs held Savannah back as Kritter continued to poke at the purple squidling in the sink. The pixie wielded a meat cleaver larger than her torso.

Will grabbed the cleaver from Kritter's hand. "Dear God! Give it here and I'll do it!" he ordered as Fawn reached the top of the stairs and turned toward the bachelor's bedroom before hearing a familiar chop.

***

Will finally finished scrubbing the squid ink from his hands and dried them off. With a sigh, he threw the towel on the counter and headed out towards the bar. There was some relief in everything that happened. The rush was officially over.

"I'm off tonight so you're in charge. I'm going to take a long hot shower and catch a few minutes sleep while I can," he called out to Legs, who was still wiping down tables.

Legs nodded her head. Her long hair was still pulled back in a tight bun. "Go for it," she wiped her brow with her upper arm before continuing, "I think I'm going to send Savannah home too for the evening. Me and Kritter should have it under control."

Will entered the four-digit number on his keypad outside the office. "That's fine. Tell her to keep her phone on just in case it gets busy tonight. We might need her help again."

Opening the door, he turned and locked it behind him. He walked up the spiral staircase, taking the stairs two at a time in hopes to find the soapy female alien waiting.

He looked around his bedroom, eyeing the dark wooden king sized bed and the immaculately built white stone fireplace. Satisfied that everything was in its proper place and Fawn was nowhere to be seen, Will quietly walked to the cracked bathroom door.

White steam poured from the gray bathroom. Heat radiated with the steam as a soft hum came from the far corner where Will's shower sat.

He knocked gently. "Can I come in?"

"Sure," Fawn answered cheerfully over the sound of the running water.

Will walked into the over-sized bathroom, eyeing the silhouette through the steam and fogged glass of the shower stall big enough to hold three. It took his breath away as he watched Fawn dip her head under the dual shower heads with a lust for the hot water. As she closed her eyes, she allowed it to cascade down her cotton candy hair to the curve of her back with a sigh.

"Will, this bathroom is phenomenal!" she said laughing into the water.

"Thanks. It took a while to get it just right. Apparently prior to me hiring them, the construction dwarfs thought all bathrooms were supposed to be… mini. Just don't use up all my hot water. I need a shower now after that chaotic lunch rush."

"Better get it while it's hot!" Fawn laughed again. She embraced the warm bliss as she spun under the water pressure.

True, genuine water pressure!

Having spent the last week in her home realm, which was abundant in many rich resources but still unaware of indoor plumbing, she couldn't help her own giddiness. Will's gray marble shower and wide variety of body washes was more than any woman could ask for. She closed her eyes and let the jets beat against her back, the soapy suds that had clung to her breasts flow down her stomach.

This was much nicer than the lake she used last week, avoiding moontooths as she attempted to wash her hair in the murky water.

"Oh, squid ink stains by the way," she added opening her eyes and noticing that she was still alone in the shower.

Will shrugged, not needing any more invitation than that. Taking off his shirt and pants, he laid them neatly on the hamper against the wall. He opened the glass door and was quickly enveloped by the steam that left the compact area. Stepping in, he quickly shut the door behind him.

Beauty was held in the plentiful scars that covered the young woman's body. White lines covered her arms and legs, exposing strength and courage few could match. Wider gashes on her stomach and legs displayed persistence and determination.

Sliding under the opposite shower head, he turned away from her. Her body was erotic and beautiful. He hoped with his back turned, she wouldn't see his growing erection. "How many times have you re-spawned over the years? I can tell it hasn't been too long since your last one."

"Fourteen hundred and," she paused in thought, looking up at the water spout, "Seventy-two." Fawn calculated, giving a nod of confirmation at her answer. "The last one was about three weeks ago, got myself in a bind with an aggronation. I called to Worvacs for help, but he was in Caly and well—" she pointed to a large gash, the scar tissue still tender and pink beneath her right breast, "I was surprised. A wound like that usually takes longer to heal. That yarrow you gave me works miracles."

"Fifty gold a pound but it does the trick," Will admired the large gash, healing nicely against her tanned skin. Being a male, he couldn't help but admire her large breasts as well.

"They broke my rib cage and next thing I know, I'm back at the revival terminal. Had a killer migraine and a bad limp, but... it happens." Shrugging off what most would consider a horrible experience the professional hunter laughed and broadcast her injuries with pride.

"Impressive. Must be nice having a reset and being able to die any time the mobs get too strong. I don't envy the hangover you get though. You can keep that." He pointed to a jagged scar on his right shoulder. The scar was lightning shaped and dipped a quarter inch into his skin.

"Spider bullet did this one. Nasty little bastards. They hit you like a normal round, but they aren't through and through. Once inside, the bullet expanded and started digging its way through the muscle. Worvacs had to cut the little bastard out for me."

"Sounds nasty. Caly doesn't have anything like that one. Luckily, friendly fire is only allowed in certain territories, otherwise the bullet... doesn't recognize you?" Fawn mumbled, failing to find the right words. It was always difficult how a bullet fired from a friendly setting on their weapons could go straight through their bodies on Caly without penetration. Earth was an odd realm in that aspect. Her eyes trailed down to Will's firm hind quarters.

She fought back an animalistic growl as she bit her lip at the thoughts that quickly filled her mind. *Scratch marks that I can add to the scars covering my back. Bite marks I can leave with the light colors of his own. Doing as nature intended with mating calls that echo off the marble tile...*

"Wash my back?" she asked with a smile, placing a wash cloth in Will's hand.

Will took the rag from her and began scrubbing her back with it. White suds dripped from her shoulders down the dip in her back, leaving trails of bubbles along her pink hair.

Fawn buried her head in the water. As it covered her face, the gills on the side of her jawline opened.

"You know I usually charge for this level of attention. But since you're a regular customer and all, I think this one's on the house." He placed his other hand on her hip and slowly scrubbed the blood from her back, admiring her firm ass and rounded hips.

"Need more water," he insisted as he slipped up behind her and run the rag under the shower head. He glided between her cheeks. Fawn caught her breath. Her core ached, pleading for more of the muscular man's attention.

The soft, rounded flesh against Will's member was almost more than he could handle but he had to continue the charade. He wanted the foreigner to need him.

Fawn flinched against the tense muscle on her side as a jab of pain kidnapped her thoughts. Caving to it and allowing the muscle to ease, she quickly realized the gesture only brought her closer to the man's solid abs, his firm abdomen and his…

"Old wounds, right?" Will asked as Fawn leaned against him for support. He followed instinct, wrapping his arm around her chest to support her weight.

His member pressed firmly between the cheeks of her ass. There was no denying the effects the beautiful woman had on him.

Fawn bit her lip. Nature reminded her what she wanted most as Will slid his hips back and forth, using her body to stroke him as he held her upright.

"Yeah," Fawn moaned at the feel of Will, hard with excitement. Rotating her hips, they glided with the hot water.

She couldn't fight the animalistic urges any longer. Turning around in Will's arms, she pressed her body to his.

Her mouth covered Will's in a passionate kiss as she pushed

him up against the shower wall with a loud thud. As his mouth met hers, he instantly tasted her sweet, intoxicating kiss.

Will grabbed the back of Fawn's tanned thighs and lifted her. Fawn bit at Will's lip as she wrapped her legs around his waist. She moaned as she slid down his length. Her breasts grazed against his chest with only water in-between.

She was surprisingly soft for someone who's skin was as scarred as his own. He wanted to enter her sacred temple, hoping to indulge in her pleasures before his own.

He filled her completely, still an inch of his own girth left.

"Oh no, this just won't do." Using his biceps, Will lifted her petite body up so her knees were held by his arms, her back against the wall. He pulled her hair, the silky conditioner rinsing out and gliding between their two bodies, now formed as one. Fawn's head leaned back against the shower wall as his lips and tongue teased the beautiful alien's ample tits. He sucked on her nipples, the most delicious thing he'd ever tasted.

Pulling out, he changed his angle. With the help of the lubricating conditioner, Will buried himself into her once more.

"Will!" Fawn screamed out, grabbing at the marble shower wall. She panted with lustful want.

"Still not there yet, Fawn. Let's see if we can loosen you up a bit." Savagely, he pounded into her. He watched as her head fell back in ecstasy. Her moans echoed throughout the room, seeping out into his bedroom with the warm steam of the shower raining down on them.

Grabbing onto Will's shoulders, her nails dug into his skin. She bit down on his chest.

"Fuck!" she screamed out as the bachelor stud filled her more, stretching her walls. "Will, I can't take anymore!" she moaned into his chest.

The water turned cold, raining a chill on their hot embrace.

"Not yet, I've still got a half an inch to go." Letting go of her legs, Will placed Fawn's feet on the shower floor and quickly spun her around. Bending her over the water faucet, he slid himself back inside her. "Now that's better, isn't it?"

CHAPTER SEVENTEEN

A STRANGER COMES TO TOWN

Evelyn Connor knew her first stop before she even passed the city limit sign. She drove down Renaud Street by her young nephew's place. Its over-sized windows with golden curtains covered the front of the two-story home.

She couldn't believe Knowhere hadn't changed since she left. Or maybe she could. It was a small Nebraska town. And like many small Nebraska towns, no one ever came or left. Nothing ever changed.

The same businesses were still open. Not even the curtains covering their showcase windows appeared any different, minus the colors fading in the sunlight.

In the three years she had been gone, Evelyn Connor still knew the small town like the back of her hand. She would still hear the same gossip at the beauty shop. Missus Wooten's board meetings as she worked on Jackie Licata's weekly manicures. Jackie would fill the salon with her chatter about everything little Joey was learning in school.

Evelyn turned the familiar corner of the coffee shop, turning again at the grocery store. No, it's not time to go home yet, she thought to herself as she pulled into the parking lot. She knew where her husband would be this time of day. In a town that didn't know change, neither did her husband.

Walking into the tavern, Evelyn Connor took off her designer sunglasses. She made sure not to mess up her hair. Perms weren't cheap and neither was the dye, highlights, or low-lights that she had gotten the week prior.

The minute the front door to the establishment slammed shut, everyone in the Misfitz Tavern looked to see who was coming in so late after the lunch rush. Mouths dropped in shock and awe at the beautiful woman who entered. Contented sighs and low whistles filled the room at the mysterious vixen, as though she had graced the old tavern with her presence.

Some simply looked. Others ogled at the blonde's voracious curves and devious smile. Everyone wondered just what tricks she possessed.

Closing her eyes for a moment, Evelyn allowed herself to adjust from the bright sunlight to the darkened interior of the bar before opening them again and looking around.

She was happy to see she wasn't the only one in this tiny town who had an eye for something new and exciting as she looked at the improved design of the tavern with glee. Though the stone walls remained the same, the bar top was no longer the warped and water-damaged cherry that had once lined a single wall.

Instead a solid oak bar filled the center of the room, surrounded by the comfort of newly added bar stools. Where once hideous chipped tiles had covered the floor, it was now replaced with the natural planks of dark walnut. The blue stone fireplace warmed what was once a damp and dingy room, now instead brightly lit.

Evelyn looked around with a strange satisfaction. It was good to see that the Misfitz Tavern was no longer a sanctuary to men whose breath reeked of whiskey. Instead, Will had made it a getaway to play pool and darts. It even catered a poker table with a sophisticated painting covering the wall behind it, as if to set the mood.

Maybe improvements could be made in this horrid, closed-minded town. Missus Connor's sparkling eyes lit up even more as she quickly recognized faces.

Her nephew had just been able to legally drink, now he was a grown man. His once chubby cheeks had thinned out slightly, making him more the adult he now was. Cole's spiked hair turned bright red. His charming smile glowed, filling the room, as his Aunt Evelyn neared him.

"My nephew!" Evelyn Connor squealed as she ran up to the young man. She pinched Cole's cheek with loving affection. "I haven't seen you in forever!"

Cole rubbed his cheek gently as he stared with puppy dog eyes up at the beautiful soccer-mom.

The woman's attention turned to the man beside him, her once joyous smile quickly widening with wicked, darkened pleasure. "And Sir!" Sir moved with enthusiasm not usually shown by such a tense man. He stood quickly, looking at his feet. "How is my little…"

Sir waited. He both anticipated and despised the word that would send a chill down his spine. One he knew was on the tip of his mistress' bloodthirsty tongue.

"Puppet?" She whispered the word and immediately sent Sir back to a long-forgotten submissive state. Though it had been years since he had last heard the name spoken, servitude coursed through his veins.

Sir answered promptly. His tone was obedient towards the woman before him. His posture, though still straight and orderly, became compliant and subdued. "Very well Mistress, thank you. You are well I hope, Mistress?"

The tavern went silent. All eyes turned from the beauty of the woman to look at the proper man who held his head high. They watched as he bowed before her very words. Sir's pride grieved.

No, some things never change. Evelyn raised her chin slightly and gave a pleased smile at her puppet's quick and eager obedience. It was good to be back.

"I hear you have a..." she thought her words out with careful precision, "disciple of your own now? Yes?"

"Yes, Mistress. When our agreement was at its end, I decided I still needed more training," he kept his head lowered, as had been the terms of their contract, "I decided after another it was time for me to take on the role I had been trained for. My first pet is still my current one. My most prized. Would you like to meet her, Mistress?" Sir asked, hopeful to both impress and please the woman before him.

The rest of the boys strained their heads, hoping to catch every word of the conversation. Everyone knew information was power. Very little, if any, information on Sir was public knowledge. This could be big.

"In due time, my Puppet," Missus Connor answered, satisfied that he had continued with the world she welcomed him. She kissed his cheek in reward before turning her attention.

The familiar face she saw next warmed her own cold heart. Though the man's hair was shaggier than the last time the two had crossed paths, she could still recognize his cold gray eyes from across the room. The mustache he grew as a disguise failed miserably in hiding the attorney's identity. Evelyn chuckled with loving affection.

"You damn idiot!" she laughed, shaking her head at Christopher, "They haven't put you in the electric chair yet?" She moved towards the brute man and hugged him tightly. Her blonde hair grazed his face.

"Me? Never! They can't catch me, much less hold me in place long enough! Welcome back, Trouble. This place has been awfully boring without you strutting around town." He pulled back from the hug and admired the woman's tight figure. Her skinny waist and child-bearing hips were mouthwatering, her flattened stomach and large breasts irresistible. Oh, how he missed seeing her strut. "Maxx know your back yet? I've had the pleasure of your girls, meeting them I mean," he released a dangerous wink.

Sir felt liquid steel filling his veins. He clenched his jaw, watching Christopher interact with his former dominant. It had been years since he had to practice this kind of self-control and, personally, he thought he was doing excellent.

"I'm sure there were only pleasures in meeting my daughters," Missus Connor answered. A deadly glare of warning flashed through her eyes at Christopher before a sigh escaped her. “I don't know how to tell Maxximillian," she confessed, "Figured I'd come here first and see who was still in town. Get a few drinks in me before…"

She looked out the glass door that led to the tavern's patio. In the distance, she could see her suburban home with a two-car garage.

They had needed something bigger. Something they could grow into. When Maxx had gotten the late-night call, he rushed to the hospital. As he had returned with mourning eyes and Cole, six-years-old and sobbing, they knew the small bungalow they had would do no more.

It was then that they found the house that her and Maxx had decided on as a young couple. One they had built on hopes and dreams.

The girls' treehouse still stood in the old oak behind the house. It was a distant reminder of when Sage and Savannah had once played together in harmony. Their laughs that warmed the neighborhood were now haunting ghosts of Evelyn Connor’s past.

"I thought it might be easier if I meet him at the house. One on one." Eyeing Christopher from across the bar, Sir lifted his drink to take another sip.

"Down, Puppet!" the dominant snapped her fingers and barked to Sir. She didn’t need to turn around as his tension radiated behind her.

"Yes, Mistress." The man held onto his anger as he leaned back in his chair. Best to put on a blank face and hide his fury.

Worvacs looked on in wide-eyed shock. How did the woman married to a man as calm and laid back as Maxx Connor entertain herself? With the company of two of the most tense, dangerous men in the tavern? The woman had greeted them both with open arms and tight hugs? She caught up on their lives before asking about her own husband?

As it always does in a small town, rumors of Evelyn Connor were shared in hushed whispers. Pitied head shakes were given for the still married man raising two daughters on his own. Though Worvacs had never asked Maxx about the sensitive subject, he knew she had left her husband without warning. While the girls were in school, she packed her bags.

He had heard of the mother's dead-end promises to keep in touch. Sage's wild behavior and Savannah's naive innocence were both blamed on the situation as elderly women *tsked* out their disapproval. Worvacs had seen Maxx's broken heart first-hand, followed by endless nights of drinking for months on end.

Worvacs stared at the woman who had given Sage her red hair. She carried Savannah's teal eyes. He tried to place how she and Maxx had ever been happily married like people described. And then, she felt his stares and the woman's attention quickly turned.

Evelyn eyed the strong set of muscles and odd-colored skin. Now that was a blue piece of meat she could sink her teeth into. She smiled, her eyes staring into Worvacs'. An indescribable thrill ran up his spine as lust crept into his loins. The woman smiled.

"William, so much has been done with the tavern. Was the upstairs remodeled as well?" Evelyn asked as she sat in one of the barstools. "And I love the hardwood floors!" she looked at the upgrade, moaning out the words with a nearly orgasmic voice.

"We aim to please Missus Connor. Your presence has always been a bright spot in this darkened void of dismal existence." Will leaned back against the bar. The other men snickered at his failed attempts to remain calm. "What can I get for you?"

"The usual, apple martini with a slice of orange William. Oh! And this one," She pointed at the man with cobalt muscles next to her, grabbing Worvacs' attention. His cheeks grew warm as he tried to fight against the embarrassing purple blush. "Gift wrapped on my bed. A single red bow will do nicely." She winked at Will, who turned around and grabbed a martini glass, starting on her drink.

"Missus Evelyn Connor, correct?" Worvacs asked politely. He tried to remain calm against the woman's bold references. His shy demeanor didn't know quite how to handle such a statement. "A pleasure to meet you ma'am. How has your return home been?" He snuck a glance around, making sure Legs wasn't around to notice him talking to the beautiful woman. When he was sure of her absence, Worvacs turned his chair slightly. What was it about this temptress that awakened his sexual beast?

"Same as always. Nothing changes, minus the number of handsome men running around of course."

Worvacs cleared his throat. He could feel his soft blush with her compliment. "So... Umm... Where did you go on your travels, if you don't mind me asking?" His eyes couldn't help but drift to the woman's exposed cleavage.

"California," she answered with a smile, finding pleasure in the man's nervousness around women. Oh, how much fun this one would be. Something about the innocent man just seemed… tasty.

Evelyn licked her lips, eyeing his biceps before allowing them to wander onward to his firm chest. "Sunny weather every day, beautiful beaches. Bikinis," she added the last one with a raised eyebrow and watched for a response.

Worvacs' pulse quickened at the thought of the married woman's body in a revealing bikini.

"But, there's no place like..." she fought the urge to snarl her nose with the word that brought a bitter taste to her mouth, "Nebraska. Nothing like seeing my girls again. And my boys." With a smile of luscious red lips, she leaned closer to Worvacs. "So tell me, what brought you to Knowhere?"

He cleared his throat again and leaned in with a whisper, "I was in a bit of trouble."

The turn of phrase quickly caught the woman's attention. *Trouble, eh?* This was least expected out of a man she could so easily send a shiver through. And yet it enticed her. She could work with trouble.

"I needed a place to hide," he continued, "A place where, if I was found, it didn't matter who they were. They couldn't do anything. I ran across an old traveler at a bar on Caly that said I should come here." Worvacs shrugged his shoulders. "I've long since been cleared of the trouble, but I found this place had grown on me. I have a place down the road. It's not much, but it's nice."

"Really?" she asked with an interested smile as Will delivered her drink.

Will wondered if perhaps he should warn his friend of Evelyn's deadly temptations before shaking his head. He knew Worvacs better than that.

A man who took down beasts three times his own size had a heart that rested peacefully on Leg's pillow. His foreign friend wasn't the type to follow the trouble Evelyn Connor had to offer.

"You should show me some time," she whispered, her hand drifting onto Worvacs' knee. Her manicured nails trailed with a close-to-painful pleasure before a quick, loud stomp rushed down the stairs.

The hustling noise interrupted the woman's seduction and quickly brought Worvacs back to Earth. He turned towards the staircase and adjusted his body as Evelyn's hand slid from his knee.

With a wink, he whispered, "Maybe some other time."

Legs entered the bar room and threw on an apron. "Sorry I'm late Will. Overslept. It won't happen again," she apologized, panting out her breaths. Her ponytail was frizzed and her clothes wrinkled.

Will waved his hand. He always knew when Worvacs was in town it left his reliable help scatterbrained. "Never you mind. Me and the boys are the only ones here, besides Missus Connor. I'm not sure if you two have met."

He nodded toward the woman sitting across from him. Picking up the tall martini glass, he swiftly mixed another fruit flavored malt. "This is Missus Evelyn Connor, Maxx's wife."

"Oh," Legs answered quickly, suddenly awake and alert. Her mind went to her young co-worker sleeping directly above them. Maxx was likely lying next to the courtesan in a peaceful slumber.

Legs' green eyes darted to Will momentarily. With a soft, confused nod, a smile formed to cover her concerns. She turned to face Evelyn.

Her eyes trailed from the woman's perfectly straightened, colored hair to her manicured nails. Evelyn's whitened smile shined as Legs' eyes moved to the contained cleavage bursting out of a tank top two sizes too small.

Legs had never before had any interest in other women and yet, she had to force her stare away. "Pleasure to meet you, Missus Connor." She quickly looked into the woman's warm, caring eyes, "I'm Legs, the Misfitz' bar manager."

"Pleasure's all mine," Evelyn answered with a warm smile, having no interest in the woman that distracted the cobalt blue meat with fidelity.

Instead, Evelyn turned back to Christopher. She knew he would be the only one careless enough to be honest with her.

"How is Maxximillian?" she asked as she tilted her head in the direction of her home.

Christopher shrugged, "Was all fuckered up after you left. But I guess after you had been gone for so long, he decided he had needs that had to be fulfilled. She's a real nice piece though. Good to him and not too high on her prices."

Raising his glass, he took a sip of his darkened whiskey before a smirk appeared beneath his mustache. He eyed the housewife up and down. *Two can play at this game. Yes, I remember you very distinctly, Evelyn. You make a better friend than an enemy. I know things you don't and information is power, bitch.*

"Good. He deserved to move on," she answered with a loving sigh. "So long as he has a warm body next to him."

Sir bristled at the conversation. He knew Christopher would only reveal what he wanted to. It was the attorney's way of keeping the upper hand. A growl escaped his lips, quickly hushed with his Mistress' glance. He needed a drink. He had to show his independence from his mistress and sooner rather than later if she planned on returning to Knowhere for an extended stay.

Though their agreement had ended, someone's first master or mistress always retained a thread of control; control that was beaten into a submissive through months, years, and sometimes decades of training.

Sir stood up and straightened his suit. He held a mutual glare of warning with Christopher before turning and walking to the other side of Worvacs. He gave the blue man a respectful nod and ordered his drink.

"Whiskey sour, please William," he slid two gold coins over to show his need for a stronger drink.

"You never get a Whiskey sour, Sir," Legs' voice held honest confusion as she typed it onto the touch screen, "A special occasion?"

Sir eyed the glass thoughtfully. Picking it up and taking a sip, he let the sweet and sour concoction roll across his tongue. He embraced its cold burn.

Worvacs lit a cigarette and passed it to Sir before pulling out one for himself. He understood the man's situation. He had a mentor once upon a time.

The stern man took a drag off his cigarette before looking at Worvacs. He tried to think of how best to answer as his mistress sat within earshot, "Just wanted a taste of old memories."

Evelyn's body tensed at Sir's comment. She closed her eyes to refocus her thoughts.

She could pretend if she pleased. Sir knew that she heard every word he'd spoken. Being aware of one's surroundings was one of the many things she had trained him to do years prior.

"Thank you, William dear. These hardwood floors, you will have to share all the juicy details of how you ran across them. Then, you should come see mine."

"Umm... umph... I look forward to the first opportunity," Will choked as he handed her another full martini glass, the orange settling perfectly on top. "You free this evening?"

"Hmmm..." Missus Connor thought, as though her schedule were already full. "You know, I just don't know." She shook her head, "It really all depends on what Maxximillian has planned. I suppose we do have a lot to talk about, but you are growing up so fast. I remember when even you were crawling around on this bar floor. So, how close is my husband to this 'piece' I'm hearing about?" She leaned over the bar for secrecy, her breasts nearly busting out of the top of her shirt against Will's oak bar.

Will leaned forward across the bar to share the secrecy she wanted, "Close enough he doesn't pay for her attention. Angel is younger, but well trained in her craft." He felt a bit of discomfort in confessing her name.

Evelyn covered her mouth with a laugh of realization. "Little Angel Mahogany?" she asked in disbelief, laughing again. "She was in cheerleading with Savannah. Her and Sage sold Girl

Scout cookies together. How funny!" She wiped a tear from her eye delicately, careful not to smear her eyeliner.

Will nodded. "She is good to him. Haven't seen him smile like that in, well, a long time."

"Good for him. I'm glad his smile has returned. Well, I would love to stay and chat, fellas. But my husband will be home soon and a good wife must keep up with her wifely duties," she said as though she had been at the bar all the days prior. "Let me know when you will be stopping by to discuss the wood, William," she added with a wink.

"Of course Missus Connor," he replied, wiping down the bar. He hoped that the time would become available quite soon.

***

Cole heard a familiar giggle outside the bar; one that made the hair on the back of his neck stand on end.

His mind raced to the thought of Sage running into her mother as his Aunt Evelyn finished her martini and set her glass on the bar.

Cole headed towards the front door. He tried to appear nonchalant, as though he'd forgotten something in his car. Barely reaching the door to the tavern in time, he pushed it outward in hopes to block Sage's path.

Lady Luck was with him as he stepped outside and shut the door behind him. Sage's outstretched hand had been reaching for the door handle that now dug into his back.

"Cole!" Sage answered quickly in shock, "Baby! Hey! I was looking for you!"

"Save it! We need to get out of here… Now! Let's go to my place. You're not going to believe this!" He leaned in close and whispered, "Aunt Evelyn is back in town." Watching the rebel's face, he hoped to gauge whether to hold her or run for the deepest bunker he could find.

"Yea, okay," she laughed in disbelief, "I give you credit for finding the yellow-bellied mushrooms I left here last night but seriously? You need to lay off the drugs," she mocked. "You are hallucinating some serious shit. And let me guess, she was drinking and trying to get some cock in her mouth, right? Before she had to pick us girls up from school? Just like the good ole' days."

The blood drained from Cole's face as Sage recanted almost perfectly what had just occurred inside the bar. He looked at her as though she'd grown a third eye in the middle of her forehead and was using it to probe his mind. "I'm not kidding she's ins—"

His sentence was muted by heeled footsteps approaching from the other side of the door before the double doors gave way behind him.

"Oh!" Evelyn said in shock as she crashed into Cole's back and found herself face to face with her oldest daughter. A smile crept across her face.

The smile quickly diminished and was replaced with rage as she realized what time it was and where her daughter should be instead. "Sage—"

"Get out of my way. I'm not dealing with this!" Sage bit back, knowing where such a tone usually led to. She pushed past Cole and her mother, heading into the bar. "If I needed a fucking babysitter—"

"That is enough Sage Elizabe—"

"Don't!" Sage glared at the woman with threat. "You left, not me," she growled, "I am not Goody-Two-Shoes-Savannah who's going to act like your presence is welcoming." She stepped towards the bar, successfully grabbing everyone's attention.

"You're grounded!" Evelyn yelled, "William, as her mother, I demand that you don't serve her!"

Sage's face turned red, quickly matching her hair as she clenched her fists. A furious fire burned in her eyes, enough to force the demon that sat by the window to pay his tab and dart out the side door. Goosebumps covered the being's red hand as he shut the door behind him with a quick glance back.

Sage turned on her heels towards Will's office. She yanked open the office door. "Let Daddy tell you, there's no point!"

"Your father will hear about this!" Evelyn shrieked. *What had Maxx been doing? Did he just let Sage do as she please?*

"Good!" Sage screamed. She slammed the door to Will's office shut, causing the purple stained glass to shake.

Kritter rushed from the kitchen with the outburst."Kritter is so sorry! Master Will, Kritter meant to re-lock Master Will's office. Kritter was cleaning, Master Will. Kritter will never let it happen again. Kritter messed up. Please don't fire Kritter!" the pixie pled, falling to her knees in a sobbing frenzy.

Legs put her hand on Will's shoulder. "Sage could probably use someone to talk to," she whispered, knowing no one wanted to go in there and get Sage out, but it needed done. It was deadly leaving Sage in there, for the business as well as the office itself.

Will looked down at Kritter kneeling on the floor, begging for her job. He was a bit upset about his door being left unlocked, but it wasn't anything he needed to fire her over. Not when she was such devoted help.

Will sighed, "Kritter get up. You're not fired, okay? Just please remember to lock the door behind you next time."

He turned to legs, "Fine, but normally this would be your job as bar manager. The only reason I'm stepping in is because it's my office and I don't want it destroyed."

Will hopped over the bar. Walking up to Evelyn, he placed his hand on her shoulder. "However I would remind you that even though you've been gone for quite some time the rules have not changed. MisFitz Tavern is neutral ground. Now I'll talk to Sage and send her home as quickly as possible. In the meantime, you should really go talk to Maxx. You leaving affected everyone."

CHAPTER EIGHTEEN

CAN WE CHANGE THIS?

"So, you didn't tell Will that we fuck," Christopher chuckled as he looked Tatianna over. Wrapped up in a towel, she put her wet curly hair back in a ponytail and leaned back against the kitchen counter in their tiny alcove. "I'm honored."

"Ha!" Tatianna laughed. "Don't be. It was for my reputation, not yours. You know, eavesdropping is frowned upon," She added with an eye roll. As if Christopher would ever care.

"Yet it is still employed as a useful tactic by governments, police, military, and politicians. It's an American pastime," Christopher chuckled at his joke as he poured brandy into a high-ball glass on his end table and sipped it slowly.

"So now that we've failed, how long do you think Earth has? We've been hiding out in Knowhere for damn near a year now."

Tatianna sighed. She knew this conversation would eventually surface.

Truth was she couldn't fathom the results of the failed task. It had been serious enough to have angels and demons working in harmony.

"Who fucking knows," she finally groaned in defeat. "I've been trying to figure it out for months now. Trying to get back in touch with them. Replaying every word they told me. It..."

Tatianna pushed the light glow and serene peace back,

convincing herself the pained memories were just a dream. She could no longer think of the pearly gates and harmonic tunes that had once filled her daily life. She was back on Earth now.

"Angels don't just fall from grace and nothing happen. That's how hell freezes over!"

Christopher grimaced in thought of the icy domain he would eventually return to, no matter what he did. "It's already done that," he growled, "We both know what's coming. It's coming soon and it's because we failed. This is unquestionably our fault. So quit bitching and drink up."

Christopher offered Tatianna the darkened bottle. Her thick curls shook from side to side beneath the chaotic ponytail as she shook her head.

"I quit that shit! Our fault?!" Tatianna exclaimed, taken aback by the joint blame. "Excuse me, Mister Let's-Get-Back-To-Life, I wasn't the one who— " she stopped.

The list of Christopher's moral inadequacies since his return to Earth filled her mind in large filing cabinets, each one listed in alphabetical order.

She paused and clenched her eyes shut. Her frustration was released in a heavy growl through gritted teeth and pursed lips. "This was supposed to be different."

"What did goat-man say about if your dick got in the way? What did she say? They knew your temptations! They had to have!"

"As if my temptations are enough to bring the universe to an end! Not when there are multiple celestial beings, two in particular, that could have stopped this calamity. But no! We can't interfere, so we'll send a couple of dead guppy fuck-ups to do our dirty work. I was all for saving the universe and having a little fun along the way, but it shouldn't have been our job in the first place," Christopher panted heavily as he finished his rant. Downing the rest of his brandy with a single gulp, he poured himself another.

"Thanks by the way, for Miami and Cincinnati. I would have died in Pittsburgh. I guess you do have some use," Tatianna mumbled, forcing a half-hearted smile.

"Don't matter anyway. Besides, it's not like you didn't save my ass in Atlanta and L.A. The way I see it, we're square. The only reason we're still together now is we still have a use for each other. Don't we?" He wiggled his eyebrow suggestively.

She searched for the word, looking at the man with regular blood staining his hands. Nope, no attraction to the man she consistently found herself an alibi for. Time and time again, he represented himself in court with confident ease. She bit her tongue against the insult begging to be released, instead turning to the issue at hand. "Will thinks it's close."

Christopher raised an eyebrow before shrugging. "So did we, remember? It's now been almost a year and still no apocalypse. Maybe we're wrong. Maybe it'll happen years from now. Will doesn't know his ass from a black hole." Christopher looked out the window behind her and peered at the tavern's rooftop. "It doesn't matter. He can't stop it the same as we couldn't."

Tatianna sighed. She jumped up on the counter of their mini-kitchenette. She lifted a single leg and allowed her foot to rest on the counter. Laying her head on her caramel-colored knee, her doe-like brown eyes went wide. "If he is right, Christopher... I can't face them again," she added, fearful of the purity she once held, destroyed by her companion's brutal honesty.

"Would you rather I kill you first and send you packing? It would be an honor to watch an angel turn purple. It hurts for a little while, then your back to the fluffy white clouds and unicorns shitting rainbows. We both know where I'm going afterwards. I get to keep suffering. Forever. So, don't sit there and tell me you can't face them again. I don't have a goddamn choice in the matter."

"Like you didn't have a choice?" she stifled back a laugh. "You're fucking kidding me, right? We all have a choice. Maybe if you weren't a complete slime ball of an attorney! Or… oh, here's one, stop luring pigtails—"

"Shut it! Like you're so high and mighty still. Like you don't have dark desires buried deep in your soul? You know what? It doesn't fucking matter! None of this does." He downed the last of his brandy and slammed it against the counter, causing the glass to crack. Standing up, he moved closer to the woman.

He could see her pulse race as his fist clenched. His heart raced with deadly urges. Unforgivable sins that sent alarms off in the back of his mind. Christopher could almost feel her pulse weaken; hear as she gasped for her last breath. As she clawed at his wrist before her eyes slowly closed and her body grew limp.

And then, he saw another fallen angel's seductive smile forming in his mind.

"We failed!" he barked, grabbing his jacket from the coat rack by the door. Yanking the door open, he paused for a moment and turned back to his roommate, "If the end is coming, I'm going to enjoy the fuck out of myself before it gets here. Do what you want, but don't come crying to me. I've got no sympathy for anyone anymore." He slammed the door behind him and left Tatianna alone in the tiny confinement of their hiding place.

Tatianna jumped from the counter and walked to the door. Locking it, she tossed Christopher's cracked glass in the trash.

Which left her blood boiling more? Christopher's outburst? Or that she knew he was right?

Survival of the fittest and… dammit, why did he have to be right? Why must he always remind me there's no room for sympathy? her mind screamed.

A shadowed figure slid past the window. Its reflection followed her every movement as she got dressed, reminding her why they were here.

"Fuck it!" she growled as she grabbed her leather jacket and followed Christopher out. If she was going to die tomorrow, then tonight was for raising hell.

***

Evelyn pulled up in the visitor parking lot of the Inter-Realm Shipping Company. It was late in the afternoon, but surely her husband would still be in his office finishing up emails.

Fixing her lipstick in the rear-view mirror, the woman adjusted her breasts and unbuttoned the top button of her blouse. She stepped out of her minivan and walked up the gray stairs. A glass arm rail lined the way for Evelyn to enter the double glass doors.

Her husband, or perhaps his pencil-skirt, had done the lobby up nicely. Teal tiles lined the shiny floor leading to a glass chandelier and large reception area. Lobby seating lined the side for potential clients awaiting their meetings. A rock waterfall lined the far desk as Evelyn paid no attention to the sign-in sheet. She noticed the women behind the large desk trying to hide their shock before one of them picked up her phone and quickly dialed. Missus Connor figured she would save the larger woman the hassle and went to the office she knew belonged to her own husband.

As she entered a smaller, modestly decorated receptionist area with elegant wall art, a young redhead stood up quickly. "Missus Connor, your husband is—"

"Of my own concern," she answered, glaring at the twenty-year-old secretary.

"But he's—" the girl continued.

"My husband," Evelyn bit, letting herself into his office.

Having worked for the Inter-Realm Shipping Company for years, Maxx had seen crazy things both enter and leave the warehouse. They sent packages to any realm reachable by Hydrogeneral Tenetics, Phototravel Vigintiwings, even Black Hole Express in larger quantities than all three others companies could provide. Packages of all shapes and sizes, living and non, traveled through their warehouse, but nothing prepared him for what came in his door next.

Maxx's wife of twenty years had been unreachable since she'd left. Now, before him, her five-foot-four, hundred and fifty-pound figure hadn't changed at all. Her shining cleavage still nearly burst from her blouse. Black heels showed off her firm legs that led to a rounded rear, barely covered by some flimsy fabric.

"Maxximillian," she said with a smile. The single word sent a chill down the man's spine as she made herself at home in his large office with two fireplaces. Pictures of Savannah and Sage sat behind the man's desk that he soon found his wife sitting on.

Her tone quickly changed, returning to the voice she had used three years prior; a loving, affectionate voice that she only shared when she wanted an extravagant purchase, "I've missed you love. I'm home."

CHAPTER NINETEEN

LET ME TALK WITH SAGE

"Maxx!" a voice called out from behind the man as he left the grocery store and headed in the direction of his two-story suburban home. Turning around, thick curly hair and doe-like eyes ran to catch up with him.

He stopped, waiting for Tatianna. The girl had been friends with his oldest daughter ever since she first came to town, but rarely talked to him and was typically up to no good. He had no reason to suspect this time was any different.

"So, I had a question. Umm... I was hoping I could talk to Sage. About Missus Connor, I mean."

Maxx raised an eye-brow. He knew it was a tender subject for Sage, who wasn't ready for her mother to return.

"Mmm hmmm," Maxx answered. He couldn't trust Tatianna any further than he could throw the young woman who stood at his height. "And what's it going to cost me?"

Tatianna's mouth dropped open. He was willing to pay her?

No, do a good dead. You can still fix this. There is still time, she reminded herself, *and this could be your way back in.*

"You're kidding me, right?" she laughed, "No Mister Connor, Sage is my best friend. This one's on me. I'm just trying to be respectful, for once, and ask first."

"Yes, you can talk to Sage," he answered, timidly granting her permission before adding, "But I want to know everything that is said."

Tatianna bit her lip. That would be difficult. Sage wouldn't listen if her dad was around.

"Umm… I'm kinda' against no-mags," she answered, scrunching her nose in disgust.

"Yeah, I know," Maxx replied.

He had noticed the same look of disgust at the electronics throughout his home every time she came to visit. The way Tatianna snarled her nose at his big screen TV in the living room. The look of utter confusion on her face the first time she watched Sage load the dishwasher. The laundry room was completely avoided.

"So umm... Well, fine. I guess you could wire me." She held her arms out in defeat, as if expecting him to place it on her right then.

It was now his turn to laugh. "No need for that," he answered, shaking his head, "I'll take your word for it. This time." Maxx's eyes, usually warm and caring, gave the woman a warning, "But I expect full honesty about anything I ask."

"I can do that," Tatianna answered before looking at her feet. "I normally only do this in my pj's but…" She leaned up and kissed the older man's cheek as if she were one of his own daughters. "Thank you," she whispered against his course skin before starting to walk off.

"You know how to get to me, just like my girls," he laughed, "Conniving and deceitful."

"No," Tatianna laughed, turning around with a spin on her heel. "My roommate is conniving and deceitful. I prefer alert and logical." She turned the corner and headed back to her apartment.

***

A few hours later, Sage let herself into the tiny two-bedroom apartment. She made no attempt to knock before opening the door of the dingy living room. She knocked on Tatianna's bedroom door and plopped down in an outdated chair from the 70's.

"You got out of school early?" Tatianna asked curiously as she walked out of her bedroom. She turned the corner to the kitchen, reaching into a mini-fridge and pulling out two beers. She opened one, handing it to Sage.

"Bitch tried grounding me," Sage bit back. "I'm a fucking adult!" She kicked her feet up against the arm of the chair only to have Tatianna knock them down as she made her way to Christopher's gray recliner.

"Skipping school is the only time I get away from that place. So, Dad said you wanted to talk to me. If it's about Cole, I'm not—"

"I don't care if you two are kissing cousins!" Tatianna laughed, "That's your business. No, this is about your mom being back in town."

Sage groaned, chugging the rest of her beer. She stood up and went for another. "I don't know why everyone acts like this is a big deal," she said into the fridge, "I don't give a shit." She opened the new bottle and took a drink before plopping back in the seat. Her leg with tattered jeans flung over the arm of the chair. Tatianna knocked it off without saying a word. "I mean, yeah. It doesn't help the family reputation at all—"

Tatianna let out a roaring laugh, "Sage, it's me you're talking to. You don't give a fuck about the family reputation."

Tatianna certainly didn't agree with her friend's choices in drug use or her relationship with Cole, who only seemed to encourage the drug use. "Why can't you be happy that she's back?"

"Ummm... because she left," Sage answered as if it were obvious. "Hello? Have you ever even met the woman?!"

Tatianna rubbed her eyes before looking down at her beer. She finished it and said something she hadn't in a long time, "I need something stronger."

Standing up, she walked into Christopher's room. Stolen merchandise surrounded her, not even fazing her with normality, as she walked over to his bed and lifted the mattress. She ignored large wads of cash, bags of diamonds, drugs, and a Taser, grabbing only a darkened bottle before letting the mattress drop. She shut the door to make it appear untouched, the same way she was certain he did with her own.

Going into the kitchen, she grabbed a glass and filled it with ice, pouring the golden liquid over the cubes. She sighed, looking down at it and, before she could second guess herself, took a drink.

The dangerous poison danced across her tongue as a bitter reminder of drunken nights, stumbling mornings, and negative bank accounts. Sage remained silent, either out of shock or respect, as her best friend slid down the wall and threw her head back. The burn of an old frenemy drifted down her throat and warmed her stomach.

Tatianna had promised herself years ago, this wouldn't happen again. Now here she was. Opening her eyes, she faced the tiny kitchen, a reminder of where the drink had gotten her up to this point.

"You're fucking lucky!" she growled, glaring at the young woman that sat on the other side of the room.

"What?" Sage asked with a snarl. "You don't even—"

"I don't have to!" Tatianna yelled, cutting Sage off with fury at both herself and the girl in front of her. Sage jumped at the rise in her best friend's voice. "Your mom fucking cares! She gives a shit!" she spat viciously. "My mother? I wished for months, for years that my mother would leave me!" she screamed into the room, filling it with her painful envy, "Anything to get away from that bitch's hypocrisy! To not have to wonder from day to fucking day if I was going to come home and find the house bare, and hope, *hope* that maybe one day it would happen!" She didn't allow her mind to process what she said, to stop her from what Sage needed to hear, "To sleep, for a single night, and not have to wonder if her latest boyfriend was… was like fucking Christopher!" She pointed at the door she had just entered. "You want to know how I can live with him? I can live with… that, because it's familiar! It's the same hell I was in before! Your mom fucking gives a shit! Stop pushing her away!"

"You don't know her!" Sage hollered as she stood up, furious and ready for a fight.

"Sit down," Tatianna threatened, without raising her voice. Doe-like eyes flashed a savage danger towards the other woman.

Sage looked at Tatianna, testing whether it was worth rebelling before she decided do as the woman said.

Sage had fought many times without any thought of the repercussions. Tatianna wasn't one of those people. She had seen the damage Tatianna could do, so she decided do as the woman said.

Sage plopped back down with an exasperated sigh before Tatianna continued, "I don't need to know your mother. Yeah, she was gone for three years and you know what? That sucks! She left you and Savannah and she left your dad but she came back. And what was the first thing she did?"

"She fucking told me what to do!" Sage hollered, pointing towards the tavern where the incident had occurred. "She just happened to show up on a day that I skip school—"

"Sage, you skip school every day. That's why you're twenty-one and haven't graduated!" Tatianna groaned, rolling her eyes as she took another swig of the poison.

"And she started to tell me what to do? She fucking grounded me!"

"Ummm... yeah, she's your mom," Tatianna answered as if it were obvious, "Last I knew, you were still her daughter and you are still living in a house that, whether she lives in or not, her name is on. Therefore, she can."

"Hmph," Sage huffed, "She didn't seem to care enough to ground me every time Daddy bailed me out of jail."

"Which is probably best," Tatianna replied, "If she grounded you for skipping school, she probably would have just let you sit in jail."

"Parents actually do that?" Sage asked, her jaw dropping in shock.

Tatianna shook her head. Taking one last swig off the bottle that had once ruined her life, she poured the rest down the drain. She jumped up and sat on the mini-fridge, looking at the insolent woman before her. How was the best way to explain this to a girl with a nose ring, red hair, her shirt two sizes too small, and jeans ripped enough that they left no room for even the dimmest of imagination.

"Sage, how long did Maxx try before he gave up on grounding you?" she asked. Tatianna knew that despite Sage's constant attitude and disrespect towards her father, she had a lot of respect for him.

"I don't know," Sage answered looking down, uncomfortable now that the conversation had been switched to her father's discipline techniques.

"Bullshit!" Tatianna interrupted immediately. "There are bars on your windows. How long?"

"At least two years," Sage replied softly. She looked down at her feet.

"Two years after your mom left?" Tatianna raised an eyebrow. "Because I've been hiding out in this damned town for a year and I remember when those bars were put up. It was right after what's his name?"

"Joey," Sage whispered under her breath, remembering her

father's fury that the boy that she had let in the house while he was gone on a business trip.

The same boy that left mud all over the coffee table, invaded her father's tool box, and left Maxx without a single flathead screwdriver.

"Joey," Tatianna answered, nodding in recollection of the outburst that occurred in Will's Pub once Maxx got back. Maxx had exposed a temper unlike any she had ever seen out of the usually mellow man. "Your dad really tried after that one."

"I had to sleep on the floor in his room for three months after that," Sage mumbled to her feet in honesty.

"I wish my mom had cared enough to ground me like that," Tatianna confessed.

It was enough to force her best friend to lift her head, to look Tatianna in the eyes. “Really?” she asked with disbelief.

Tatianna nodded. "Usually hers was ill-attempted screaming before she told me what a whore I was. Your mom’s trying, Sage," she added with heartfelt concern for her friend.

"But she has no place to!" Sage growled defensively.

"Why?" Tatianna’s voice was calm once more, "Because your dad already has? Don't they both deserve to try, even if it doesn’t work."

Sage looked up at her best friend, realizing what it was that Tatianna was saying. She wasn't telling Sage to not be herself. To suddenly listen to an adult who randomly decided to step in and discipline her.

Instead, Tatianna was simply telling Sage to be herself; to let her mom try, even if it was a failed attempt.

Sage forced a smile, nodding her head. "Fine," she laughed as the grin became devious. She would accept the attempts as a challenge. "She can try."

CHAPTER TWENTY

COULD THIS BE LOVE?

Will leaned against the bar and cradled his beer like an infant suckling his mother's sweet milk. After the weekend's party rush, he was tired. He was happy at the number of patrons who had shown up, but the 'come down blues' were starting to wear on him with Sunday's unforgiving silence.

"Legs, pour me another one please," he asked politely, sliding his mug across the bar. "I'm glad you're still here. Everyone leaves after a heavy weekend and you get lonely, ya' know?"

Legs lifted the silver nozzle and filled his mug with foamy liquid. "I know what you mean," she answered with a heavy sigh of her own.

The young bachelor was forced to spend more time in the bar than anyone else. It was a curse he couldn't run from.

She imagined that it made it hard for the man to date. He was easy on the eyes, with a built frame and charming smile that left the cutest of dimples glowing from his cheeks. Quick comebacks and smooth pick-up lines left women melting into puddles when he walked by, but his housekeeping left room to be desired.

"You get used to the rush. Then, the silence makes you think 'what now'. Still, sometimes being alone with your thoughts is nice too." She smiled softly, "I'm glad I'm here too. It's become home."

Will nodded in agreement, drinking away his sorrows with the golden liquid. "Where are Worvacs and Fawn?" he asked finally, filling the void of silence once more, "Out on another run?"

Legs nodded her head before sighing, "Worvacs said this one was mandatory. Something about a massive goldmine of a cave on Fomar. Then they were going to Caly, Worvacs needed help with his place. Can I ask you something?" Her green eyes met his and he could see the question had been weighing heavily on her mind.

"You just did, didn't you?" he asked in attempts to lighten her mood before finishing his beer. Grabbing a bottle from across the bar, he pulled out two shot glasses and set them on the bar top. "I'll trade you a question for a question. Sound fair?" He poured them both a shot and waited.

This was a familiar game in the Misfitz Tavern. One that sometimes ended in bar fights, treason, and revolution, but just as often resulted in crazy romances and life-long friendships.

"Deal," Legs laughed. She moved around and sat beside him, ready to ask the question that left her sleepless more nights than not. "Fawn and Worvacs, has she said anything to you about them?" She took the shot to swallow her fear of the answer.

Will raised a questioning eyebrow and wondered if he should be concerned before shrugging. He downed his shot. "Fawn's told me a lot about her and Worvacs."

"That's cheating! You knew exactly what I meant and fully avoided the question," she growled, taking another shot out of frustration. Why even try questioning the professional bartender on what he heard from his best friend. She should have known better.

"My turn," Will laughed, "What has Worvacs told you?" He poured another shot and waited for the dreaded truth he already knew.

"He says they are just travel partners. He's known Fawn since she was young and naive and that I have nothing to worry about. But if I had nothing to worry about, why would he say I had nothing to worry about? I don't know how relationship stuff works, Will," she groaned, running her hands through her hair in frustration.

Will picked up his shot glass and eyed it carefully to avoid her gaze. Choosing his words carefully, he replied, "I believe he's telling you the truth. As far as what they do on their runs…"

Will pictured the petite, tanned beauty lying back on his bed. Her pink hair spread out like a halo around her as the sheets covered her bare skin.

"I think when you're away for an extended time, like they are, that a person has needs that should be fulfilled. Physical needs. You and I aren't physical people, not in the same sense of Fawn and Worvacs, so I don't think we could ever fully understand how their relationship works." He looked at her and thought, *There you go, be easy on the poor girl.* "But I trust my friend. If he says you have nothing to worry about, then you have nothing to worry about. My turn. Do you think Fawn can have a relationship?"

Legs took Will's question as her opportunity to avoid eye contact. She looked to the fireplace in the corner. Raising her finger slowly, the flame rose with it and filled the room with a more comfortable heat.

"I think she could, but only for the right guy. Fawn has been coming to this bar for what? At least the last two years I've been here. During that time, I've never seen her show consistent interest in a man, but I also spent most of that time going from my room to the front door."

"In the last few months, that changed. This is the first place she goes when they get back. Worvacs goes home and drops off some his guns before stopping in. Fawn's here the second they land. Do you really think that's for your shower?" Legs asked with a laugh, taking a shot.

Pale realization swept over the bachelor's face. It was true. Fawn did find her way back to the tavern the minute she hit realmside. Always smiling and bubbly, she would come in and always asked for him. Her smiling face would force one to creep across his own as she pulled out a trinket, ore, gun, or even a new rocket launcher to show him. Perhaps he should add another toothbrush to his bathroom?

"It's either my shower or the crab salad," Will answered in denial. "So, your question then," he added quickly, taking the spotlight off himself.

Legs' eyes gleamed bright green as she giggled with childlike glee. The warm shots of whiskey calmed her nerves and dropped her need for serious conversation. Leaning forward, Legs looked Will in the eyes. "Do you love her?"

The question filled the empty pub. The fire cackled in the background, clean dishes clanked in the kitchen. Will's eyebrows furrowed as he tried to delve deeper into his own mind.

"I don't know. It's been so long since I was in love that it's hard to remember what it felt like. I always look forward to seeing her when I know she's coming home. I miss her like crazy when she's gone. I get tongue tied every time she asks me something. Do I love her? It feels like it. But I'm not sure she's ready for love." He shrugged again and filled the shot glasses. "Do you love him?"

Legs should have known the question was coming and yet still found herself unprepared and speechless. Her mind raced.

It was one thing to ask herself that as she curled up to her pillow on lonely nights. When she lay there wondering if Worvacs could even see the same moon she was. If he was really that far away. How gone he was and when would he be coming home?

"I don't know," a glowing smile dominated her face, "He's the one I tell everything to. Good news, bad news. It doesn't matter. Part of me wants to share everything with him."

"If he isn't at the tavern, just knowing he's back on Earth makes me feel whole. When he's gone, I wonder where he is. I wonder what he's doing."

"I ask myself if he misses the sunny days. If once he returns, he will embrace the sight of a deer crossing the road rather than a dakibant," she looked down as a blush filled her cheeks, "I'm not really sure if that's what love is, but maybe I am."

"Hmmm... and it's my question." She wanted to ask about Worvacs' past, even about Will's, but knew it was best not to. She would rather not get asked about her own and decided to play it safe. Will was one of Worvacs' friends. She had access to a glimpse of Worvacs' mind.

"Has he ever dated before?" she asked nervously.

"Oooh, good question," Will replied as he raised his shot glass in toast. Downing it quickly, he gave himself a moment to think.

The shot burned down his throat as he recalled years of history. Women who had been with the men, and between them, before he opened his eyes.

"Yes. Worvacs has dated before. I answered your question. I could answer that with much more, but I think we are getting a bit deep here. Deeper conversation would require a higher price so let's keep it simple. Has Fawn ever dated before? I'm sure even if you haven't seen it yourself, girls talk." He wiggled his eyebrows teasingly at her and poured another shot.

Legs laughed. She and Fawn had, in fact, giggled about first kisses that were clumsy and inexperienced. They joked about their first times with men and how nothing could prepare them for what to expect. Reminiscing of long ago was joined with shots of heavy liquor, and much like Legs assumed the men did, her and Fawn teased and poked fun. And once, after one of Fawn's less than successful trips back from Caly, did she mention her first love.

"Yeah," Legs chuckled to herself as she thought back to the conversation. How Fawn had made her promise to never speak of the man's name who, though she loved, hadn't yet kissed. "Fawn's dated before, but it was never anything serious. She could know monogamy, with the right guy."

***

"You owe me for this," Fawn groaned, wiping her brow from the top of the ladder. She was helping Worvacs build onto his home on Caly, a project they had been working on for months. "Take a break and tell me what you think."

Worvacs wiped the sweat from his eyes as he looked up at the two-story structure. "Plenty of space and plenty of safety. Solid support beams. I think she'll do nicely." He wiped his hands on a dirty rag and placed them on his hips, admiring their day's handiwork.

The two-story house was made from Earth's white birch. It included a balcony inside and held torches lining the top level. A neat cobblestone gate guarded the front walkway to the door.

"A woman's touch is nice occasionally. And you're right I do owe you for this one."

"Yeah, you do," Fawn sighed, sitting down on the ground. She looked up at the magnificent structure they had put blood, sweat, and swear words into constructing during their last three travels to the realm. It had been taking away from their hunting time and was quickly putting a hefty dent in both their wallets.

"So, are you and Legs serious enough for you to bring her out here?" she asked, batting her pink eyelashes playfully. "You sure do go running to her place as soon as you get to Earth."

"Is that jealousy? Besides, Will's shower seems to be getting considerably more use lately, the way I understand it," he teased back, sitting down beside her. He pulled two beers from the cooling unit that sat on the other side of him. He handed one to Fawn. She took a drink before looking up at the sun. She loved Caly's single springtime season.

Worvacs closed his eyes, inhaling the fresh air surrounding them. It beat the chill winters they faced in Nebraska and Fawn's home biome was wet and rainy. The Quad sat in a clearing just past the wood shed, polished and ready for their return.

"I'm not jealous. What happens on Earth, is Earthly business. Same with any other realm. I don't care what you do. I just think it's cute. As for Will's shower, you've seen my place," she added, referring to the single room she rented from George, "Sorry Worvacs, it's not Will I love. It's the water pressure."

Worvacs shrugged at Fawn's back as the woman headed to her next task. He wasn't so sure about her love being solely for the comforts of Will's shower.

"Is there enough water?" Fawn called as she jumped into the claustrophobic ravine that would soon be a watering hole for Worvacs' newest livestock, "They aren't kerberos, you know. These are low maintenance mammals."

"Of course my merpin are low maintenance," Worvacs laughed incredulously, "I'd hate to see what trying to breed your kerberos would be like."

Worvacs could just see the large, three-headed dogs nipping at one another before they jumped into a territorial dog fight. It would result in multiple gash wounds and injuries that would be in dire need of medical attention. Yes, in comparison to that, perhaps his two-headed piglets were low maintenance.

Fawn stuck her head out of the tunnel and spit out a mouthful of the yellow cake-like clay. She growled up at the bank where Worvacs stood.

"Let's not test that, okay? You're lucky I'm letting you keep the damn chickens. Those things plot to escape. You want two testosterone filled dakibants in the pen next to them? I can't wait to see what happens!"

A wet trickle touched Fawn's ankle and stopped her train of thought. She gasped as the cold water reached her naval and grabbed at the muddy walls of the opening, she tried to pull away. Worvacs erupted with a roar of laughter at Fawn's exasperated face before dodging a mud pie thrown at him.

"Hey! Easy I just got my boots cleaned. Come on out. The water pit should fill quickly now. We can eat while we wait."

"Well… must be nice," she groaned, shimming back and forth as she tried to pull loose from the hole that now suctioned to her. The mustard-colored mud clung to her boots, holding on tightly. With a hard tug, Fawn jerked herself free. "Food sounds great. What's for lunch?" she asked as she climbed out and wiped the clay from her forehead.

"I don't know. What do you feel like making?" Worvacs teased, dropping his head quickly to avoid the next assault of mud pies.

He held his hands up in surrender. "Chicken, jeez it's chicken," he laughed, walking towards the barn at the top of the hill.

"Mmm mmm… and baked potatoes," Fawn called after him, "And those stewed carrots you do!"

Fawn quickly followed Worvacs to the barn. Her pants weighed down on her hips as she felt fine gravel line the insides of her socks. "I miss my shower."

"You and that indoor plumbing crap. I don't know why you're so in love with it. You could just as easily use the purification chamber the teleports offer," he replied with sarcasm.

"The same reason you love the shine of emeralds," Fawn hinted playfully.

Worvacs sighed as he looked at his polished rock floor then back up at Fawn, who was still leaking mud everywhere. "Go get cleaned up. I'll have lunch ready before you get back."

"Thanks."

Fawn closed the barn door and walked down the hill to the river. It wasn't the same as the shower Will provided her with, but would do in a pinch.

It wasn't long before the peaceful silence of Worvacs' foreign home was shattered by a scream from Fawn.

"Worvacs! You and your damn 'I'm going to be a farmer' shit! Get! Get! Get!"

The door flew open and Fawn stood before him. Soaking wet and wrapped only in a blanket, she glared at Worvacs with an unmistakable fury. Her pink hair clung to her face, matted with yellow mud. White feathers, likely from Worvacs' chickens, stuck out of the globs as her orange eyes burned like molten lava.

Worvacs momentarily wondered if she was a loot-able creature and was ready to make the ideal reference. He opened his mouth with a laugh already in his voice.

"Not a fucking word," Fawn growled as she stomped to her storage compartment. Pulling out her plasma rifle, she flung the door to the barn open.

"Here chickie, chickie, chickie!"

CHAPTER TWENTY-ONE

OH, TO BE WILL...

Genine Prepares for Fifth World War

The planet of Genine in the Parcarson Realm officially announced its Fifth World War on Saturday. "The violence against our people has gone on too long." Gernada Marsqual, Genine Representative in the 295th House states. "It is time we take back our land that was peaceful and kind. I ask all of you to help us in this act."

So far, thirty-five of the seventy-two representatives have agreed and another twelve are offering financial support in the on-going battle between fire and water.

Nanina Parson of the Caly Republic seems to disagree stating, "Sending assistance in this battle is useless. They ask for help, and then allow themselves into the same predicament. Caly will not be choosing sides in this endless battle. We are staying neutral, as I would suggest the rest of you do. If all we do is focus on other realms, what good does it do our own?"

Realms will each choose for themselves whether they would like to send armed forces or financial assistance before the next meeting, which is to occur with Zachariah's next rotation.

Will sat at his desk and read through the headlines, as he so often did in the morning. He didn't know what he was looking for as he chewed on the end of a toothpick, but there was something.

He could feel it; a dark, ominous something. For years, he felt this dangerous shadow lurking overhead and yet, he could never pin down what exactly the omen was.

So, he acquired this new hobby over a decade ago when the feeling had first washed over him. It also included prepping for what he called 'The End'.

He was prepared, ready to survive. It didn't matter to him what it was or how it showed up. It symbolized the only thing William Pearson truly feared, death.

The part that upset Will the most was that the feeling had steadily grown stronger over the last few months. Now it plagued his every waking moment, every silent thought to himself involved planning.

"Kritter, come into the office please," Will called into the talk box that was located on his desk.

Kritter rushed into the office, her terrified eyes went wide. "Kritter is sorry, Master Will. Kritter didn't mean to," she stammered apologetically, "Kritter was only meaning to clean under the stairs, Master Will. Kritter didn't know mouseling had made a home beneath the stairs. Kritter didn't mean to destroy mouseling's home, Master Will." The pixie continued with rapid apologies as she shut the door behind her. Her hands shook with fear that Will had seen her when she flew onto the bar top with loud squeals as the mouse had come running out of the darkened corner.

"Never mind that, Kritter. I want you to post a notice on the front door that the Misfitz Tavern will be closed Monday evening. We will be having a feast Monday night for everyone who's on the payroll. Find out what our employees' favorite dishes are and go collect some of the best ingredients you can find. I don't care how much it costs or what realms you have to get them from."

Will eyed her over the edge of his desk. The mint green pixie wrung her hands fearfully. "And that includes you," he added with hopes of relieving her nerves.

"Thank you, Master Will," Kritter answered, nodding with appreciation. "Kritter will start on the list immediately, Master Will. Kritter will invite everyone on payroll to the feast. Kritter will close the tavern Monday. Master Will, may Kritter ask the special occasion?"

"No, you may not!" Will barked harshly.

Tears immediately filled the pixie's eyes at his sudden outburst. She shook with fear causing her wings to tremble at her sides.

Will ran a hand over his face. "What I mean is I don't want to spoil anybody's… oh never mind. Kritter, please just do as I ask." He looked at her and prayed for a simple acknowledgment. Somewhere in the back of Will's mind, he knew he wouldn't receive one.

"Master Will," Kritter spoke more softly, her tone delicate tone with fear of another outburst, "Master Will has bad news for staff? Is the Misfitz Tavern shutting down, Master Will?"

"Kritter has nowhere else to go. Kritter is a misfit. Kritter is home. Master Will can't make Kritter leave home. Kritter will do anything. Kritter will serve favorite foods. Kritter won't say such things. Kritter will do what Master Will says. Kritter will do anything. Don't make Kritter leave, Master Will."

Will shook his head, stifling a chuckle the best he could. "No Kritter, we're not shutting down. I doubt that the tavern itself would let us, much less our rowdy group of patrons. Besides, how many times must I tell you Kritter? You can stay or go as you please. You should know by now that there will always, *always*, be a place for you at the Misfitz Tavern. At least as long as I'm running the place."

Kritter put her hands on her tiny hips as a motherly scowl came out. "Master Will should not scare Kritter like that!" she scolded as her miniature hands grabbed at her chest, "Kritter was worried Kritter would have to return to pixies. Kritter can't return to pixies, Master Will. Pixies were very upset with Kritter's decision to stay here."

"Now, where were we?" Will leaned back in his chair and closed his eyes. He pinched the bridge of his nose as he tried to stem the headache that slowly grew stronger beneath his skull.

"Kritter must advise bad news is usually not served best over good food," she warned, "Kritter's pixies used to believe that to be an omen, Master Will. Kritter is to obey Master Will. Kritter just feels as though Kritter should advise." Her eyes darted everywhere as she avoided looking at Will behind his desk.

"That's right! You're supposed to be telling me a better way to deliver the bad news, remember?" He cracked one eye and looked at Kritter with a smile.

She wiped the sweat droplets from her brow before continuing, "Pixies deliver bad news with more bad news following. Then when pixie cries over first bad news, pixie gets second bad news and first bad news isn't so bad, Master Will. Pixies also deliver bad news with death, though Kritter would suggest against that, Master Will."

Will sighed heavily and covered his eyes in defeat. With a deep inhale, he chose his words wisely before speaking them, "How about we just stick with favorite dishes and loaded guns to start with? Push comes to shove, we'll decide if we want to give them more bad news or just shoot everyone after dessert." He lifted his hands from his eyes and looked at Kritter.

"And bring me something from the kitchen, I'm starved." He mockingly sucked in his stomach to appear thinner before sticking his tongue out at her.

"Kritter will bring Master Will leftovers," the pixie answered with a laugh. "Kritter believes there are falcon wings still. Kritter will add Master Will's favorite sauce."

Will watched as the pixie left his office, eager to feed him.

Her green skin clashed against her bright orange wings as she bobbed with quick movements.

Soft patter was heard from upstairs, followed by footsteps as a scarred ankle exposed itself at the top of Will's stairs.

"A meeting followed by an assassination?" Fawn laughed, wrapped only in Will's thick comforter as she walked down and sat in the clear chair across from him. "Care to explain?" she asked, her pink hair scattered in every direction.

"Just my crazy idea that the universe is coming to an end. You going to be here for dinner? I'll have Kritter add you to the list." Will eyed the beauty before him and could only picture a child's troll doll with hair splayed everywhere. "You look like you slept well. Hair of the dog?" he asked as he moved over to the mini-fridge in the corner of the room.

"In my coffee, please. Something creamy," Fawn answered as she rubbed her eye with a loud yawn, as if still trying to wake up. "And that sounds like an excellent idea. The world is coming to an end so we tell everyone and then we kill them. Very much like the oil rigs on Caly," she laughed.

"No! No! Hair of the dog, not drunk again!" Fawn exclaimed when she saw Will pour a hefty amount of the liqueur in the bottom of her cup. "As far as dinner goes, I suppose that depends on where we sit with this morning's light, don't it?" she asked, hopeful that Will would forfeit how he felt after their first night sharing a bed.

Will corked the bottle and topped her cup with coffee. Stirring the liquid to a light tan, he handed it to Fawn before making his.

He contemplated what she was asking as he sat behind his desk and leaned back in his chair. "Well, if you promise to do that thing with your ankles again, you can come back anytime you like." With a chuckle, Will winked at her and took a sip to savor the warmth of the drink, "What can I say? It was entertaining to say the least."

"Ahhh... the thing with my ankles," Fawn laughed as she wrapped her hands around the warm mug. "It helps when your hips have been broken as many times as mine have. Dinner it is!" she exclaimed before leaning forward. She pulled the blue comforter closer to her bosom. "So, what's the bad news?"

Will eyed Fawn sitting across from him. With her tangled mess of hair, she was a natural beauty. One he wondered if he could wake up to every morning. Or maybe that was just the coffee talking.

Did he really want to tell her what he knew? Was she ready to hear the truth?

He sighed heavily. "The end is near. No, I don't know what it is. I don't know how it will happen or when it will hit." He sipped his coffee again before adding, "But I know it's close. I can feel it in my soul. It's the end of everything." Will sat in silence for a moment and waited for her reaction.

Fawn looked back at Will and wondered if the man was questioning her sanity. She nearly questioned her own sanity after such an orgasmic night. She raised a pink eyebrow and waited for him to burst out in laughter. When he didn't, Fawn shrugged.

"I suppose it doesn't surprise me," she stated honestly, "I mean there have been plenty of times that the teleport refused to send me or Worvacs to Dual Peaks. Camp Icy can be a bitch to get to in the winter. The world may as well end when you can't go to your trading portals. If they were that way, even here, I mean," she stopped and couldn't help but laugh at the thought of such an absurdity. "I die on a weekly basis. I know it's not the same on Earth, but it happens Will. Sometimes it's just in larger quantities."

Will smirked at her response and felt a sense of relief that she believed him, though he wondered if she fully understood.

"I don't think this is the same thing. I have a feeling, and this is just a feeling mind you, that whatever 'The End' is... It's big.

That it's going to affect all of us, on every realm.

"I've known that it was coming for years, but the feeling is stronger now. Stronger than it's ever been."

He pressed the intercom button on his desk, "Kritter, grab me the daily papers please. All of them." He released the button and turned back to Fawn, "I've been prepping for years. I'm not sure whether it will do any good. Hell, I don't know if any of us will survive at all, but I'm going to try."

"What do you think is going to happen?" Fawn asked nervously, her purple eyes wide. She was concerned that Will was so adamant on his idea.

Kritter entered the office silently, dragging a large wooden chest from the stairway storage behind her. It stood every bit of her four-foot height as she yanked, pulling it into the office.

As soon as the chest was past the doorway, the pixie left. She never spoke a word and kept her wings wrapped tightly around herself.

This isn't just a crazy idea, Fawn thought to herself as she looked at the heavy chest, *It's an obsession.*

"Natural disaster?"

"Maybe, but I doubt it," Will answered, "If it were a natural disaster, it would have to be on a universal scale to affect everyone.

"A black hole would—"

"Not the way I'm talking." Will slid the chest next to his desk. Opening the lid, he spread the papers out across the desk.

Fawn's eyes scanned the variety of news articles in various languages. Multiple articles discussed grotesque heart failure, mass casualties and empty tombs.

"This is Caly!" she exclaimed, looking at the familiar red print that covered the top of one of the pages, "And this one is Resurstorm!"

The multiple realms each had different textures of paper and stone that reported the news, yet they all told the same thing.

Facts that a local reader in any realm would consider an inconvenience, a tragedy even. But here, like this, Will's theory added up.

"This is big," Fawn sighed in disbelief as she leaned back in the clear chair. She pulled the blanket close for comfort. "I... some of these realms I've never even heard of."

Will nodded. He sat back in his leather chair as he saw the truth sink in. "Once upon a time, I used to get around. The worst part is I don't know when. It could be today. It could be six months from now, if we're that lucky."

Will frowned as he looked at the calendar on his desk. He didn't like how close the winter months were.

"If we're lucky?" Fawn asked as her mouth dropped open. "Will, that doesn't leave any time at all! Anyone snowed in will be lucky! They'll have protection." Her mind drifted to her and Worvacs constant travels.

Fear swept through the brave woman at the thought of what uncivilized realm she might be stuck on when everything fell through. What sort of mobs she may find herself up against? Or worse, what locals!

"This is casual, us I mean," she whispered in reference to their relationship. "If I'm here, I would like to stay. If I'm not, don't be a hero. Save your own ass."

"No skin off my back, love," Will answered with a shrug, "I'll be here one way or the other." He swirled his finger with a sigh before confessing, "It's almost enough to make me want to crawl back under the blankets and have a good cry. I'd settle for kinky sex, though." He winked at her suggestively.

Pushing against the chest, he slid it to the wall next to the door of his office. "Either way Fawn, so long as this place is standing, you'll always be welcome."

"Greatly appreciated," Fawn nodded respectfully.

Standing up, she opened the blanket and exposed her bare body in front of Will at his desk. The soft succulence of her skin flashed into his view before she pulled the blanket tighter around her body.

Flashing Will a smile that said more than words, Fawn silently turned around and walked back up the spiral staircase that led to his bedroom.

***

"Suck it!" Sage screamed with a howling laugh. She jumped around the pool table with excitement as the last of her solid balls rolled into the far pocket. "Eight ball, corner pocket," she called out as she leaned over the pool table to make her shot.

Meanwhile, Fawn sat at the bar and flipped a gold coin. Her last trip off-world was good. This morning was even better.

Now the foreigner had gold in her pocket, iron in her inventory, and showcased a new pair of green leather pants. The smile on her face was irreplaceable.

"Nice threads. I assume you had a good run?" Will asked. He smiled at Fawn as he wiped down the bar. Doing his best to hide the shivers that still rolled down his spine from their escapades earlier that morning, he attempted to remain casual.

"The green looks good on you. A bit spikey but hey, cacti might make good security against some of the scum floating in here." Winking at her playfully, he refilled her drink and slid it across the bar.

"Thank you," Fawn answered with a proud smile.

"Thanks to Worvacs here," she laughed as she nudged the cobalt man next to her. "If it wasn't for him overhearing those older miners, we never would have run across that gold mine," she boasted with excitement, "And here, I thought we were going to have to ask my investor for juice just to make it back to Earth."

Worvacs opened his inventory bag and dug around, finally finding the small metal box he'd been looking for. A proud smile covered his face as he held it out for both Will and Fawn to see. As he lifted the lid, a large green emerald came into view. It shined in the bright lights of the tavern. Each cut of the octagon gem sparkled with its own unique beauty.

"I kept this back from one of my runs," Worvacs announced with pride, "I'm going to give it to Legs. Do you guys think she'll like it?"

"It's a bit flashy if you ask me. Hey, green's not really my color though," Will shrugged.

"I think Legs will love it," Fawn told Worvacs proudly, "But I have to agree with Will. Take it home, cut it down, and use the multiple emeralds to make her something." She pursed her lips in thought. She tried to think of what Legs might like before deciding that picking on Worvacs would be more fun. "Are you going to ask her to marry you?" she mocked, pinching his cheek.

Will's attention was turned from the conversation as the front door of the tavern opened. Sir silently strutted to the bar. This time, however, Pet did not follow.

"William, Worvacs," the stern man acknowledged with a nod of his head before he turned and nodded politely at Fawn, "Madam, I find myself curious as to the pants you're wearing. They seem a bit… thorny?"

"The dye was cactus leaves," Fawn answered, laughing at the man's raised eyebrow of questioning. "I tried to get all of the thorns out but—" She shrugged playfully, "I guess it's just another one of life's painful pleasures."

"You know Sir, green isn't the only color I can dye leather," Fawn added with pride, flashing her business smile. "I have a very nice rose red that would look stunning on Pet." Sir pursed his lips in consideration of Fawn's offer.

"Perhaps, but first, I would like to see the color in person. Prepare some samples and then we shall discuss a price." Giving the trader a polite nod, he turned back to Will.

"Are we prepared to work William? I do have a schedule to

keep."

"As do I. We're waiting on Legs to come down and take over. In the meantime, sit and have a drink. Don't worry, we've got plenty of work to do so you may want to be loosened up before you have to hunch over for hours on end." He poured Sir a martini and slid it across the bar. The man moved, occupying an empty bar stool next to Worvacs.

"I don't hunch, William," Sir informed Will as he straightened his suit jacket. He eyed the large emerald Worvacs was putting away and cleared his throat.

"Perhaps you and Fawn could work together on a piece for my Pet? Emeralds are no interest of mine. However, a ruby studded collar would look stunning on my Pet. Wouldn't you agree, Mister Worvacs?"

"I'm sure Fawn and I can whip something up for you. Something you will find most satisfying for Pet; for an equivalent price, of course," Worvacs added quickly, not nearly as willing as Fawn to make a deal with the man.

"Money is no consequence to me, Mister Worvacs. I only concern myself with the happiness of my Pet. See to my request and you both shall be amply rewarded for your efforts." Sir waved his hand nonchalantly. As he lifted his martini glass, Sir sipped it delicately with his pinky extended.

"We'll discuss price later," Fawn agreed with a nod. She shined an ignored glare at her blue co-traveler.

A blue chandelier above the bar shook as Legs rushed down the stairs, taking them two at a time. Her namesake, followed by a black pencil skirt and white button up shirt became apparent as she turned the corner of the stairwell.

A smile covered the bartender's face at the welcoming atmosphere the old tavern held. Two corner tables were taken by a group of elves enjoying the last of their chipmunk nachos. A gargoyle sat on the seat cushion next to the stone fireplace, in an attempt to stay warm while Sage danced merrily around the pool table, gleaming with her win.

Fawn and Worvacs were the only two patrons at the bar, aside from Sir. Their familiar faces she could pleasantly serve drinks to for the duration of her shift.

"Sorry Will," Legs stammered quickly. She smiled briefly at Worvacs as she clocked in. She typed her code onto the flat screen behind the wooden bar. "In my defense, I still clocked in on time."

Will waved his hand nonchalantly. "You're here, that's all that matters. The elves still need to pay and the gargoyle wants a hot toddy for the gravel in his throat. He's an old friend so his drinks are on me."

He placed his towel on the bar and keyed the orders over to her on the flat screen. "Kritter's going to be here in about an hour. George took her unicorn hunting again."

Grabbing his keys from the ice chest, Will looked at Sir. "Are you ready, Sir? There are plants to be harvested."

Sir nodded.

Will winked at Legs and Fawn both, leading the way to the staircase near the banquet room as Sir followed.

***

He unlocked the metal door and clicked on the light switch. With a soft buzz, a white fluorescent glow illuminated the staircase. Will descended the stairs two at a time as Sir turned and locked the door behind him.

"How many shall we harvest today, William? The upper class are not keen on waiting and the soccer moms request new and exotic strains."

"Two today, we should have two more the day after tomorrow, if we're lucky. Your client base growing larger is a wonderful thing, I won't argue, but..." Will turned at the bottom of the staircase and held his hand to the palm reader on the wall.

The hydroponics bay doors slid open with ease. "Be careful how quickly you grow or we won't have the supply to meet the demand."

Stepping into the room, Will inhaled deeply. A smile covered his face as he walked over to a work bench along the far wall. Clicking on the small desk lamp, he quickly opened the top drawer and pulled out two pairs of gloves and two sets of shears.

"Leave your worries with me, William," Sir answered as he moved to Will's side and slid on his gloves, "You have my solemn vow. Nothing adverse shall happen to our happy little entrepreneurship." The older man picked up his sheers and ran his finger across the blade, ensuring it was sharpened.

"I don't trust anybody that much," Will answered. He stepped over to the first hydro bay. Admiring the blooms of the purple and green, Will reached out with his shears and gently clipped the first pick at the stem. He then placed the bud in a plastic bag and moved on to the next.

"Purple Dragon's Hair. This has to be one of the best strains we've had all season," Will announced with pride as he clipped another.

Sir stepped up to the second bay and started on his plants. "I would argue that the Nyphim's Tears was quite a pleasant cross strain. However, the yield wasn't nearly as generous," the man replied as he clipped buds from another large plant. The burn of the narrow sun-lamp warmed his skin, slowly toasting it to a light pink burn.

The two men continued to clip in a comfortable silence until Sir cleared his throat.

"Pet is with child."

Sir dropped the bombshell in Will's lap, leaving him at a loss of words. His shears slipped from his hand and clipped an entire branch of a plant as Will blinked his eyes repeatedly.

"Oh... umm, well these things do tend to happen," Will

answered as he tried to hide his discomfort. He thought about the many tales that Sir had shared with him over the years and found it difficult to imagine Sir as a father.

Sir placed the last flower from his golden leafed plant into a bag. "What an obtuse observation, William," he retorted, "Yes, of course they tend to happen. Must I explain to you how it takes place or shall we just crack-on then?"

Sir returned to clipping the plant as he continued, "I, too, was unprepared for this eventuality. I find myself anxious at what the future may hold. My father wasn't a very forth-coming man."

"Mine had this place as a tavern. He drank away half of my childhood and smoked away the rest. When he died, there was still unfinished business between us," Will shrugged his shoulders as he moved on to the next plant, "No one's parents are perfect. All we can hope to do is try to shape a generation better than our own."

"That is not all that worries me. How to best proceed with my Pet is most important at this point. I find myself at a loss for direction." Sir stopped, pausing long enough to meet Will's gaze before he continued with his chore.

"Do you love her?" Will asked as he moved on to the second set of plants.

"She is my Pet," Sir stated, "Of course I love her. Our relationship is not that simple, however. Pet requires a firm hand. If the child were to take after her mother, then things may become difficult."

"What makes you think it will be a girl?" Will closed his bag and walked to the dehydrator against the back wall.

"Do you even remember whom my Pet was prior to her collar?" Sir snapped, "Of course the child will be female and it is certain that she will be just as dangerous should Pet's attitude and traits continue forth in our bloodline. Yet, there is another issue at hand that I feel must be addressed, William." Sir clipped the last bud from his plant. Closing his bag, he moved to join

Will.

"Oh? And what is that?" Will wasn't sure he was prepared for any other issues Sir might be facing.

"I am not a young man anymore. I want to ensure that whomever my child may be, that I leave them a proud legacy. If something ill should befall of me, I need someone I can trust to ensure that my Pet and my child are well cared for." Sir placed his bag inside the dehydrator next to Will's and closed the door. He watched as Will set the timer.

"And you want me to guarantee that? I'm not stupid, Sir. I know what you're asking of me. What makes you think I could, even if I wanted to?" Will turned to Sir as he listened to the tick of the timer's countdown.

"I ask it of you, William, because should the situation become dire, I know you are not one to hesitate in doing what must be done," Sir replied solemnly.

"I hate you. You're such a buzzkill."

CHAPTER TWENTY-TWO

ANGEL NEEDS A VACATION

Angel entered the tavern and scanned the room. A dark winged dragon played darts in the far corner while Legs collected a tray of food from the kitchen window. Legs smiled and gave Angel a nod as she walked over to serve Worvacs and Fawn their plate of nachos by the fireplace.

Angel politely waved back. Walking across the bar room to the purple stained glass door, she pressed the buzzer.

"You have been staring at the same thing for an hour," she called into Will's office. She didn't have to see the bachelor to know what she said was true. "Come have a drink!" She turned around before Will had a chance to respond. Walking up to the wooden bar, she sat at one of the bar stools and waited.

Will knew Angel was right. Payroll was never easy and always required the most attention. It appeared no one liked to work for free.

He threw his pen onto the stack of papers that covered his large desk. Sighing deeply, he stood and stretched the ache from his back.

Grabbing the gray suit jacket from behind him, Will threw it on over his casual t-shirt and sprayed himself down with musky cologne before heading out to the bar.

"You know I hate it when you're right," he growled as he

stepped behind the bar and pulled down two glasses.

"Only because you can't argue when I am," Angel answered matter-of-factly with a playful smile.

Taking a clear shot glass, she flipped it over for him to pour. "You're going to need this," she warned, sliding the glass in his direction.

"Oh boy..." He reached beneath the bar and grabbed a bottle of red liquor with swirling silver flakes. "What now?" he asked, pouring them both a shot and then raising his, "Cheers."

Angel tossed back the shot. An icy fire trailed down her throat causing her to shake her head against the taste. "I know you have the meeting planned and I have to speak with a potential client first, but..." She looked down at the glass. Her eyes avoided the bartender. Her chest rose and fell with a heavy sigh as she met his stare. "I need to take a week off."

She finalized the statement with another shot. Letting the burn fill her stomach, she wiped a remaining drip from her ruby red lips.

Will groaned. He took down a larger glass from above the bar and started to mix a chaser for the Roman Brandy. When he finished the mixture, he sipped it gently. "A whole week?" Will cringed at the thought.

Angel was valuable. She had increased his business dramatically and brought in new regular customers.

"Business may drop while you're gone," he informed her honestly, "Where are you going? I can't guarantee your safety out there right now, you know that." His thoughts raced to what the headlines said. What the warning signs were.

"It hasn't happened yet and Salem," she answered with another heavy sigh. Her bosom rose and fell beneath her black and gold corset. "My mom and dad. My grandmother and brother. It's... it's getting cold. If you are right..."

Angel couldn't bring herself to mention Revelations. She knew word-for-word what it spoke of. Will nodded in understanding of the courtesan's silent Sunday evenings alone.

"I should go see family while I can," she added, fearful of his predictions. "Since you can't guarantee my safety, I need to go while the truck can still make it." She worried about how her blue low-rider would handle the Appalachian snows if she waited. "I'm sorry."

Will waved his hand, brushing away her sincere apology. He understood. "If I had family worth seeing, I'd find a way too."

As he took another sip of his drink, Will tossed an idea back and forth in his mind before he swallowed the liquor. "I can't guarantee your safety, but I may be able to cut down your risk." He held up a finger and motioned for her to follow him to the basement.

The pair walked to the door and headed down the spiral wooden staircase. Angel looked around in awe at the Jacuzzi tub with a floor to ceiling television that sat next to the stairwell.

Will led her to a large steel-plated door that filled a far wall of the stone basement. He used his body to block Angel's view of the keypad as he typed in '1620'. Engines roared, causing the rock floor to vibrate as the motor kicked in and moved the door to reveal a beast of a truck.

The cab was one she would have to jump into. Spiked tires that were waxed and polished led up to black titanium armor that covered the over-sized pickup.

"I… I can't," she whispered in awe, trailing her fingers down the titanium steel. Will reached into his jeans pocket and pushed a single button that caused deep vibrations of the motor beneath her hand.

"Why not?" Will laughed. His dimples shined as his blue eyes glowed with pride.

"She has dual tanks that are run by a switch on the dash. Four-wheel drive and the body is weighted down with cast iron weights under each of the tires, thanks to the goblins at the mechanic shop."

Angel continued to stare in awe at the truck's thick metal shine under the lights. She stepped up to the grated, shatterproof windows that stood at eye-level.

What would her parents think if she showed up to their old-fashioned home in this monster? Her mother would faint. Her father would hold his head high and smile with pride. He would wave at the neighbors as he waxed the hood, buffing it to a shine.

The three-inch tread on the tires promised guaranteed travel through mud and snow.

"Oh!" Will added with a smile, "Just don't push the red button."

"I just can't!" Angel reminded herself, even though she knew this would make her trip through the mountains so much easier. "Not this!" she exclaimed, pointing to the truck, "Not with the strain I'm already putting on you and the tavern by going."

"Soon enough, money isn't going to matter anyways," Will shrugged.

Angel shook her head at the apocalypse-obsessed man. She could see how hobbies were a necessity when Will was bound to the tavern, but this one was becoming extreme to say the least.

"I'd be more put-out if my favorite vixen didn't make it back," the bachelor added with a wink. Pulling the keys from his pocket, he hit another button on the remote and unlocked the doors.

"Can you drive a stick?" he asked curiously.

It was Angel's turn to laugh as she threw her head back in humor. She climbed into the driver's seat. The brown leather conformed to her body with comfortable ease. It hugged her hips as the seat sent waves of heat to her most invested places.

"I drive sticks for a living, Will. I ride them too. Now, let me hear her purr," she begged.

"Be careful what you ask for, Angel," Will eyed the young courtesan in her tight fitting black and gold corset. A short skirt that matched nearly exposed the curve of her cheeks.

He allowed his mind to drift to a back, gravel road where her legs would be high in his cab before he shook it off.

"I might cash in that favor you owe me still from when I bailed you out of jail. But first…" Will grabbed onto the handrail as Angel moved to the center seat.

Pulling himself up, Will climbed in behind the wheel. "Hit the garage door opener on the visor. It'll open up the wall there," he pointed in front of the truck. Smiling with boyish charm that was enough to drive the girls wild, he continued, "to the field behind the tavern."

"Brilliant!" Angel hit the button as Will had insisted.

The button turned a glowing red as the garage door slowly lifted open. Exposed was the dark night sky, filled with twinkling stars as it draped over the fields of tall grass. Angel stared at the beauty before her. Throwing on the five-point harness, she gently placed her hand on Will's knee.

"And feel free to cash my debt in at any time, Mister Pearson. Your wish is my command."

CHAPTER TWENTY-THREE

THE MEETING

Kritter scurried to the front of the tavern. The small pixie turned off the neon light with the fading sunset. Her wide eyes looked back to Legs.

"Kritter closed the Misfitz Tavern, Miss Chara. Kritter is ready for Master Will's meeting."

"Yeah, what's this meeting about?" Legs asked casually as she wiped down the bar.

Kritter feverishly shook her head from side to side as her large leaf-like ears swung to and fro. "No! No! Kritter is to keep Master Will's secret meeting secret!" she barked at Legs as her tiny body shook with tremors.

The pixie still believed the bad news was that she had just turned the open sign to closed for the last time. She feared Master Will was closing the doors and that she would be left out on her own. Or worse, that she would be forced to live with the other pixies once more.

Outside, Evelyn pulled up in her gold minivan.

"You girls be careful," she said with chipper motherly love as Sage jumped out of the front seat, rolling her eyes. The young woman couldn't get away from her mother fast enough.

"I'm twenty-one fucking years old, not twelve! I can drive Chrome," she snapped in fury, rolling her eyes.

Her younger sister leaned forward to kiss her mommy's cheek.

"Thank you, Mommy," Savannah chimed with glee. Evelyn smiled with pride as her youngest daughter quickly jumped from the van and rushed inside.

"Come straight home afterwards girls!" She called out after them, putting her designer sunglasses on to block her sparkling blue eyes from the setting sun.

"Yeah, right!" Sage growled under her breath, flinging the door to the tavern open.

***

Will sat behind his desk and reread the numerous articles from over a dozen different realms. He bit the end of his blue highlighter as he scanned over Ark's most recent article on malfunctioning respawn terminals.

The door chime in his office activated, pulling him from the article as he looked up and saw the Connor sisters, a near yin and yang of one another, walk through the front door.

Savannah pranced into the tavern as if she were a fairy from the green pastures of Valhalla. Sage, on the other hand, nearly passed as a devil succubus with a darkened desire to take over the world. *How did they come from the same parents?* Sighing deeply, Will gathered a few articles that seemed most promising to show the crew and walked out of his office.

"You two are early. I'm guessing your mother had another hair appointment?" Will smiled as the girls carried their school bags in hand.

"Yeah, something like that," Sage bit as she threw herself into a bar stool. "Whiskey, bartender!" she hollered to Legs. "I'm assuming drinks are covered too?" she asked Will, not giving him a chance to answer before she continued with her rant.

"Monday night book club. Thirteen chapters of getting hot

and bothered over Jose's muscular abs and luscious hair." Sage flung her head back with a sarcastic, romantic sigh, "Can you believe they ran away together?" Legs turned her back so the girl couldn't see her roll her eyes.

Will shook his head, doing his best to hide the smirk that slowly crept across his lips. "Not my circus, not my monkeys," he chuckled as he held up his hands and stepped back towards the bar.

Throwing some ice and a few crazy liquids into the blender, his finger punched down on the pulse button a few times. Will turned the blender off and poured the grossly unjustified Pina Colada mix into a margarita glass. He took a sip. It would have to do.

"So Kritter, what live creature will I have to stab with a fork tonight so it doesn't crawl off my plate before I eat it?"

"Master Will said to make favorite foods. Kritter made favorite foods," the pixie answered quickly as she scurried under the stairwell into the bar. "Kritter's making Miss Fawn's crab leg salad, Master Will. Miss Fawn's crab leg salad is chilling. Kritter is making Young Savannah's peanut butter cookies, Master Will. Young Savannah's peanut butter cookies need another five minutes. Kritter is making Mister Sir's five-star lasagna. Mister Sir's lasagna is baking and nearly ready, Master Will. With digging, Kritter found Goddess Sage and God Cole—"

"That's a surprise Kritter!" Sage interrupted, causing the pixie to seal her lips.

"It's brownies," Angel answered knowingly as she entered the room from the banquet hall and sat down beside Savannah. "Sir will be coming shortly," she informed Will with a wink.

"Brownies, eh?" Maxx asked thoughtfully, walking down the stairs. He knew when his daughter was up to no good. He also knew to never eat any brownies the rebellious woman left out on the counter.

"I won't tell your mother if you don't," he told Sage, playfully winking at Savannah. He took a seat at the bar next to Angel.

"Where were you?" Angel asked with a warm smile. She leaned back into Maxx's arms as he pulled her close.

"Sorry, love. I had to put a few things away upstairs. Don't worry, I made sure to lock up before I came back down." Maxx wrapped his arms around Angel and buried his face in her hair. He inhaled the courtesan's sweet, beautiful scent. "You look beautiful tonight, by the way. What did you order? I'd been meaning to ask you all weekend."

"Roasted cod with wine and herb butter, and cappuccino crème brûlée," Angel answered with a heavy euphoric moan.

"Now that sounds delicious," Maxx answered, smiling down at her. He felt her hand land on his knee. "You'll have to let me try a bite. It sounds sinful."

"Yeah! Yeah!" Will waved a hand that told Kritter to get on with the dinner arrangements. "I'm sure it's all going to be quite delicious. Did you manage to get my T-Rex T-bone from TimeLeap Foods?" His mouth watered at the thought of such a delicious hunk of juicy tender meat.

"Kritter did pick up Master Will's T-Rex T-bone, Master Will. Kritter is cooking Master Will's T-bone to medium rare, just like Master Will likes T-bone."

"Excellent. Thank you Kritter."

"T-Rex? Roasted Cod? Man, I got screwed!" Cole exclaimed as the double doors of the tavern closed behind him, "All I asked for was a bacon cheeseburger and fries. If I'd known, I would have at least ordered an ostrich omelet or something. I always wanted to try one of those things."

"I missed you, my goddess. The disciples send their love in the form of large quantities of gold." Pulling a large leather bag from his belt, he dropped it into her hands.

"Payday!" Sage exclaimed with excitement, "A bottle of tequila William. No! Two, make that two," she laughed, "and the poker tables! C'mon boys! Lady Luck's taking me out to eat."

"Not tonight, she's not," Fawn answered as she walked in the door. Still in her armor, the woman's pink hair was up in a messy ponytail. She walked over to Will and gave the man a subtle wink. "We'll take your money after the important stuff."

"One could say the same of you, Miss Fawn, if you're not careful in how you deal your cards!" Sir's cold voice rang out, appearing without the notice of the bar's occupants. His black suit contrasted with the white dress and see through lace he'd picked out as Pet's evening attire. She stood up straight at his side. Her eyes were pointed to the floor. "Still, I feel as though cards won't be played anytime soon this evening. Best not to dawdle. Come Pet, let us head to the banquet hall." Sir passed by the group of patrons with his head held high

Will nodded to the loyal patrons, "You guys go ahead." Mixing drinks once more, he loaded them onto a server tray as Fawn remained at his side.

"Where's Worvacs?" Legs asked the other half of the traveling pair with concern. He had promised Legs he would be there this evening. She had worn his favorite perfume.

"Oh, still showering most likely," Fawn laughed. Using her body to block the sight, she slid her hand under the bar towards Will's. Her touch comforted the tavern owner in the difficult conversation to come. "Nothing like snableshot snot to make you want to get back to indoor plumbing."

"Exactly!" Worvacs groaned. Walking into the tavern, he closed the door behind him and ran a hand through his orange hair. "Those little bastard's slime will eat through armor, clothing, and then to skin and bone. At that point, I usually just say to hell with it and respawn." He shrugged. Walking across the bar, he swept Legs up in his arms.

With a low dip, Worvacs' lips planted against her glowing smile. She kicked her leg up in the air as a squeal left the woman.

"Still, nothing like a bunch of no looters to bring your life into perspective. I missed you, love," he smiled into Legs' sparkling emerald eyes before placing her upright, "Give me a beer, Will. It was a bad run today so I hope you have good news."

"He won't tell us," Legs informed Worvacs as she looked at Will, "and Kritter hasn't slipped any information either. I've been trying all day."

"Did he give you the lecture about loose lips sinking ships?" Worvacs asked with a chuckle, "Don't worry, I've never known Will to keep a secret for long and if he's going through the trouble of serving us all our favorite dinners. Either it's really good, or it's really bad." He slipped his arm around Legs' waist.

Walking towards the back room, she laid her head against Worvacs' muscular chest. "Oh, that makes me feel so much better."

"He's been in his office all week. All he does is ask us to bring him the daily papers. Then he writes down numbers and circles letters. Who knows?" she sighed in confusion.

***

"It's just weird," Fawn whispered softly to Cole as they followed behind Pet and Sir. "Do you think they do it at home too? The whole silence thing? All the time?" she asked as she slid her hand into his before holding it out for gold in return.

"They do," Savannah answered softly from behind them, causing Fawn to jerk her hand away. The girl walked ahead of them, seemingly oblivious.

"Pay up," Fawn growled, shaken by the close call.

Cole grinned and handed the gold across to Fawn. He looked around, making sure he hadn't drawn any attention.

"Thanks," he whispered as they walked into the banquet hall.

"Your welcome, Cheeky," Fawn pinched Cole's rounded cheek and sat at the middle of the table. Legs sat across from her.

"Will probably has some crazy flavor of the week plan. It's going to make us all insanely rich and none of us will ever have to work again." Worvacs laughed sarcastically. Pulling out the chair next to Legs, he sat down. "But I'm not canceling my next teleport out. How's business been? Good tips this week?"

"Not bad," Legs replied with a smile, "Better than most weeks actually. Angel and I have been working together. I keep her drink filled and the guy she's talking to feels the need to keep up. It's been working out in the tavern's favor." She leaned her chair towards the window to the kitchen. "Are you sure you don't need help, Will?"

"We've got it," Will answered, shooing Legs with his hand. "Take the evening off." He turned and headed into the kitchen, gathering everyone's plates.

"Kritter helps too," Kritter responded urgently. She took Cole's plate from the silver prep table. Grabbing a bottle of ketchup, the pixie stuck it between her wings and held them close to her back as she rushed into the banquet hall.

"Where shall I sit, Sir?" Pet asked softly.

Sir nodded in the direction of two chairs closest to Will's. "We shall sit there, my Pet. If William went through all this trouble, we should at least be close enough to hear him speak." He walked the length of the table and pulled a chair out for Pet to sit beside him.

She glanced up momentarily and saw the bulletin board that she had feared would be present. The fact that it was empty troubled Pet even more. Threats of the unknown screamed out to her as an unwelcoming chill swept up her spine. It warned of foreboding misery.

Her periwinkle eyes stared, unable to look away from the cork-board that was filled with holes. Once holding memos and notes, the blank canvas would likely be coated once more by the end of the meeting. Pet's legs trembled beneath her, causing her knees to go weak.

Angel sat beside Fawn. She patted the seat on the other side of her for Maxx, "Here, love."

Will walked in, carrying a drink tray on one arm and a tray filled with plates, bowls, and an unusual array of cutlery on the other. Kritter followed close behind with a tray of her own. Everyone stopped talking long enough to watch as Will and Kritter filled the table.

With mouths watering in anticipation, lids hovered high into the air. An exotic variety of smells filled the room. Colorful dishes lined the table as people leaned over their own plates and complimented others. Will cleared his throat to gain the group's attention. "Dinner is served," he announced with the wave of his hand.

"Wait!" Angel insisted, interrupting the union of forks and mouths as she cleared her throat. "This may sound odd coming from me, since I have seen almost all of you naked," she chuckled to herself, "And the other half of you have paid me to see others naked as a Christmas present." She looked down with a blush that matched the ruby red of her lips. Batting her long eyelashes, she looked back up at the table's occupants.

"I just wanted to say that everyone here is like family to me... in a sick, unrelated incestualized way," Angel added quickly with a snort of a laugh that caused her to cover her mouth in embarrassment. "I had a small request. Can we have a moment of silence before Will makes this meal a toast to our lives? Be that as kings or peasants, from here on out." Angel bowed her head and beneath her breath, whispered a silent prayer of thanks.

Sage quickly reached over to grab her strawberry milkshake. She slurped loudly through her straw.

Savannah glared at Sage on the opposite end of the table. "You are so rude!" she bit at her older sister in disbelief.

Sage opened her mouth in response and exposed a tongue-full of half-chewed brownies and French fries.

Maxx didn't pay any mind to his daughters' bickering. Smiling with pride, he placed his hand on Angel's, dutifully bowing his head. He whispered a silent prayer and hoped some divine being listened.

Sir nodded politely in Angel's direction. He closed his eyes and lowered his head. After a respectful moment, his head raised.

"Am I to speak freely during the meeting Sir?" Pet whispered. Her words were barely audible to her master and silent to everyone else in the room. "Or inform you later, Sir?"

He smiled before leaning in close so only she could hear. "Pet, you may speak your mind freely. If you have information one may consider valuable, however, withhold it until later. I shall determine then who should receive it." Sir sat up straight once more. Tucking the cloth napkin into his collar, he started to cut into the large lasagna pan with a spatula.

"I thought Angel's speech was great!" Fawn chimed in. Her words jumbled as her cheeks looked like those of a chipmunk.

***

As empty plates were pushed away, everyone leaned back in their chairs, stomachs full and content. Satisfied groans were dispersed along with the occasional masculine belch.

"Well, dinner was great," Sage announced once she finished her brownies. Her eyes were glazed and bloodshot as she stood up, ready to leave. "Thanks Boss!"

"He wasn't just feeding us," Savannah whispered softly. "Sit back down, Sage." The young girl insisted as she looked to daddy in confirmation of her request.

"Will, I know you shouldn't bite the hand that feeds you, but what's the special occasion?" Angel asked. She leaned forward on her hands with one of her warmest smiles. Her dark brown hair surrounded her glowing face.

All eyes turned towards the tavern owner. The question on everyone's mind quickly resurfaced.

"Now that we're all just so attentive! Sage, sit down," Will scorned until the rebel huffed, collapsing into her seat. "Once upon a time a long time ago—"

Sage tapped her foot from the far end of the room, strumming her fingers on the table. "Blah de blah! Come on already," she groaned, "I have a case of beer and a jay with my name on it."

"Shut up Sage," Maxx and Savannah scolded in unison.

"Make me," Sage bit back viciously.

"You're just being a brat!" Worvacs chimed in, "Shut up and let the man speak!"

"If you would just hush and let Will speak—" Angel started.

"Coming from someone who never knows how to shut her legs!" Sage hollered.

"Really Miss Sage!" Sir commented, shaking his head with disapproval.

"She's the cum dumpster that—"

"Sage!" Legs exclaimed in disgust.

Fawn glared at the spoiled brat, always persistent in having the last word, before she turned towards Pet.

"You hold her down. I'll cut her tongue out and then we can all enjoy some silence," Fawn explained

Pet turned to look up at Sir with hopeful eyes. Upset with Sage's level of disrespect, Pet wanted nothing more than a chance at her old ways. To release the control that she had placed in her master's hands as a smile formed along the corner of her lips.

"No Pet, that won't be necessary. I'm rather certain Miss Sage enjoys being able to taste things. However, should she feel the need to open her mouth again, feel free to shut it for her." His gray eyes studied Sage as they held true to their warning.

When the woman finally broke the stare, Sir turned his attention back to Will. "Please William, do continue"

"I gathered you all here as regulars and compatriots of the Misfitz Tavern to, in not so eloquent terms, offer you sanctuary."

"Sanctuary from what?" Savannah tilted her head to the side as her blonde pigtails moved with her confusion.

"Has something changed with Karma?" Sage was suddenly concerned and attentive.

"No more than usual. She's as moody as she's ever been. As far as from what... 'The End', not to put too fine a point on it," Will chuckled to himself at the skeptical looks he received from some, bewilderment from others, "The end of humanity anyways."

The subdued voice of Pet piped up and quickly turned everyone's attention.

"It does feel close. It's heavy in the air. The plants in our garden have all been hardier this year than in the past. They are preparing," she whispered softly, causing Sage to roll her eyes.

"That's fucking bullshit!" she hollered, "Plants don't know shit. At least, not the ones you grow."

"It's not," Fawn answered in Pet's defense, "Plants are always the first to prepare. Remember that ice age on Rock?" she asked, looking at Worvacs for confirmation. She knew he would remember the iceberg that had drifted into the teleport pad's floating concrete island.

"Well, I'm glad to see at least some of you are taking this with more than a grain of salt and a shot of tequila," Will stated sincerely, "The end is coming, I've known for almost a decade now, but it's approaching sooner than I had expected." He looked at each of them in turn, resting his hands on the table.

"Once upon a time, a long time ago..." Will repeated. He shot a glare at Sage, who quickly shut her mouth as she glanced from Pet to Will with pursed lips. "I had a feeling that in the flash of a moment, consumed every fiber of my being and then it was gone. But the feeling was simple. The end is coming. Prepare now." Will shuddered at the memory. He motioned to Kritter.

"Yes, Master Will," Kritter answered promptly, leaving the room. She returned with a wagon full of newspapers and snapped her fingers. Just as Pet had feared, the bulletin board filled with newspaper articles, maps, and weather reports. All the information Will had collected over the different realms. "Here, Master Will. The articles needed, Master Will. Kritter kept it filed, Master Will."

"Thank you, Kritter. Now, run down to the basement and fetch me the Chateau Le DeCleur eighteen-eighty-five please. I think we are all going to need a drink for this."

As Kritter disappeared from the room once more, Will pointed out the different articles that coated the bulletin board. Connections that, to the untrained eye, appeared as nothing more than coincidence. Placed together, however, they made an obvious string of information that couldn't be ignored.

Savannah rose from her chair and walked up to the board. Her blue eyes scanned one article, and then another. She read each of the headlines, connected by colorful strings, with attentive concentration.

Studies show tooth decay to be a thing of the past
Swine Flu: The new leading cause in respiratory failure
Caly local respawns as cannibal, four attacked

"Daddy, look at this one!" she pointed to a picture in black and white. It showed a one-eared alien foaming at the mouth, reminding Savannah of the rabid raccoon they had found by the trash can on her seventh birthday.

"You've been a busy boy, haven't you William?" Sir inclined, "I can see you gathered your news from reputable sources. Some of these papers aren't even legal on Earth. That's very impressive. These here…" Sir pointed to a few of the articles that appeared to be written in triangles, squares, and occasionally a diamond, "are all quite reputable. I happen to read two of them myself."

"I'd say Will's a smart man, if you ask me," Worvacs stepped forward and observed posters that held graphs of multiple endgame scenarios, each listed with percentages, odds, and likelihoods.

Nuclear fallout leaving entire realms as nothing more than rock and ash. Worldwide pandemics that carried symptoms of the common cold. Solar flares causing polarized winters.

"I'm not that smart, but when you lay it out like this. Dude, this stuff is kind of hard to ignore!" Worvacs nodded his head to Will in respect, awed by damages that would affect thousands of realms, across multiple dimensions. Legs stepped up behind Worvacs and wrapped her arms around his waist.

"Some of these are pretty local too," an article she had seen last week caught her attention. A neighboring town had made front page when a group of campers witnessed a moose eating salmon from the river. "I remember the old golems chewing the fat over this one."

Angel silently whispered a prayer as she looked up at the statistics, not in favor of survival. They exposed what her grandmother had once told her of Revelations. Pictures of dead birds lining fields, bats coating the floors of caverns as far as the eye could see. Tsunamis on Zacharias. Earthquakes in New Zealand. Her eyes finally fell on the war declared on Genine that would leave thousands dying from violence and starvation. "And there will be signs in the sun, the moon, the stars and on Earth," she muttered as she remembered the book of Luke. Her heart wept.

"Ha!" Sage laughed from the back, propping her feet on the table. "As if we have anything to worry about! April Fucking Fools!" she yelled. Leaning her chair back, she placed her hands behind her head.

CHAPTER TWENTY-FOUR

I MUST GO

Angel turned off the motor with shaking hands before climbing out of her truck. She stared up at the two-story suburban home. A minivan was parked out front, proof that the gossip she heard from one of her clients was true.

The high school principal told her Missus Connor had called and made sure Sage arrived at school. He verified to the student's mother that, though she was late, Sage had made it in time for lunch.

Angel turned around and got back in her truck. Allowing the motor of the low-rider to hum quietly, with tears in her eyes, she drove away.

***

"I would like to speak with Mister Connor, please," the woman stated, a wide smile exposed past her bright red lips. Her black sequin dress hugged tightly to her legs and landed mid-calf. "I am here to discuss the transport of my goods," she added with professionalism. Leaning over the registration desk, her perfume filled young blonde receptionist's senses.

The receptionist closed a manila envelope and stood up to file it away. When she returned to her seat, she smiled up at the guest. “I can schedule you for an appointment if you like. Mister Connor is a rather busy man, unfortunately. I have a two o’clock?”

"I would rather not be kept waiting," the woman stated as she reached into her tall boot. Pulling out a fifty-dollar bill, she slid it across to the receptionist before signing in on the clipboard. She signed her name as Chara Black, knowing that Legs wouldn't mind.

The receptionist looked around the room, pocketing the money before she glanced at the name on the clipboard. "I understand, madam. I'll see to it that he knows you are here. Just a moment, please."

The young blonde stood up and walked down the hall that led to his office. Knocking on the door, she cracked it open slowly and peeked her head in.

"Mister Connor? A young woman is here to see you. She made it seem urgent."

"Send her in. If it sounded that way and it’s not one of my daughters, it must be." Maxx motioned the young secretary away and waited for his visitor to come in, hoping it was Angel.

He meant to stop by and see her yesterday. However, business had been slow this week. That left him with extra marketing paperwork to boost the company’s sales.

"Mister Connor will see you now. Please follow me," the young secretary said as she entered the lobby. She quickly turned back around and led Angel back towards Maxx’s office.

"Here you are, Ma'am. Let me know if there's anything else you need." With a light smirk, the receptionist hurried off.

Angel turned and watched the blonde in the pencil skirt walk back to the rounded desk. She faced Maxx and, with a warm smile and graceful flow, moved to the chair that sat in front of his desk. Crossing her legs, the rise of Angel’s sequin dress exposed her toned thighs. It granted Maxx the ability to guess the color of her undies with accuracy.

"I heard," her voice was faint, hushed, and… pained?

"I figured you would," Maxx sighed, rubbing his eyes in frustration, "I'm sorry you didn't hear it from me directly. I guess this means we need to discuss some things." Pressing a button on his desk, his office door swung shut electronically. With a loud clank, it locked itself in place to ensure their privacy.

He held out his arms, motioning for her to join him in the leather chair. Angel obliged with a smile, sitting on Maxx's lap as she wrapped her arms around his neck.

"Discussion is such a serious word," she answered, pursing her lips in mock seriousness.

"Well, it's a serious matter when a man gives his heart to the woman he loves. Much like the way I do for you, Miss Angel. It doesn't matter who lives in my house, you are the only one for me."

When a blush filled Angel's cheeks, he quickly added, "Now… when you are in my position, with so many woman around, it's hard not to get distracted or have particular urges. However, with your career, I think certain accommodations can and should be made." Maxx smiled as he looked at the courtesan.

Lifting her chin with his fingertips, he planted a delicate kiss on her lips. His hand grazed her thigh, stroking her tender skin. A heavy sigh escaped Angel with the touch, her body yearning for him. She knew that she must focus if she wanted to sort this out.

"Umm… So, what does that mean?" she was challenged while collecting her thoughts. Angel wanted to tell Maxx the recent plans she had made. She needed to.

"Are you merely a client again, Mister Connor?" she asked nervously, her heart raced. Her stomach twisted and turned, seconds seeming like hours, as she waited to hear the man's answer.

"I would like to be much more. If I am limited to only one

woman, it would be you. However, I don't know if that's possible with so much 'T n A' running around, as your generation calls it. It's difficult when I can't have you around all the time and... a man has needs."

"Understood!" Angel laughed as she tried not to roll her eyes at the man's meager attempts to keep up with the current slang, "Then, perhaps we should discuss the next order at hand as whatever this is." She nervously looked down at her dress. The news weighed on the edge of her tongue, begging to be released as her heart broke.

"My services will be unavailable for a week. That also includes my company," she informed Maxx with hopes that he would understand, "For all of Knowhere."

"It is a small town in a very big universe. So, you will be traveling? How long did you say again? A week? Are you sure you'll be safe? I'm not saying that Will is right, but he is my friend. I have never doubted his confidence in the past."

"I'm going to Salem," Angel confessed, "It's a city full of history." She knew the explanation left Maxx little room for inquires. "The drive itself is actually quite beautiful. Besides, Will's been saying this for months, years even. His meeting just allowed him to tell all of us at once."

Picking her up, Maxx placed Angel on the desk in front of him. He slowly spread her legs open, his fingers trailing her thighs. "I have missed you these last couple days." He lifted the bottom of her dress to expose the silken beauty of the panties underneath.

"A very interesting town to choose, my love. You should bring me back a souvenir," Maxx suggested as his lips traced the bend in the courtesan's knee.

"I... I will!" she promised, her voice steamy with anticipation.

CHAPTER TWENTY-FIVE

AN ANGEL DELIVERS A MESSAGE

Tatianna barged into the tavern, storming up to the bar as the door slammed behind her. "Where's Will!?" she demanded.

"It's a Tuesday morning," Legs, who was mixing a drink for the lone gnome who sat at the bar, answered in confusion. She passed the gnome his drink, accepting his payment of gold. She tucked a strand of hair behind her ear as she casually entered the order into the system. "He's doing inventory in the back of his office. Why?"

"I need to talk to him," Tatianna answered firmly, noticing Legs was in no hurry to notify her boss. "Oh, for Merlin's sake!" she growled as she leaned over the bar and pushed the intercom button herself.

After a brief pause, Will answered, "What is it Legs? I'm only halfway through the inventory."

What could she possibly need? It wasn't like the bar is crowded, other than the little pervert with green hair who always showed up.

"It's Tatianna, William! Let me in! This is important!" she insisted with urgency, "I've been in your room of inventory. You can take a moment out of counting for this."

Will sighed into the intercom and paused the game on his big screen television. "Come on back, the door's unlocked."

"Give me a second guys," he said into his headset, "No, turn right! Right! Jerome, lead them into that room. I'll catch up." With a growl, Will threw off his headset and set down the controller next to his clipboard.

Tatianna smirked at Legs, who rolled her eyes in response. Standing up straight, Tatianna tugged at her leather jacket, symbolizing dominance, and walked into Will's office.

She sat in the clear chair across from his desk, waiting anxiously.

Will took his time before he stepped out from the back room that kept him so occupied on Tuesday mornings. He looked the woman up and down, watching as she jittered in her seat. "What has your panties all in a bunch this morning? Panic is not usually a word I would use to describe you, but right now it fits perfect."

Tatianna stood back up the moment she heard Will's voice behind her. "What were you doing in there? Please tell me you were watching the news!" She let her guard down enough for fear to shine in her hardened eyes.

Fear? That's a new one for Tat, Will thought to himself.

"Inventory, like I said. Why? What's on the news?" He suddenly became uneasy. Though he read the papers, Will rarely watched anything on the news. Most of it was guided by politicians and didn't affect Knowhere directly.

"Sit down!" she demanded, pointing to his leather chair behind the desk. Will raises an eyebrow at her questioningly. "Now. Sit. Please!" she corrected quickly.

Shrugging his shoulders, Will took his seat behind the desk. "There, I'm sitting. Happy now? What has got you all riled up?"

"The apocalypse has hit. Sooner than expected and fast. It's already crossed multiple realms. Some of them have already given up on finding survivors. It's here, on Earth! Great Britain, China, and Russia have closed their borders," she paused for a second, not wanting to bear the rest of the news, "The dead are walking, Will. Ark's shut down their teleport station."

Will looked at Tatianna and slowly started to chuckle before releasing a roar of laughter at the preposterous claim. "Did Kritter put you up to this? Ten years without showing a sense of humor and now she decides to get one."

"What? I'm not kidding!" Tatianna screamed. She stood up in fury. Her blood boiled that Will was calling her a liar. "Here I am trying to do the right thing! To save your ass and you laugh at me? Look it up on your own you damn no-mag!" She pointed at his computer. "Christopher was right! We should have just packed and left town, but I wanted to give someone with half-a-brain a head's up!"

Will's laugh dropped at her sudden outburst. He clenched his jaw and turned to his computer. Flipping it on, he switched tabs over to the leading realm news.

"The outbreak is most heavily..." He clicked the channel to another station.

"It was first spotted on Chandliener..." He continued clicking through channels, all carried the same headline and none of them were very helpful.

Will turned back to Tatianna. His face was pale. Nodding solemnly, he held up a finger for her to wait while he pressed the button that sent him to Kritter's talk box.

"Shut it down Kritter. Get everybody out. Now. We are officially on lock-down. Shitstorm has started. Move." Will unclicked the mic and ran his hand through his hair. "You guys have a plan?"

"Nothing solid," Tatianna lied, her jaw tense and words short. "We..." she paused in thought, "We can survive."

Will leaned back in his chair and looked at her for a moment. He released a heavy sigh, "I don't like Christopher. You know that, but if you can keep your dog on a leash, and that's a big if, then you can stay here. I swear to Odin! He breathes the wrong way I'll put so many holes in him he'll look like the theory of evolution." Will eyed Tatianna.

Tatianna nodded her head. "We're going south," she confided, knowing a finger couldn't pinpoint on the vast number of places they could be headed, "I can't guarantee what we may find once we get there, though. Is it fair to ask if I can hold you to that, should things not work?"

Will rubbed his chin for a second. "I'll tell you what. If you make it back alive and uninfected, I'll let you in. I might add to that later, but that's the risks you take by leaving and coming back. Are we clear?"

"Perfectly," Tatianna answered with a nod of respect for the tavern owner. "I haven't seen or heard anyone since the news spread. Other than Sage..." she added with a heavy sigh towards her best friend, "Her exact words were 'bring it mother fuckers'."

Will shook his head. He moved from his desk and started to pull out his weapons of choice. "There are two kinds of people," he informed her, loading a pistol, "The hunters and the prey. Be a hunter." She wondered how much thought she should put into Will's offer.

"If you trust me in your sanctuary, I'll assume you also trust me with a gun. Want some help?"

Will raised an eyebrow. "Do you have time? From the way things look..." he pointed his thumb at the computer, "Time is something none of us will have here soon. What exactly would I owe you for such an act of generosity?"

"Christopher and I live with our bags packed and ready. Besides, you're offering us shelter in the one place where good and bad are viewed the same; the only place. I can help you prepare in keeping it safe," Tatianna answered honestly as she reached for a handgun. She loaded the gun with ammo, handing it back to Will.

Will accepted the gun from her tenderly. "Thank you. The armory is downstairs. We need to be as quick as possible. Come on." He opened the office door, stepping out with Tatianna following behind him. He quickly locked the door behind him.

"Kritter, are we locked down yet?" he called, walking towards the basement.

"Yes, Master Will," Kritter answered promptly, "Kritter asked all guests to leave. Kritter sent young Savannah home, Master Will."

Tatianna looked from Will to the pixie. She raised an eyebrow at the pixie's quick and accurate behavior. *He had been preparing for this!*

"Kritter locked the doors and set the alarms, Master Will. Kritter has sent Miss Chara to Miss Chara's bedroom. Kritter did not tell Miss Chara or Young Savannah about the intercom, Master Will. Kritter kept Master Will's secret safe."

"Good. Keep Legs in her room for now. Tell her I'll cover her wages for today. Spoil her to keep her occupied, if you must. Absolutely do *not* let Legs see the news. Shitstorm has hit. I'm taking Tatianna down to the armory to get some prep work done."

"Notify all our regulars that until future notice the bar is shut down. If anyone who was in the meeting Monday is staying here, they have to teleport in. Check everyone for injuries." Will looked at Tatianna. Jerking his thumb towards the basement door, he led her in that direction.

"You're allowing people to teleport in?" Tatianna asked, shocked by the conversation that had just taken place.

Letting people in? Spoiling the girls? Giving them a paid day off? Tatianna questioned if Will lost his mind upon hearing the news. She had feared this happening to the contained man, but expected him to last the first week at least. "Shitstorm? Do you care to explain?"

"Shitstorm is the code word for the humanities of the realms falling. Kritter and I had a feeling a major catastrophe was on the horizon. We just didn't have a timeline. We didn't know how widespread it would be. I had her start prepping for a general catastrophe a long time ago," Will shrugged.

He took the steps two at a time, hoping Tatianna was quick to follow behind. "I'll leave the teleport open until either everyone checks in or I'm forced to close it, whichever happens first. It's going to be a shitty existence for a while, least I can do is offer a warm bed and a cold beer." He headed to the armory door and quickly typed in the code to crack the airlock.

"Like the regulars? Maxximillian Connor, CEO of Inter-Realm Shipping Company? Sage and Savannah? Cole?" Tatianna looked at Will, questioning his sanity even more. She chuckled to herself, "I'm sure they are all safe in their own fortresses, from the size of those houses. Maxx likely already has his girls on lockdown."

"Fawn and Worvacs are an entire realm away. Who knows what condition they're in! Respawn isn't working correctly so I highly doubt your girlfriend's going to make it for the crab salad this week. Oh, but you know," she added with apparent sarcasm as she raised a finger in thought, "Sir and Pet could probably use some shelter."

Will turned around and glared at her. "You're kidding, right? The only way anyone has a chance is to be armed with both magic and weapons!" Will flipped the light switch, allowing the many rows of lights to flicker to life dramatically, "and lots of both."

Tatianna's mouth dropped. She stared into the room with safes hanging along the four white walls. Floor to ceiling, guns of various shapes, sizes, and destruction level waited behind bulletproof glass. Each held a gold-plated label, marking their ammo size and home realm.

Tables formed aisles in the room, each covered with maps, disassembled rifles, and piles of ammo. Ammo boxes stacked beneath the tables carried extra ammunition, grenades, and smoke bombs.

"The spell over the tavern should keep it safe for a while," Will continued. He walked down the aisle, searching through the gun racks until he found the one that contained his auto-gun turrets. "That doesn't mean it won't fail eventually, though."

Tatianna froze in place at the thought before she rushed to keep up with Will. "What do you mean it won't hold up forever? This is the oldest building in all of time, over all the realms. If it doesn't hold up, nowhere will! Besides, you're bound here," she added quickly in reminder, "Your lying!"

"HA! I wish!" Will retorted, "Don't know much about plagues, do you? When the dead walk and shit hits the fan, the plagues become a black hole to all the magic around them. They absorb it. Suck it up well... honestly, about like you do. Eventually enough dark energy bounces against the barrier and it falls. It's only a matter of time. That's why I need these..."

Will hefted the large weapon onto his shoulder. He grabbed the barrel of a second one and slowly trudged towards the door. "The longer I can keep them off the barrier, the longer it will hold and the longer I will survive. As far as my binding is concerned, I don't think The Creator had an apocalypse in mind when this place was created. I don't think anyone did."

"Our... our magic won't work?" Her stomach dropped and fear shone through the fallen angel's eyes.

"Your magic will work from a distance. Say about," Will thought to himself for a few moments before continuing, "a meter. After that, they'll slowly pull the life force out of you. Then, you won't be able to use your spells. You will be just as no-mag as anyone else. Now, three feet may sound like a lot. But, what if you get ten or fifteen of those things on you at once?"

She looked down at the floor, unable to believe what she was hearing. What their odds really were. This was impossible. Sure, at first, they would survive. In due time, however, her and Christopher would be powerless without the magic that got them out of sticky situations in the past. Situations they never should have survived.

"You have to help then! We don't have weapons, ammo!" she lied, hopeful that Will would believe her. Her handgun weighed heavy in its holster against her thigh.

Will lifted the second gun onto the table with a groan. Bending down, he flipped it onto his other shoulder to carry both. He walked towards the door, a bit slower than before. "I don't have to do anything. I do what I choose or have you forgotten who owns this place? Now be a dear. Grab a few boxes of the .50 caliber rounds over there."

Tatianna picked up the box, eyeing the rounds in her hand before she looked back up at Will. "We slept together," she answered quickly, "You wouldn't just leave me out there helpless, would you? With Christopher?"

Will stopped in the doorway and turned around, nodded his head towards the direction of the far wall. "When we get done setting up, you can pick one. Count them *one,* off of my shelves. Not because we slept together, that you did of your own accord the same as I did. I'm giving it to you because I hope you'll be smart and put that dog down before he turns on you. Which I think is twice as likely now that it's a matter of survival." He turned sideways, shimming himself through the doorway that led upstairs.

"Thank you," Tatianna answered with respect for Will, "And if he does, I'll do what needs to be done. Not a second before."

Will shrugged. "It's your life. If I were you, I would put him down now. Save myself the headache later but hey, that's me."

CHAPTER TWENTY-SIX

THE END?

Legs knocked on the door to Will's office. Her hair sat down around her face. Soft curls at the bottom gave off a natural look that wouldn't hold until the end of her shift. Her sleek, straight hair never could hold curls.

"Come in," Will answered, removing his feet from where he had them propped up on his desk. He sat up straight as a chill flowed through his bones. *Who could be knocking on my office door this early? And of all mornings, this one?*

The shiver of fear escaped him as Legs opened the door. "We need to talk," she stated formally as she sat down in the chair across from him, "About business."

"Yes?" Will answered with a smile of relief. She obviously didn't know of the news yet. "That we do, Miss Chara."

Legs pursed her lips at the name. If Will was using her real name, the one she held before becoming a bartender, either this was very serious or Will was simply trying to make it a rough conversation.

"I understand that Kritter keeps the place clean," She started with a heavy gulp, "And I know that you have the fancy desk. You run the show, Will."

"Yes?" Will answered, curious as to where Legs was going with this.

"But the bar needs a wider variety of inventory for the diverse groups that come in here. The fairies would go crazy over orgasms. I can make a vampire's dream, and if I give the dwarves blue balls, it will double our income. The shots of course."

Will nodded his head, "You're right."

"I am?" Legs asked, shocked that Will agreed so easily.

"The bar does need more inventory, but you're wrong about the type. You haven't seen the news lately, have you?" He pulled out a stack of newspapers that he'd gone and picked up earlier that morning, handing them to her.

"Want a morning treat?" Will made his way out to the bar. "You may need one after you read that."

"Hold the hot sauce!" Legs insisted. She carried the papers with her to sit at one of the bar stools in the darkened tavern.

She tried to read the paper regularly with an interest in how the magical interacted with no-mags. However, she never went out of her way to purchase the black and white news, instead occasionally overhearing articles from the older drunks who came in.

Will poured a generous share of liquor into both glasses, stirring them to a good mixture. "This should help wash down the news." He smiled, taking a sip of his. The effects of his hangover from the night before quickly evaporated.

"Thank you," Legs took a sip that eased her unsettled stomach. "It tastes perfect. So, what did the news say?" She picked up the paper from her lap and leaned back to read it while sipping on the liquid relief.

"The world is coming to an end… again," Will murmured with a deep sigh. He leaned back against the bar. Quickly changing his mind for a more comfortable position, he jumped up and sat on the bar top. "Large multitudes of the dead are walking in our world, as well as with the no-mags."

"They've done that in the past. There was the Black Plague

and the Egyptians. What makes this time any different?" she stuttered in confusion, "We burn the bodies to prevent spread of infection, we tomb them. Occasionally someone sees something they shouldn't, but then it's blamed on trauma, mourning, or feverish hallucinations."

"This one is already roaming. Detroit got hit with a massive earthquake last night, Chicago had thousands of undead this morning. Boise hospitals are already full and Vegas shut down completely after a black blizzard wiped out the Las Vegas Strip. More than a quarter of the U.S population has already been affected adversely," Will explained, opening the paper to show her a map that was printed by Knowhere's Wizarding Press.

Red blotches covered most of the West Coast, creeping inland to Arizona, New Mexico, and Nevada. The tip of Texas and panhandle of Oklahoma were both red, though the main portions of the states were still unaffected.

In the south, all the Gulf States held casualties caused by humanoid attacks and flooding. Florida's southern tip remained white, despite the fact that it was surrounded. Legs' eyes quickly glanced towards the North East and found that though Minnesota, Ohio, and Indiana were reddened, Angel's destination appeared safe for the time-being. Before her very eyes, the northern tip of Illinois' red tint bled further south.

"It's moving inward," she whispered as her stomach suddenly dropped, "When was it noticed? I need times, dates, symptoms." She insisted before her emerald eyes scanned across the words of truth, written in black print.

"Two days?" she exclaimed in disbelief. Looking up at Will, there was genuine fear in her eyes. "This is after two days?!"

"Unfortunately. The way I see it, we have a day and a half at most before it's all over us. We don't have time to bail out, even if I could, so our best bet is to board up and lock down. But first, we need to stock up and resupply." Will sipped his drink. He needed something stronger to swallow down the truth, but thought it may be best to stay sober as he prepared for this.

"I have faith in our survival. Downstairs, in the basement, my parents made a small survival stash. I've steadily been growing it since I took over. We should only need a few more things to seal this place up."

"My question is what about you? Do you want to stay here and risk the end with me and Kritter? Or do you want to risk trying to make it out on the road?"

Legs didn't have to contemplate it. Even without Will's amusing quims or Kritter's delicious food, her room was still her own.

She couldn't imagine going on the run and leaving the safety of her purple bedroom walls and plush blankets. She enjoyed reading on her own personal couch in her private room. The Misfitz Tavern had grown on her. It was now her home.

"I'm staying. If you don't mind, of course!"

"I don't mind in the least. Good news is, we'll have plenty of fun."

A blush filled Legs' cheeks as she looked around the fully stocked bar, unsure of what exactly the bachelor was referencing to.

"What we don't have are boards," he explained, frowning as he set down his glass.

"Why not?" Legs asked with curiosity. "You have two pool tables, two bars, two desks, nine tables, and six spare bedrooms fully furnished. How do we not have extra boards?"

"We need to seal up the doors and windows. I will not sacrifice the integrity of my tavern, my home, or any of its contents for some widespread, realm-destroying disease. We still have at least one day before it hits us. So, we're going to do some shopping. A lot of shopping. Do you know how to spend a lot of money in a short time?" He smiled at her, almost sure he already knew the answer.

"Do I what?" Legs sputtered, "Not nearly as well as Angel or

Evelyn, I'm sure."

She looked down at the picture of the United States, over a quarter of the nation reddened out. The bright ink spread by the minute. "These spots are gone?"

Will nodded solemnly.

"Ark?" she asked, her voice nearly mute as tears welled up in her emerald eyes. Her thoughts drifted to Worvacs, how desperately she needed his big, blue arms wrapped around her after hearing this news.

Will sighed heavily. He knew it was a question Legs was going to ask and there was no easy way for him to answer. He had no words of comfort.

"Their teleport station is closed," he informed her, his heart going out to the young bartender. He was fearful for his own lover, and his best friend, "but they aren't touched yet. Ark is trying to keep the infection from coming in, for now. All contact was severed when they found out Earth was infected." There was hope, the two of them just had to hold onto that for now.

Frowning, Will walked over to one of the walls of the tavern and pulled a painting from the wall to reveal a safe behind it. With a wave of his hand, the safe's dial turned and the heavy metal door sprung open. Will started to pull out large stacks of money.

Legs tried to hide her shock at the multitude of currency Will pulled out, lining the inner pockets of his jacket. She had never seen so much money before in her life.

"What are we buying?"

"Anything we want. I was saving for a rainy day. Well, the skies are gloomy and it looks like we're about to have the shit-storm of the century." He handed four stacks to her. "I'm going to have some contractors come in and do some quick installations. Solar panels, deep freezers, etc. You, my dear, are in charge of picking up supplies. Don't worry about weapons, I have plenty. Do pick us up some entertainment. We may be stuck in here for a while until the dust settles. Literally."

Legs nodded, still in shock of what he was asking her to do. *The West Coast is gone? All the people? No more sunny California? No more lights-filled Las Vegas? Illinois is slowly being taken over and... Chicago?* She shook the thought from her head. *None of that matters anymore. They are gone. You are still alive and that's what matters.*

"I can handle entertainment," she said with a smile.

"Oh, I'm sure you can. If you run across something you can't afford, call me. I'll come take a look." He finished loading up his pockets and held out his hand for her to take. "Care to have a bite of breakfast at the cafe?"

"I would like that very much," Legs answered with a smile as she took his hand. Will looked at her hand in his, finding the cold that rested in her fingertips soothing against the warmth of his own before her voice pulled him from his thoughts. "What about the bar?"

"Don't worry about that. Kritter's going to cover the morning shift. I've already got her prepping for the contractors." He led Legs toward the stained-glass window that rested above his office door and placed his fingers on it.

"The Misfitz Tavern has closed its doors?" she asked in shock, trying to wrap her mind around it all. "Will? What if we get hit early? What if there's already chaos out there?"

"It hasn't yet. I've already been out this morning. Most of the places around town are shutting down and there are people leaving town tonight. A few people that I've checked in with are also holing up."

"Anyone you trust?" she questioned, hopeful that they would offer support. She tried thinking of who she knew to warn, but no one in particular came to mind, aside from the ache that rested in her heart.

Worvacs was the only one she wanted to talk to right now. She needed to see his comforting smile as he promised her that they would both stay safe.

Will knew she was referring to the regulars of the tavern. "Sir said he and Pet were still uncertain about their plans," Will answered, counting another stack of cash before he handed it to Legs, "But Pet was scurrying around when I got there and it looked like she was packing. There was a teleport flash in their backyard last night and their house was locked up when I drove by this morning. Angel's already left town."

Another bombshell Will wasn't ready to drop yet. "She said she should be in New York by the end of tonight." His eyes drifted to the state, slowly bleeding red. Infection had started in Brooklyn, Staten Island was underwater. Bear attacks lined most major interstates. "Maxx said Inter-Realm's sensors detected an abnormality in the cleansing stations. The building went into lock down. Most of the workers were still inside." He added gravely, "Him and Evelyn are boarding up with the girls. Evelyn tried to get Cole to join them but… he's insistent that he figure out a way to attach a cannon to the roof of his house."

Will reached a hand into his pocket, pulling out a wand and tapping it against the stained glass.

"Elven hardware," he called out. Bright sparks flew from the frame of the window. Legs closed her eyes to the blinding light as she walked through the doorway. Her stomach dropped as the hidden teleport swirled around them. Gravity lost control and her feet lifted off the ground momentarily before she felt the comfort of the tile in the back of the hardware store.

Her heart raced, pounding against her chest with a painful ache as she followed Will to the front of the store.

People were dead. More were dying and they all would return to walk among the living. Soon, danger would lurk around every corner. Soon, nowhere would be safe.

Legs kept her head high as she attempted to hold herself together. Her throat grew tense as she fought back tears that choked her; tears that would leave her gasping for air.

Nodding to the pointy-eared elf at the front register, Will held the door to the hardware store open for Legs to walk out. It was the door of a cage and she found herself a bird, dying to fly as far away as possible.

Looking around the nearly empty street Will sighed, "Let's skip breakfast. I'll see you for lunch. Chinese?"

Fret rested in the woman's watery eyes. Her long hair was still pulled back for the morning she had prepared to spend behind the bar, serving drinks to early morning customers with a smile on her face.

Legs simply nodded her head, unable to speak. She feared that if she did, her self-control would be lost. That she would find herself breaking down in front of the witches that hustled past them in preparation for the danger that awaited the tiny magical town of Knowhere, Nebraska.

Will nodded. He felt an unexplained defeat in the fact that Legs' was now in deafening silence. He worried about how Legs would respond in public, without him around to comfort her. *Can she handle facing others right now? Talking to them? Knowing that, in a matter of days, they too will be lifeless forms, some lining the streets? Others walking them?*

It was a foreboding truth that he also faced, but thanks to a family curse, couldn't run from. All Will could do was board up and hope that the magic within the tavern was enough to keep him safe.

***

Angel looked through the rear-view mirror at the distant view of Knowhere, Nebraska. It was nearly unrecognizable now, disappearing with the miles that trailed behind her. She couldn't even see the tavern anymore, its brick and mortar a blurred mirage.

She turned her attention back to the gravel road ahead as she passed a small white church lined with a picket fence. An apple tree sat in front of the whitened steeple, a cemetery rested out back. The church became just another mile marker of the past, causing Angel to release a heavy sigh.

She turned the steering wheel sharply and felt herself bend with the curve of the truck, driving back in the direction of Knowhere. She didn't bother to turn on her blinker, knowing there was no one to see it, as she pulled into the vacant parking lot of the quiet church.

Straightening her dress, Angel hopped out of the truck. She made sure to take her keys with her, just in case, as she faced the large cross above the double doors. A welcome sign sat out front with service hours listed.

The wet ground gave way beneath her heels as Angel felt her legs move forward. Without thought, she pulled on the large doors that were always unlocked, protected only by God's presence and grace.

The misguided courtesan walked among the pews, the sweetened aroma of cedar surrounding her. Stained-glass windows that carried pictures of saints lined the walls and allowed the sunlight to shine into the darkened cathedral. Angel's eyes stared ahead, never leaving the wooden statue of a man who had sacrificed his own life for her sins.

Angel dropped to her knees and allowed herself a moment of silence. "I don't know if you can hear me," she brushed a ringlet of hair away from her face as another presence filled the single room of worship, one she couldn't explain.

The sunlight that shined through grew warmer as a strange feeling of serenity filled the air. A small gust of wind brushed past Angel and blew the curl of hair back in front of her shoulder. She closed her eyes with relief and continued with her prayer.

***

Legs' eyes darted down the road in the direction of the tavern. Its parking lot was empty, minus Will's burgundy Corvette, across the street sat the cerulean house that held the memories of love. Memories of laughter that she choked back with painful tears.

She had to see for herself. She needed to know that what Will said wasn't true as she saw her blue monster sitting on his couch, waiting with open arms. Her heart pleaded that he would be there, willing to take this nightmare away.

As she felt Will's eyes watching her, Legs' gaze quickly moved to the grocery store that sat on the opposite corner of the tavern. A valid excuse to be walking that direction.

"We need food," Legs whispered with every ounce of strength left in her. The words spoke more truth than anything else that morning had. Her voice crackled as she looked down at her open toed heels.

Will nodded his head. Legs' voice was music to his ears. It meant she would be okay.

"Good luck. I'll see you at lunch," he said before turning around. Her green eyes watched as he walked down the road opposite of her, towards the dwarves' home.

Legs walked toward the grocery store. Her knees trembled as she held her arms against the chill of warning in the morning air.

She approached the sliding glass doors of the grocery store. A set of stairs leading to the two-bedroom apartment above had clothes hanging, left behind and forgotten. The door to Christopher and Tatianna's apartment was open, abandoned and welcome to anyone passing by. Legs turned around, glancing up the road to search for her boss. Not seeing him, she kicked off her heels and picked them up in her hand.

She ran as fast as she could towards the hexagon house, shaped unlike any other in the tiny town.

The pavement bit at each step the woman made until she reached the consoling homestead. The Quad, Worvacs' giant teleport pad, typically sat on the roof, it's motors buzzing as it awaited his command. It was silent, forgotten.

Her eyes begged to see matching hover-bikes sitting out front only to find those missing as well. Him and Fawn must have taken the bikes with them on their last trip to Ark.

Reaching into her bra, Legs hands tremored as she fumbled with the spare key she wore around her neck. Tears welled up in her eyes as she stopped in defeat after her third try at forcing the key into the tiny hole on the gray door.

Taking a deep breath, Legs refocused her thoughts and slid the key into its assigned hole. She turned the key and heard the door unlock. Her trembling hand touched the doorknob, the metal cold and merciless beneath her palm as she opened the door and exposed the darkened front room with plaid wallpaper.

It took every ounce of strength Legs had to step onto the stained carpet as she dropped her shoes by the door. Dread filled her at the sight of the empty couch. The damned light with a bull skull lamp shade, one Worvacs refused to get rid of, hung above a single end table.

The smell of man, soil, and musk filled her nostrils as tears gathered in her eyes. No… this wasn't possible.

Legs raced from one room to another, seeing the man's presence everywhere. A pan remained on Worvacs' stove from his last night in town, when she had come over after work and made his favorite meal of Alfredo. A good luck gift before he left.

Socks, a t-shirt, jeans, and boxers lined the bending hallway from the kitchen to his unmade bed, where they had spent the night making love in each other's arms. Her mouth pressed against his in passionate embrace of their bodies joined as one, connecting with true love.

A single towel sat on the bathroom floor in front of the green shower curtain that Legs was insistent he put up. If she was going to use his bathroom, she demanded privacy in the home without doors.

Denial swept over her. The agonizing pain became too much as she grabbed his pillow from the bed. She inhaled deeply, breathing in the man's familiar scent, wrapped in memories of happiness and laughter, taking in every ounce of the man. She finally exhaled the deep, heavy sobs she had been holding in for so long.

Her chest heaved with the painful truth. He was gone. Forever gone from her life. Through blurred eyes, she looked up at his nightstand that held two empty glasses of wine, her own lipstick resting on one.

It was plum. The same lipstick that had also covered his neck that night. There was hope. One last place where he might be. Darting through the tiny doorway next to Worvacs' black nightstand, Legs held her breath as she came out at the other end of the hallway.

The sight of the empty ammo room was too much. The lamenting beat of her breaking heart sent Legs to her knees. It was tormenting. She clenched tightly to Worvacs' pillow, still in her arms, as she landed on the concrete floor. Her chest felt as if her heart would explode as the tears fell freely.

Empty gun cabinets lined the six walls of the hexagon room. Not a single bullet remained in the secret ammo room, not a single rifle or handgun to relieve Legs' fears that surfaced in the deadly waters.

The abandoned room confirmed that the man was missing in action. Her false hopes were nothing more. There was no sign of the foreign alien on Earth. Worvacs was on Ark and the dead were here.

Knowhere was on its own.

EPILOGUE

She walked with a grace that mirrored the power she wielded. She smiled, exposing her pearly teeth as she stepped foot onto a cloud surrounded by gold-colored marble pillars holding vines of shiny silver leaves. As her magenta hair fell down her back, a grin swept her face that could just as easily mean danger as happiness.

"Zues," she said, her head was held high with pride as her eyes shone at the god before her, "Allow me to introduce myself, I'm Karma." She sarcastically bowed before him as her tight-fitting golden dress caved to her contours.

"Yeah, yeah, I remember who you are. I'm surprised it took you this long to show up. If you're looking for Jesus he's down the hall on your left, Buddha is the door on the right." Zeus nubbed out his cigarette on the marble pillar he was leaning against. His long, white hair covered his shoulders down to his light blue robes. "It took the end of existence for you to stop by so I can't say anybody's going to be real excited to see you."

Karma laughed in response as her eyes sparkled. "I have already visited with Buddha and Jesus. Very pleasant visits in fact. We had a few laughs over good times. You on the other hand Zeus…" A shiver crept down Zeus' immoral spine. "It is no surprise that you are not pleased by my company. Adultery does have nasty consequences," she added with a wink, "But, to be discussed at another time, I suppose. Never know when I might show my shining face."

She sat down before him, stretching her arms. "Remember last time we spoke I requested the Misfitz Tavern be a place where only I governed? I brought it up to you, to Jehovah and Mother Nature. It was discussed with Hades and Grim, too. And Buddha. Even the Kachinas agreed. It's crumbling now… why?"

Zeus pulled another cigarette from inside his shining chest plate and lit it with a snap of his fingertips. "Yeah well I don't know if you've noticed or not, but that's not the only thing that's crumbling around here you know." An echo rumbled from beneath them as small chunks of marble and gold fell from the ceiling and landed at their feet. "Without people to believe in us, there isn't much left that's not crumbling at this point. It's taking most of the power any of us have left just to keep the ones who are still breathing around long enough to tell of us. To keep us from disappearing too. Speaking of which, if you're in charge of keeping the balance, I have a question for you. What beautifully magnificent deed was done that you had to balance out by killing off almost every living thing in existence? Is this payback for the beginning of time?" He exhaled, blowing out a floating one eyed gorgon of smoke that began swinging its giant mallet around.

"This?" she asked in disbelief before coughing at the smoke that quickly surrounded them. "This wasn't me. Well…" she shrugged her shoulders in thought, "Maybe part of it was. Part of it was Jehovah and Lucifer too. When they sent those two idiots to Earth. And then, the humans were focused on whatever the flaming bottoms Nephthys had let loose. I couldn't allow that chaos running free. Windigo gave Hades the idea for the disease. Do you really think we expected it to go this widespread, this fast? Look," she raised her hands in her own defense, "It's out of my hands now. Pandora gave someone an idea for some damned box. Said it wasn't fit for gods and goddesses. Now we have these young sproutlings of a god and goddess roaming around.

What if they *actually* knew they had powers? Do something Zeus!" she insisted with fury.

"What do you expect me to do about it? I don't know how you created it, much less how to control it. The only thing I could think to do was lock off a couple of dimensions in a side realm out in the boonies for the few survivors there are left to restart on." He sighed in frustration before tossing his cigarette to the ground and stomping on it with his foot causing a crack to form in the marble flooring. "At this point the only, *the only*, thing I can think to do to put a stop to this mess is for everyone to combine what divine power we have left and try to stop it that way. Even then, I don't know what might happen, or what we might become for that matter, if everyone did."

"You want *me* to work with some of *them*?" Karma asked before laughing, "Do you know what Hades and Lucifer have to do to keep me from ruining... well, anything that they do? Jesus and Buddha, them I can work with. Even Cupid and I can come to an understanding on occasion, but Mars? Aphrodite?" She raised an eyebrow, as if the thought were unrealistic before seeing that Zeus wasn't backing down. She let out a heavy sigh. "Fine!" she pouted before asking, "Does that include the sproutlings?"

"Ha! The sproutlings aren't even bright enough to pull their collective heads out of the dirt long enough to see what's going on around them. If you think you can get them to come, by all means go for it. But where we're going, it's not exactly a nice place."

"Oh no, if they want the title, they can have the responsibility," Karma grinned. The expression on her face quickly became demented as she wrung her hands together with joy. "I know just the person to tell them of their precious followers."

"They were right," Zeus cringed, quickly turning around as his mind wandered. Karma was deep, with dark, demented caverns that held the creepy crawlies that infested homes, kitchen cabinets, and sinks of rotten food. She had mountain tops, soaring high and bright to surround those who tossed a quarter to the bum on the street.

“Karma apparently can very much be a bitch," he huffed before turning and walking over to the wall of armor that stood overlooking the lobby. He slowly began unstrapping his boots and shin guards. "We still have to let everyone know what the current plan of action is and then get them all to agree. Much less getting to where we have to go." He slung his boots and shin plates on the armor stand before him before removing his armored pants and chest plate.

Karma nodded her head before sighing, "I suppose that means that for now the Misfitz Tavern, and everywhere else ran by the likes of us, is on its own."

THE AUTHORS

Matthew was born in Mississippi. Being raised in a military family, traveling and reading have always been passions of his. Upon graduating from Maury High School, Matthew joined the Navy and spent four years serving in both Guam and Cuba as a Master at Arms. After leaving the Navy, he moved to Missouri where he was blessed with a son, Zayne, in 2010. When he is not writing, Matthew enjoys video games, hiking, and pyrography.

LaTasha was born and raised in Missouri. She developed a love for reading early on, which was greatly influenced by her Grandmother and Great-Grandmother. In 2006, her poem "Perfect" earned the Editor's Choice Award through Poetry.com and the International Library of Poetry. In 2015, she was published in the *My ABQ Guide* with an article on the Albuquerque Film Studios. When LaTasha is not writing, she enjoys spending time with her family, pyrography, and playing with her chickens that she has hand-trained.

Follow the authors at www.facebook.com/matthewandlatashalee and feel free to leave them a message.